WOLF PASS

Also by Steve Thayer

The Wheat Field

Moon Over Lake Elmo

Silent Snow

The Weatherman

Saint Mudd

WOLF PASS

A Novel

STEVE THAYER

G. P. PUTNAM'S SONS
NEW YORK

This is a work of fiction. Names, characters, places, and incidents either are the product of the author's imagination or are used fictitiously, and any resemblance to actual persons, living or dead, business establishments, events, or locales is entirely coincidental.

G. P. Putnam's Sons
Publishers Since 1838
a member of
Penguin Putnam Inc.
375 Hudson Street
New York, NY 10014

Published simultaneously in Canada

Library of Congress Cataloging-in-Publication Data

Thayer, Steve.
Wolf pass : a novel / Steve Thayer.
p. cm.
ISBN 0-399-14991-0
1. World War, 1939–1945—Veterans—Fiction. 2. World War, 1939–1945—Prisoners and prisons, American—Fiction. 3. Germans—Wisconsin—Fiction. 4. Prisoners of war—Fiction. 5. Serial murders—Fiction. 6. War criminals—Fiction. 7. Wisconsin—Fiction. 8. Sheriffs—Fiction. 9. Revenge—Fiction. I. Title.
PS3570.H3477W6 2003 2002190772
813'.54—dc21

Printed in the United States of America
1 2 3 4 5 6 7 8 9 10

This book is printed on acid-free paper. ♾

Book design by Michelle McMillian

For Celeste

WOLF PASS

PROLOGUE

THE WOLF

Eighteen years we spent stalking one another. I was last in his rifle sights on the steps of the cathedral, that bloody October day. I remember it was raining. No thunder. No lightning. Nothing so dramatic. Just a bitter, dispiriting drizzle. In fact, a sickening chill still crawls up my spine when I think about standing on those cold stone steps, the top of my head frozen in the crosshairs of his rifle. I carried with me the ghosts of that day for over fifty years. Now the time has come to write about it.

He was a handsome man, in a homely sort of way. His face was pocked and scarred. His nose was long and sharp. His eyes were raven black. Lacking a soul. Heartless, but penetrating. As I write this, I have a photograph of him propped up before me. It is the same photograph I carried while hunting him after the war. The official Nazi photograph was taken as he approached forty. He had a receding hairline, his dark hair cropped short about the ears. The strangest thing about his face, what one noticed first, was his mouth. His lips were so thin he appeared to have no lips. Small menacing scars droop from the lower lip, adding weight to his evil visage. I never knew from where those scars came, but my guess back then was that they were not the scars of war, but rather the scars of disease. He was an immaculate man, posing in his highly decorated SS uniform, a swastika pinned to his tie. I remember him as tall and solid. Even today, if you were to cover up the uniform and just stare at the eyes, you would see staring back at you a frighteningly splendid example of Hitler's superman.

I am retired now. Fifty years of police work in the rearview mirror, almost all of those years spent on the roads of Kickapoo County. Still, it is an island off of a peninsula that I retired to, with my files and my memories. And my rifle. The days are slowed here, and then slowed again. The winds of Lake Michigan blow nightly through my cabin, like the cold winds of time. There is a sailboat tied to the dock, but I'm getting too old to be on the water alone.

For years I had wanted to produce a series of books that contrasted the beauty of Wisconsin with the state's long history of bizarre crimes. So now I sit at the bay window and write the chapters of my life. And the one chapter that haunts me still is a chapter I simply call "The Wolf." Looking back, it seems I spent a lifetime chasing a conspiracy that forever stayed one step ahead of me. A ghost in the morning mist.

The chain of deadly events I now relate to you actually began high in the Bavarian Alps during the last months of World War II, at a railroad junction the Allies called Wolf Pass. But for the sake of storytelling, let us begin at a later date in my beloved Wisconsin. The year was 1962. The year of the wolf.

It does seem extraordinary that novelists find it necessary to invent such tales when the appalling truth is surely far more "dramatic."

—GITTA SERENY, *Into That Darkness*

1 | THE HILLS

In all my life the hills never changed. They were born of glaciers, mountains of ice that reached two miles high. For over a million years these immense ice packs shifted back and forth, carving out the land below. The last of the prodigious glaciers were seen heading north some ten thousand years ago, leaving behind great ridges of dirt and rock, and dark and deep waters that sparkle like stars beneath the summer sun. It is geography with an unusual heft and expanse. Today, enormous boulders are scattered about, and old wooded roads of dirt dip and rise on a dramatic scale. Too rugged for development. Too isolated for big-city tourists. So the rocks and trees in the heart of Wisconsin roll on for miles, up and down, jutting in and out, acting for a thousand years like a natural protector to all creatures, great and small, who choose to live in the vast green hollows. But too often over the years, unmitigated evil found its way into those beautiful hills. Then violence would shatter this hushed and peaceful world, and spill down into the villages nestled in the valleys. Like my hometown.

I found Frank Prager hanging out of the cab of his steam locomotive, like a sodden rag doll. A swath of blood, dark and red, stained the entire side of the cab, blacking out the white of the locomotive's four-digit number. A semicircle of railroad workers stood before the train station in Kickapoo Falls, like statues in the midmorning sun. Shocked. Silent. Grieving. I stuck a foot into the steel wheel workings of the 82-ton monster, grabbed onto a handrail, and hoisted myself up to the dangling body. The cab was nothing more than a partly enclosed platform on the back of a giant, belching boiler that could exceed 2,000 degrees Fahrenheit under full steam. The dead engineer smelled of oil and coal. Grease and iron. And blood. Brain bits and skull fragments had splashed around the cab, smearing the gauges on the back of the boiler. His black and white striped overalls were tattered and worn. His cap, equally worn, lay at the track below my feet. Balancing on one foot and clinging to the handrail, I grabbed a fistful of soggy hair and lifted his head with my free hand. He'd been shot between the eyes. One shot. A large caliber. The damage to his face was extensive. Death was instantaneous. I recoiled in horror and unceremoniously let his head drop. What remained of his face made a soft bash against the side of the cab.

I jumped down to the tracks. Wiped my hands with a handkerchief. I slipped on my sunglasses and instinctively searched the high wooded hills, their peaks sheared off by ancient ice. White birches lined the lower regions just above the train station. Above that stood some of the oldest rock in North America—quartzite bluffs more than a billion years old, massive boulders that rolled into the spruce and the pine. Behind the pulpwood was a forest of maple, elm, white ash, and black oak that climbed into a steel-blue sky, where I was forced to avert my eyes from the glare. Death had found engineer Prager on a near-perfect September morning. The shot that killed him had come out of the sun.

"Tell me what happened."

Walter Beyer, the train's conductor, was standing beside me, visibly shaken. His normally pristine black uniform was askew. His coat was open wide. The tie around his neck had been yanked loose. The cap that was seldom seen off of his head was being wrung between his hands. "We were running two minutes behind," he said. "I checked my watch and called 'all aboard' and . . . I don't know . . . Frank stuck his head out the cab to look down the train, like he always did . . . then his head snapped back, real violent-like, and he dropped over the window there . . . blood running out of him like a faucet. I climbed up there to check on him, and I seen that . . . well, you saw it . . . half his face was gone."

The conductor was a good deal older than his friend Frank Prager. The stubble of hair remaining on his balding head had gone to silver and white. The proud age lines of a railroad man creased his eyes. Like the old steam locomotive behind us, he was nearing retirement.

"Did you see anything?" I asked him.

"No, nothing unusual. I thought I might have heard a shot, but you know how noisy train yards can be." He shook his head in amazement. "The thing of it is, Deputy, I was staring up into the hills when it happened . . . it was such a pretty day. I saw nothing. Had to be some kind of ghost up there. People that live here sometimes, you know, take the hills for granted. But Frank and I never did. We took this old train through these hills near every day. Never tired of the view. Guess I'll never look at them the same."

This was the first I'd ever heard of a ghost in the hills. In the summertime, the baronial hills were where we went to escape the tourists who flocked to Kickapoo Falls to frolic in the Dells, an enchanting fifteen-mile stretch of the Wisconsin River, where a melting glacier had left behind soaring cliffs and haunted gorges. The region's economy depended on those tourists, who were both a blessing and a scourge.

Walter Beyer nodded at Frank's tattered cap lying on the ground alongside the tracks. "May I?" he asked.

"Yes, go ahead."

The old conductor reached down and picked up the engineer's cap. Held it in his hands, along with his own.

A horde of passengers was strung out along the tracks, standing beside the twenty murky yellow cars that trailed the engine. The Chicago, Milwaukee, St. Paul and Pacific Railway, nicknamed the Milwaukee Road, was a popular train, a lifeline for small towns in Wisconsin. Its importance could not be overstated. Already, word had spread down Main Street. A crowd from town was gathering. Cars and pickup trucks were pulling right up to the tracks. More deputies arrived. I ordered the station sealed off. The sheriff, or rather the acting sheriff, squealed to a halt with lights twirling and a siren screaming. The mayor was with him. I walked their way.

Packy Deitz jumped from the squad. "Frank got shot?"

"Yes. He's dead."

He stared up at the corpse. "Sweet Jesus, here we go again. Do you know who did it, Mr. Pennington?"

"Not yet," I told our cherubic mayor.

In Kickapoo Falls, the office of mayor was largely ceremonial. The real power lay in the sheriff's office. "Dear God," he said, "let's hope this was a hunting accident. The last thing this town needs is another murder. Especially with you two running for sheriff." The mayor moved off toward the body.

Sheriff Zimmer stood beside me now. He surveyed the sight as his deputies tried to clear the murder scene and restore some order to the train station. He was a tall, slender man. Wore a thick mustache at a time when mustaches were not only out of fashion, but they smacked of a sinister character. Still, the thick but neatly trimmed mustache somehow looked right on him. Lent him an air of authority and respect, though I often wondered what he'd look like without it.

Normally at this point I would describe J. D. Zimmer's personality, but he didn't seem to possess one. Some deputies called him "the iceman." I remember him as a reticent man. His steely eyes often made it difficult to discern his thinking. Looking back, I don't think I ever once saw him smile. He came up from Madison to fill the sheriff's position, the governor's appointment after the unfortunate death of our beloved Sheriff Fats. It was a death some still blamed on me. And though he was sent up to our county by the governor, rumor had it Zimmer's appointment came straight out of the Kickapoo Gunn Club—a very private and very secretive organization in which Zimmer was said to be a proud member. Perhaps, it was whispered, even some kind of club officer.

Zimmer, too, was hiding behind sunglasses that end-of-summer day. Sometimes he wore them indoors. Claimed bright light bothered his eyes. Maybe it did, but it was an annoying habit. Other than that, at the time of the engineer's murder, I liked the man well enough. He wore the sheriff's uniform as proud as Fats had worn it. On Labor Day we had all switched to our winter grays. Long-sleeved, tapered shirts. Black slacks. Silver Stetsons. Our badges were pinned proudly to our chests. The emblem of the Kickapoo County Sheriff's Department was embroidered on our arms. Fats had kept us looking sharp. He hated the slovenly appearance of rural cops. J. D. Zimmer was continuing that tradition. I vowed, if elected, I too would see that our policy of sharp uniforms continued.

Zimmer spoke without glancing my way, focusing his dark glasses instead on the dead engineer dangling from the train. "When is that trip of yours to St. Paul?"

Seemed like a strange question, considering the circumstances. "Next month," I reminded him.

He nodded the victim's way. "Do you think you can wrap this up before then?"

With a homicide, Fats once told me, people want justice, and they want it fast. You want to wrap it up quick. Don't let it linger. For a hundred years, justice in Kickapoo County had been swift and harsh. Zimmer seemed to understand that.

"I can try."

"Frank was a hunter, wasn't he?"

"Yes," I told him, "Frank and Lisa were both hunters."

"Lisa hunts?"

"Yes."

I watched him chewing on a thought. "I know it's out of season, but do you think this might have been some kind of hunting accident?"

"If you were out hunting illegally, Sheriff, would you hunt in the hills above a crowded train station?"

"Kids playing with a rifle?"

"It would have to be one hell of a rifle . . . and one hell of a kid."

"And the shot came from those hills?"

"Yes, it had to."

"Let's get some Boy Scout troops up there. Comb every inch for clues."

"I'm on it, Sheriff."

I was about to turn and go, get back to work, when the sheriff stopped me with a pointed question. "Have you ever seen anything like this before, Deputy Pennington?"

I didn't answer the question, because the truth was, I had. The sheriff noticed my lack of a response. He looked directly at me for the first time. "You are the department's homicide investigator, are you not?"

Despite the upcoming election, we'd had an amicable relationship. Still, I didn't care for the way he'd put that. "Yes, Sheriff, I am."

"Well then, Deputy, it looks like you've got a homicide on your hands."

"Yes, it does. Somebody has to tell his wife. It should probably be me. I have to question her anyway."

"Yes, I understand you two are friends. You should be the one to tell her."

I didn't care for the way he phrased that, either. It would be the first homicide Zimmer and I had worked. No sheriff likes a murder on his watch, and we were off to a bad start on this one.

The morning sun felt good on my face. We were on the autumn side of summer. Labor Day had come and gone. The tourists had gone back to Chicago, or Milwaukee, or Minneapolis, or back to wherever the hell it was they had come from. I'd been looking forward to some rest and relaxation before the heat of the election. But as I walked back to my squad, I overheard several snippets of conversation that told me there would be no vacation before November.

"Gonna be a terrible blow for Lisa."

"Lisa's a pretty thing . . . she'll marry again."

But the remark that troubled me most was the observation our loud-mouthed mayor made to the sheriff when he thought I was too far away to hear. "Good Lord, that's no hunting accident, Sheriff. One shot . . . from high in the hills . . . right between the eyes. There's only one man in Kickapoo County who can shoot like that."

2 | CAMP KICKAPOO: *In the Beginning*

I tell this aspect of the story secondhand because it took place during World War II, while I was away, serving in Europe. Censorship was strict during those war years. Newspapers seldom published anything about German POWs. Photographs of German prisoners were subject to confiscation. Though often ignored, fraternization between prisoners and civilians was forbidden. After the war, government documents relating to the POWs were sealed. As a result, few Americans remember that over four hundred thousand German prisoners of war were held in more than five hundred prison camps in the United States. There were camps in every state in the union. More than a hundred fifty base camps, which spawned numerous branch camps. In fact, one of the first military sites selected for the housing of German prisoners was Camp McCoy in the heart of Wisconsin. The site was chosen because it was far from war-related industries and close to forests and farms, where laborers were badly needed. As fate would have it, one of the first branch camps out of McCoy was a small logging compound built for two hundred fifty prisoners at the foot of the Kickapoo Hills.

I feel comfortable in telling the story of Camp Kickapoo because of the trust I had in my primary source. As he told it to me, it all happened very fast and somewhat mysteriously. In early March of 1943, a Madison newspaper announced that a stockade and four watchtowers had transformed a former Civilian Conservation Corps camp into a prisoner-of-war camp—a small cluster of wooden buildings nestled beneath high bluffs three miles south of Kickapoo Falls. Across the road from the camp, wooden barracks were hastily erected in a farm field that had been leased by the army. At the end of March, soldiers who were to serve as guards arrived and moved into the barracks.

One American industry severely crippled by the labor shortage during the war was the pulpwood industry. Pulpwood states like Maine, New Hampshire, and Wisconsin suddenly found themselves in need of thousands of loggers. Since the pulpwood industry produced items essential to the war effort, the government moved quickly toward using prisoners of war to cut pulpwood, which are the softwoods such as spruce, aspen, or pine, used in the making of paper.

The hills surrounding the new camp were remote and ruggedly scenic, a seemingly endless forest of massive trees, with deep blue lakes and fast-running rivers. The small camp itself was another story. At Camp McCoy the prisoners had enjoyed accommodations similar to the best the United States provided for its own men. But the wooden buildings that formed their new camp were stark. Bleak. Barely functional. Chill winds shot through the doors and windows. The grounds were rough and muddy. The latrine was two hundred yards away. The nearest town was three miles away. The POW enclosure was divided into four compounds, three residential and one for recreation. Standard double-woven wire fencing topped with barbed-wire overhangs surrounded the whole works. At night, the haunting bright lights of the new stockade up in the hills could be seen from the town.

The first year the German prisoners were at Camp Kickapoo, hundreds of people would drive for miles on a Saturday or a Sunday to gawk at the barbed-wire enclosure. Hoping for a chance to see a real

Nazi. One of Hitler's supermen. But by the end of the war, people in the valley had lost interest and the prison camp drew little attention.

Until the murder.

One more note about the camp. Under the Geneva Convention of 1929, the International YMCA was asked to promote educational and recreational facilities in prisoner-of-war camps. The work was carried on by mutual agreement among the United States, England, Germany, and Japan. Each country was divided into sectors. Each sector had a YMCA field secretary, and each camp had a YMCA prisoners' aide, usually a local volunteer. The aide's mission seemed simple enough—provide prisoners with books. Help establish theaters, chapels, and sports teams to occupy the prisoners' free time. Get the men some material for arts and crafts. Seek donations of musical instruments and sports gear, anything to keep the prisoners occupied and content while not at work. It was not until the war's end we discovered that Germany and Japan had paid little attention to the Geneva Convention, while in the United States perhaps too much attention had been paid to the rules. Sometimes, in some American towns, the prisoners' aide paid a price for his volunteer work. In Kickapoo Falls, the prisoners' aide from the YMCA was my father.

3 | THE WIDOW

John Donne said no man is an island. Still, I came damn close. I spent my life alone, surrounded by turbulent waters. Breaking waves. Too often over my long and storied career I went knocking at death's door, only by the grace of God to be turned away at the last second. I never married. Had no children. I was a witness to love, but never a participant. Could be I never met the right woman. Perhaps I was just unlucky. Or maybe, all those years, I harbored some deep, subconscious fear of committing myself, heart and soul, to another human being for the rest of my life. A lot easier to blame war wounds.

I rang the doorbell, but there was no answer. It was a handsome house in one of our better neighborhoods. Frank had made good money. He'd worked his ass off, long hours, days away from home, and the railroad had paid him well. I prayed his insurance and his pension would take care of Lisa.

I walked around the house. When there was no sign of her in the yard, I tried the back door. It was open. I removed my hat. Stepped into the sparkling white kitchen and called her name. Still no answer. A cereal bowl lay unwashed in the kitchen sink, along with an empty cup of coffee. The crumbs and jam on a plate were left over from toast. The last breakfast of Frank Prager. Apparently, he had eaten it alone. I turned to call her name again when I noticed the newspaper article stuck with a magnet to the refrigerator door.

THE KICKAPOO FALLS REPUBLIC
Thursday, September 6, 1962

COUNTY DEPUTY TO ATTEND MASS WITH PRESIDENT
P.A. Pennington to Travel to St. Paul

Deputy P. A. Pennington of the Kickapoo County Sheriff's Department has been invited to attend Mass with the President of the United States at the Cathedral of Saint Paul in St. Paul, Minnesota, on Sunday, October 7, the White House announced today. Pennington will be one of a dozen Catholic dignitaries from the Midwest who have been invited to attend Mass with President John F. Kennedy, said Minnesota bishop Gerald O'Keefe, who is scheduled to give a sermon explaining the function of the Second Vatican Council.

The article was nearly a week old. Until the shooting, it had been the talk of the town. In heavily Protestant, heavily Republican Kickapoo County, the news that I would be attending Mass with the Democratic President was greeted with elation by some, and with deep resentment by others. Most folks were happy for me. Others thought the President was trying to interfere in a local election. Word was, the gentlemen at the Gunn Club were furious. Personally, I thought everybody was overreacting—that the President of the United States had more important things to concern himself with than a sheriff's election in the middle of Wisconsin—though I was flattered that he had remembered me.

I was still staring at my own name when a voice came from upstairs. Lisa's voice. "Is that you, Frank? Forget something?"

I moved through the living room to the foot of the stairwell. "No, Lisa, it's me. I rang the doorbell, but . . ."

She stood in the upstairs hallway staring down at me. A smile illuminated her sweet, sunny face. Between the two of us, a plush layer of cream carpeting rolled down the steps. "Deputy Pennington. My, my, what a pleasant surprise." She spoke in her flirtatious voice. "In the morning . . . and in uniform, no less. Come on up."

"I'd rather we talked down here." But she disappeared into the bedroom. I climbed the stairs after her. "Lisa . . . ," I called.

She had flopped onto her bed, on her back, one leg playfully bent over the other. Lisa was tall for a woman. Near five-ten. She had brilliant red hair. Wore it loose above the shoulders. Not much different in style from the First Lady. It was amazing how in just two short years, America's women had loosened up. In style. In dress. Even in speech and attitude. Every one of them trying to be like Jackie.

She was wearing a sky-blue blouse with tight-fitting slacks. The blouse was untucked. Bare white feet stuck out of those black slacks. It was the outfit of a woman refusing to believe the summer season was nearly over. "You're not going to quit on me, are you," she asked, "now that you're the favorite altar boy of the Pope and the President?"

"Lisa . . ."

"That's what people around town are calling you, you know . . . Pope Pennington."

"Lisa, I'm here on business."

"Pope business?" She laughed. "Oh c'mon, now, I'm Catholic, too." Lisa wanted to play. I wanted to cry. "Frank is a heathen," she said, "but I'm still a good little . . ." She could see from the blank stare on my face that I wasn't joking. "What kind of business?"

"Police business."

"Yes?"

"Lisa, Frank is dead. Somebody shot him down at the train station. I couldn't be more sorry." It was an all-purpose cliché I'd picked up on the job. Not that I didn't mean it; I did. But I found it froze people. Neutralized them. I used it on homicides. Traffic fatalities. I said it again. "Lisa, really, I couldn't be more sorry."

"Shot him how . . . why?"

"It appears someone in the hills hit him with a high-powered rifle."

"Do you mean like a sniper?"

I felt defensive. "More like a hunter, I think."

"Like an accident?"

"No, I don't think so."

"I'm not sure what you're saying . . . my Frank was murdered?"

"It looks that way."

It wasn't easy for Lisa to go white, her skin was so soft and pale. But as she sat up on the edge of the bed and tried to catch her breath, I watched her face turn white as an angel. There were no tears. Not yet, anyway. "Why? I mean . . . Frank drove a train. Who would want to kill him?"

"Lisa, where do you keep your guns?"

"In the basement. What . . . do you think I shot him?"

"No . . . but I have to check all of your guns. It's routine."

"In the basement," she said again.

I saw a near-empty glass on the nightstand. I could smell the Scotch. Alcohol, the dirty little secret of small towns. "Have you been drinking?" I wanted to know.

Suddenly, anger flashed across her face. Replaced the sorrow. "I've had a drink, Deputy. I'm not drunk."

"For Christ's sake, Lisa, it's ten thirty in the morning. What would Frank think?"

"My husband, or as you have just informed me, my dead husband, worked sixteen-hour days. Most of those days he wasn't even in the county. I had one drink . . . I think I'll have another." She reached for the glass and drained the contents. Then she lay back on the bed and squeezed her brow, as if wringing out a headache. Still, there were no tears on her face. More anger than anything. "When were you ever a friend of Frank's?" she asked. "I don't remember you having any kind of affection for him when he was alive."

"Have you ever told anybody about us?"

"What's to tell?"

"Still . . ."

"Frank asked about you once."

"What did you tell him?"

"I told him the truth . . . that you've never touched me. Why?"

"Packy Deitz is already running around town implying I might have shot Frank."

"Packy Deitz is an idiot. That's why we made him mayor."

"Yeah, well, the wheat field case is still hanging over my head. We have to be careful."

The anger in her voice was subsiding. "You came out of that case a hero. Even the President wants to meet you."

"Half the town thinks I'm a hero. The other half is not so sure. Then there's the Gunn Club. We have to find out who killed Frank. Are you going to be okay?"

"Please don't go."

"Lisa, I've got work to do."

"Yes, it probably won't be as exciting now that I'm a widow . . . always available."

"Where does your sister live?"

"St. Paul."

"I'll call her."

"Don't bother."

"I know you're not feeling good right now, but somebody should be here."

"You can't know what I'm feeling . . . you're a fucking man."

She was lying on the bed, her fire-red hair against the white pillowcase, a chenille bedspread beneath her body. Minutes passed in silence. Dead silence. Painful silence. I stood at moral attention at the foot of the bed. Watched her. At first, I thought she was going to cry, and I wanted to hang around long enough to know she'd be all right.

But she didn't cry.

She unbuttoned her blouse, that sky-blue blouse, slowly and deliberately, all of the time staring up at a ceiling made bright white with the morning sun. When the blouse was completely open and her bra and her tummy were clearly exposed, she slipped one strap of the bra down her shoulder. Pulled down on the cup. Lisa was tall and slender. Her stomach flat. The bare breast she exposed to me was round and firm, like a ripe melon. She had beautiful white breasts accented with dark red nipples. With her long fingers, she toyed with the nipple as I watched.

"Lisa, please . . ."

"You know the drill, Deputy. You're not supposed to talk," she told me. "You're supposed to watch. Do what you're told."

She unbuttoned her slacks. Pulled down the zipper. Then with both of her hands she slid the Jackie slacks over her hips and down her legs, to her ankles. She wasn't wearing panties. "Pull them off," she told me.

"Lisa . . ." I begged.

"Do what you're told, Deputy."

I reached over the foot of the bed and removed her slacks from her ankles.

Now she was half-naked before me. One tit exposed beneath her blouse and bra. Naked hips and long, athletic legs. I toyed with the Stetson in my hand. Tried to look away. But that wasn't possible. Lisa spread her thighs. "This should only take a minute," she told me. With her right hand she inserted her middle finger and forefinger inside of her. Pleasured herself while I watched.

Few women are as beautiful as brides and widows. I stood there transfixed at the foot of her bed, hat in hand, staring at Lisa Prager as she masturbated. As many times as she had performed for me in the past, I still could not conquer the draw of her natural beauty. The curves of her figure. The white of her skin. The soft and gentle way she touched herself. The sheer pleasure she derived from it. And the obvious gratification she received from my being witness to her sex. Lisa was in her early thirties when Frank was killed. It was as if she longed to know there was still one man in the world who admired her beauty. Her womanhood. That she could spend her life in Kickapoo Falls with a husband she may or may not have loved, and with a husband who may or may not have loved her, as long as there was that one man in town she could bring to a dead stop with her sexuality.

That morning was faster than usual, though I'd have waited all day to watch Lisa come. Her moaning became increasingly louder, the strokes between her legs progressively faster, almost as if she was trying to hurt herself. Then, for the first time since I'd given her the news, a tear rolled out of the corner of her eye and shot down her cheek. As she threw herself into orgasm, one tear followed another. Finally, she screamed, the loudest I'd ever heard her. The most intense. I glanced over my shoulder at the open window, worried the neighbors might hear.

The widow Prager rolled to her side. Tucked her hands between those long, gorgeous legs and buried her face in the pillow, if only to hide the flood of tears.

I wanted to go to her. Sit on the edge of the bed and wrap her in my arms. I knew in my heart that would be the right thing to do. The manly thing. But as had always been the case with us, I just stood there and watched.

Finally she poked her nose out of the pillow. Cleared her throat. "You can go now," she choked out. "I'll be okay."

4 | DEATH IN A WHEAT FIELD

I hate like hell to repeat myself. Write things already written. Still, the wheat field case bleeds into the story of Wolf Pass. So perhaps a little background is in order.

When I retired to my cabin here on this Lake Michigan island, I decided to spend the years I had left committing to paper the chapters of my life. Stories from fifty years of law enforcement in one of the most rugged and most beautiful counties in the state of Wisconsin. The first chapter I chose to write about was an obsessive chapter I simply called "Maggie."

Just two years before Frank Prager's face was blown off in the cab of his steam locomotive, a young and prominent Kickapoo Falls couple, Maggie and Michael Butler, owners of Butler Travel, were found shotgunned to death in the middle of a wheat field.

At first glance it appeared to be a murder-suicide. Maggie shot Michael for his philandering ways, then turned the gun on herself. But I quickly determined it was a double homicide. They were completely naked. Their clothes were missing. They'd just had sex. Somebody sitting nearby had smoked a cigarette and watched. Kickapoo Falls was scandalized.

I was the first deputy on the scene that day. I was the lead investigator. And as fate would have it, all of my life I had been in love with the lovely Maggie Butler. In love with a woman who was not in love with me.

Just another story of unrequited love? No, the case turned out to be a great deal more. Other forces were at work.

At the time of the murders, our county sheriff, the legendary Sheriff Fats, was nearing retirement. I was in line to replace him. His protégé. A sure bet. But the wheat field case took ugly turns.

The mystery of the handsome young couple gunned down during a sex act ran me up and down the Wisconsin Dells. Literally threw me in and out of the Wisconsin River. It dropped me into the middle of a pornography ring. Had me eye to eye with a powerful congressman who wanted to be United States senator. The investigation took me from a Nixon rally at the state capitol in Madison, to a deadly sloop off of Hyannisport, Massachusetts, on election night, 1960.

In the end, the mystery of the double murders in the wheat field was solved. The case was closed. But not before Sheriff Fats was shot and killed. And not before some bad people slipped out of Kickapoo Falls to practice their mischief in other places.

Like so many visceral issues over the years, the wheat field case divided Kickapoo Falls into two separate camps: those who thought I was some kind of hero, and those who thought I stumbled across the killers while bungling the investigation.

5 | THE SHELL GAME

Before nightfall we had found a 30.06 shell in the hills above the train station. The killer had rested a bipod on the flat of a boulder. Downward angle, the shot out of the sun. Wind to the back. The sniper had simply lined the train engineer up in the crosshairs, and then squeezed the trigger.

It hadn't rained in weeks. The area was too dry for footprints. Too rugged to track. Other than the spent shell, no other evidence could be found.

The September sun was sinking into an intensely blue sky. The warm winds of summer were giving way to an autumn breeze. The sounds of birds and wild animals could be heard above us, where they had retreated after we had trooped into their sanctuary. Boy Scouts were climbing all over the hills, having the time of their lives assisting in a real live murder investigation. It was while standing up there in the hills that the horrid feeling first washed over me. It was a frightening sensation. A premonition of sorts. Hard to describe, except to those of us who hide an unimaginable fear. My police instincts should have entertained the possibility, but my dread blocked out the thought.

"Are you all right?" It was Deputy Hess, a longtime friend. A combat veteran of the Korean War. A big, mean Marine. Sheriff Fats had hired him, too.

"Yes," I told him, "I'm fine."

"You look like you saw a ghost."

"For a second, I thought I had." The 30.06 shell was in my hand, resting over a handkerchief. I stared down at the casing, then down at the train yard. I was drowning in memories. None of them pleasant.

"Odd that our killer would leave that shell behind."

"Our killer wanted us to find it," I said.

"So it was some kind of sniper attack."

Like most good marksmen, I was quite adept at estimating distances using nothing more than the sights of my rifle. I didn't have my rifle with me, but I ventured a fairly accurate guess. "That's over six hundred yards," I muttered.

Hess glanced over at me. "Well then, we have the right man on the case."

"What does that mean?"

He wasn't the department's most provocative thinker, but Hess wasn't dumb, either. He was a husky man who carried his weight well in uniform. You could count on him. "It means you won that rifle contest five years in a row," he told me. "Christ, they changed the rules because of you. You're an expert with rifles. What did you think I meant?"

For years, after the war, the town was host to a popular shooting competition: the Kickapoo Gunn Club High-Powered Rifle Invitational. Back then, they welcomed all comers. We shooters had to hit a target at a thousand yards. The bull's-eye at which we aimed was a circle twenty inches across. It was like putting the crosshairs on the head of a pin. We had ten rounds, and ten minutes in which to fire those rounds. After I won the contest five consecutive times, the competition was limited to Gunn Club members only. Cynics called it the "Pennington Rule."

"I could name ten men in this county who could have made that shot . . . and a few women."

Deputy Hess shrugged his shoulders. "Can you name ten men who had a reason to kill Frank Prager?"

My fellow deputy had a point. In our neck of the woods, good riflemen were a dime a dozen. But I couldn't think of anybody who had reason to kill the train engineer.

In Wisconsin, our neck of the woods ranged from the Kickapoo River just east of the Mississippi, to the popular Wisconsin Dells on the Wisconsin River. It was river bluff country, and behind those bluffs lay some of the most fertile farmland in America. Our location in the Midwest was damn near ideal. By car, Chicago and Milwaukee were only two hours to the east. St. Paul and Minneapolis, three hours to the west. The University of Wisconsin was just down the road in Madison. Even the famous Mayo Clinic in Rochester, Minnesota, was within driving distance.

According to the 1960 census, there were four million people living in the state of Wisconsin. But only 52,000 of them lived in Kickapoo County. And only 10,000 of those resided in Kickapoo Falls. A lot of folks in the county came from strong German stock. Families with Scandinavian heritage followed them closely. Followed by British stock, mostly Welsh and Scots. Politicians counted ten Catholic counties in Wisconsin. Kickapoo County was not one of them. As part of the Second Congressional District, the county was heavily Protestant, and had gone handily to Richard Nixon over John Kennedy in the 1960 election.

So, yes, it was a rural county. But in the summertime when the tourists arrived, Kickapoo Falls became a circus. Besides the natural attraction of the Dells, there were strip joints out on Highway 33, that nowhere land that lay between the small towns and their ordinances. During those summer months, traffic, alcohol, and drunken teenagers with rifles were our biggest headaches. Then suddenly, with all of the tourists gone home, I found myself handling the county's second murder investigation in two years. The solution to this one wasn't looking any easier than the murders I had uncovered in the wheat field.

"Did you tell Lisa?" Hess asked.

"Yes, I told Lisa."

"How'd she take it?"

I thought of the red-haired beauty curled up on her bed. Half naked. White as a lamb. Her hands prayer-wise between her knees. Tears spilling down her face. "She took it hard."

"I went to school with Lisa," he said. "I asked her to the prom."

"Did she go?"

He was embarrassed. "Not with me."

"That's okay . . . I never went to the prom, either."

"Listen, Pennington, I didn't mean to imply anything. You know, don't take this wrong, but most of us don't give a damn which one of you wins the election. I miss Fats, too. We all do . . . but Zimmer's not a bad guy."

"Zimmer takes his orders from the Gunn Club."

"Well, maybe he does . . . maybe he doesn't. Nobody really knows for sure who's running the club these days. Either way, he's kind of got you on the spot with this one."

"How so?"

"He's put you in charge of a murder investigation. It's perfect. You solve the case before the election . . . he takes the credit. You don't solve the case . . . he assigns you the blame. Float out a few rumors about your past, and he walks away with the election without even getting his hands dirty."

"Do you think people in this county are that shallow?"

"Yes."

"So do I."

We stared down the steep, rugged hill at sleepy Kickapoo Falls, tucked neatly into the valley. The soaring white steeple of the Presbyterian church was the only structure that reached above the treetops. On the outskirts of town, where prairie grasses once stood eight feet tall and four hundred kinds of wildflowers once flourished, there were now farms. Huge farms, replete with red barns, silver silos, and white clapboard houses fronting patchwork fields that rolled serenely into the more gentle hills to the east.

Tales about me had been floating around this bucolic town since the end of the war—wild and often unfounded rumors about what exactly my wartime role had been with the Army Rangers. But it was no secret.

6 | THE PASS: *1944*

High in the Bavarian Alps was a railroad pass so narrow, and so protected by rock and forest, it was almost impervious to attack. In the last year of the war, the Nazis used this once innocuous pass to ship out of Germany millions of dollars in gold and war loot. The pass was also believed by Allied intelligence to be the future escape route for Nazi war criminals, including Adolph Hitler. The *Alpenfestung,* they called it. The Alpine fortress. Last stronghold of the Third Reich. If all else failed, the Nazi leaders planned to retreat to a complex of bunkers and ammunition dumps they had installed amid the forbidding, snow-capped peaks of western Austria. So the trains that ran through the pass were often called the "runaway trains."

This strategic mountain pass fell under the province of a ruthless SS colonel by the name of Christian Wolfgang Stangl. So zealous and successful was the Nazi colonel at protecting this stretch of train track, that the Allies named it for him: Wolf Pass. Attacks on the pass by air resulted in an unacceptable loss of pilots and aircraft, with little interruption in train traffic. In the spring of 1944, a British commando team daringly scaled the Bavarian heights. They were never heard from again. The trains kept running.

By the summer of 1944, the defeat of Nazi Germany appeared inevitable, and it was noted that train traffic through the pass had dramatically increased. Finally, the Allied command turned the problem of the runaway trains over to the American army. The army handed the problem to their Rangers. After giving it a great deal of thought, the Rangers decided the best course of action would be a sniper attack. Killing key personnel—engineers, switchmen, and high-ranking officers, backing up the trains for miles down the mountain, making them sitting ducks for an air assault. Keeping in mind the missing British commandos, the Rangers believed one man would stand a better chance of executing the mission and then evading the enemy than would a team. Nobody called it a suicide mission, but essentially, that's what it was. After searching their ranks high and low, the Rangers dropped in a lone sniper. A Wisconsin boy.

7 | THE FUNERAL

We buried Frank Prager on another warm September day. A couple hundred people gathered at the gravesite. The tall trees in Oak Hill Cemetery shielded the service from the bright sun. Only a few feet away, just over my shoulder, lay the graves of my previous mystery. Maggie and Michael Butler—the couple murdered in the wheat field.

A wrought-iron fence ran around the old burial ground. Legend had it the Kickapoo Indians once danced over the christened earth. Worshipped there themselves. The Ho-Chunk people, successors to the Kickapoo, claimed the cemetery rested on sacred land. Their land. Now their sacred land was littered with the dead bodies of Wisconsin's European pioneers and their descendents, and the grounds were surrounded by a neighborhood of large Victorian homes set back from red brick streets.

The widow was dressed in black. A sheer black dress, with her flaming red hair tucked beneath a floppy black hat. Standing before her husband's casket, Lisa Prager was the sexiest widow I'd ever seen. Sinful thoughts, for sure, to be having at a funeral, but goddamn it she was gorgeous. Every once in a while, while the preacher spoke kindly of the dead, Lisa would glance my way. Maybe I was being paranoid, but I sensed from all of the stares and furtive glances that half of the people at the funeral suspected Lisa had blown away her husband. The other half suspected me.

It's hard to imagine what Lisa was thinking at that moment, but I couldn't stop thinking about our first day together. It was only three months earlier.

Her car had been stolen. Said Frank was going to kill her if he found out. Next morning, I found the five-year-old Thunderbird in a parking lot up in the Dells. It was undamaged. Teenagers had probably taken it for a joyride. Lisa couldn't thank me enough. We agreed Frank would never know. She ended up inviting me on a picnic lunch. It sounded innocent enough, except that when you go on a date with a married woman, even a lunch date, I'm not sure there's any such thing as innocent.

So we were in the woods just north of Witches Gulch, one of those wonderfully hidden spots over the Wisconsin River that was known only to us locals. I remember it was warm, but not hot. Early summer. The river was high. We could see the dark rushing water through the trees. Our picnic lunch was spread out on a blanket. So were we. For the hundredth time, Lisa thanked me for finding her car.

"Do you and Frank ever come up here?"

"Frank and I have been married seven years," she said. "We don't do much of anything anymore."

"I'm sorry to hear that. You always seem to be wearing that sunny smile."

"That's you, Deputy Pennington. Something about you makes me smile." She paused after saying that, both of us a bit embarrassed. Me more than her.

She went on. "Frank drives his great big choo-choo train through the hills. Personally, I think it's a rolling phallic symbol. To Madison he goes, to Milwaukee and Chicago . . . to Timbuktu, and beyond. Sometimes he's gone for days. A girl gets lonely."

"Yes, I suppose."

"How about you, Deputy? Do you ever get lonely?"

I gave her what I thought to be an honest answer. "I was born lonely."

"They say you were in love with Maggie Butler?"

I didn't respond.

"She's dead now, you know. All gone, Deputy Pennington. Where do you go from here?"

Before answering, I thought about what she had just said. Dead. Gone. No more Maggie. Truth was, I'd been thinking about that chapter of my life a great deal. "When you've spent your entire life in love with a woman who's not in love with you," I told her, "you don't leave yourself a whole lot of options. Especially after she dies."

"I would think that you would find her death liberating."

"Yes, you would think."

A shy look washed over her face. Sexy shy, not embarrassed shy. She began talking softly, glancing down as she spoke, and then catching my eye at the end of each sentence. "They say you can't do anything . . . because of the war."

"Is that what they say?"

"I can do stuff. Do you want to watch?"

"Here?"

"Sure . . . why not?"

I glanced over my shoulder, making certain we were alone. "What's in it for you?"

She laughed, a provocative laugh. "You don't know much about women, do you?"

"No, quite frankly, I don't."

"Do you want to learn?"

Sometimes the wisest response to a bold statement is no response. That was the thing about Lisa, she was bold. Yes, I wanted to learn. Yes, I wanted to watch. But I kept my mouth shut. Sat there on my ass. Hoped for the best.

I guess it was a sundress she was wearing. Pale blue. Very summery. It set off her red hair. She got to her knees, with her back to me. "Unzip me," she said.

I grabbed hold of the smallest zipper I'd ever held in my fingers. Tugged on it until it began to slowly slide down the curve of her spine. All the way down to the top of her panties. The skin of her back was a sensual white I find hard to describe. I wanted to reach out and touch her, and I know she wanted me to, but I couldn't. Not yet.

"Unfasten my bra."

I hesitated.

"Do it," she told me.

I put my fingers around the white strap and began fumbling with the buttons, or the fasteners, or whatever the hell it was that held it together.

"They're hooks," she said. "Just pinch them together."

It worked. Her bra came undone, and I sat there staring at her wide-open back.

She stood on the blanket, glaring down at me, one hand just below her neckline, holding up her dress. The sun up in the sky was providing soft warmth. A soft light. All was daytime quiet. The only sounds I remember at that moment were the sounds of nature—birds celebrating summer, and squirrels poking about the woods. In the distance was the faint singsong of rushing water, the Wisconsin River shedding its winter snows.

Lisa Prager dropped her hand and let the dress fall to the blanket. It fell from her figure in such a fluid motion that it almost seemed choreographed. Without any hesitation she peeled the half-cup bra from her breasts and let it, too, drop at her feet. Now she was hovering above me in just a pair of light blue panties that matched her dress. I felt at that moment like the luckiest guy in the world, but still a little bit scared for the both of us. There we were in the woods above the river, in a clearing with a picnic lunch and a blanket. A cop and a naked married woman. In my mind, I could see the headlines screaming in the *Kickapoo Falls Republic:* COUNTY DEPUTY ARRESTED ON MORALS CHARGE, P. A. Pennington Caught Fornicating in Dells.

Yet, at the same time, it felt like we were the only two people on earth. Lisa stuck a finger beneath the tight fit of her panties and traced her waistline. "Take them off," she said.

Oh God, I wanted to. I wanted to reach out and rub my hands up and down those long white legs. Around the gentle curves of her hips. Up the flat of her tummy. I wanted to squeeze those perfectly rounded breasts.

"Do it, Deputy. Take off my panties."

I swallowed hard at the game she was playing. Got to my knees. Now I was staring straight into her naval. The nipples of her tits were brushing against my hair. I reached out and grabbed the panties at her waist. Then I slowly pulled them down to her knees. Pulled them down to her ankles. She stepped out of them.

Waves of colors were swimming through my head. The fleshy white of her unfettered breasts. The fiery glow of her red hair. I was staring down at her panties on the blanket, which lay beneath her lacy bra, which was lying atop her blue dress. All of this on the lime-green grass of summer.

She ran her fingers through my hair. She put a finger beneath my chin and lifted my face to hers. "Just watch, Deputy. That's all you have to do. Just don't look away."

With that, she kissed me, ever so lightly on the lips, without any other parts of our bodies touching. Then she was lying on her back, her toes brushing my knees. I couldn't have looked away, even if I had wanted to.

Not the least bit self-conscious, Lisa slowly opened her legs. She slipped a finger inside of her, followed by a second. Then she began stroking herself. I had never seen such a thing in real life. Every view, every sensation was better than the last. Was I expected to do something? Was she thinking of me watching her? I remembered her orders: *"Just watch, Deputy. That's all you have to do."* I was fascinated by how gentle the woman was with herself. How uninhibited. How carefully she worked the fingertips inside of her. With her eyes half closed, she began to moan with pleasure. An erotic sound amplified by the woods. As she got further and further along, and her cries of pleasure increased, she began thrusting her hips into her fingers. Her legs grew weak. Finally, when it seemed like she couldn't take it anymore, she exploded into orgasm, her legs wide open. I thought her screams would bring the entire county down upon us. But instead, all was suddenly quiet. Even the birds and the bees had stopped what they were doing to watch.

Lisa rolled to her side, her back to me. Stared off toward the river that spilled cold from an ancient glacier. I didn't know what to do, what to say. "Thank you" seemed grossly inadequate. At long last, I reached over and placed a hand on her shoulder. She kind of purred at the touch. Kind of smiled. With that bit of encouragement, I let my hand slide down the soft curve of her back until it came to gently rest on her beautiful white bottom. I swear, that was the only time I ever touched her in that way. But you know, to me, that one long caress was more erotic than all of the sex acts in Kickapoo Falls.

That's what made it so damned difficult when Lisa was killed.

8 | THE STRIPTEASE

Was it possible that in the sunny September days that followed Frank Prager's death, I actually allowed myself to think about a life with Lisa? A wife of my own? Because if I had, it would have been one of the few times in my life I truly believed I'd have a partner in life. A woman to dine with night in and night out. To sleep with. To love. A woman to bear a child. To help raise a family. Was there ever a chance I wouldn't die on this remote island, old and alone? Looking back, it's hard to say. There were only five days between Frank's murder and Lisa's.

"I love you, Lisa. Strip for me."

"Where are you calling from? . . . Out on the highway? . . . You sound far away."

"In thirty minutes . . . go to your bedroom window . . . strip for me."

"You sound funny."

"Will you strip for me?"

"Will you come over then?"

"First, strip for me in the window. Thirty minutes. I love you, Lisa."

• • •

The dispatcher called me at home. Woke me up. It was near two in the morning. I jumped out of bed and raced to County General.

Deputy Hess was in the emergency room, scribbling in his notebook. The front of his shirt was stained with blood. There was blood on the back of his neck, where he had rubbed it with his hand. "They just brought her in. It's a stomach wound," he told me, his face red with both anger and fear.

"What happened?"

"We got a call at one thirty . . . neighbor heard a shot . . . then a scream. We rolled on it. Found Lisa on the floor, half dressed. Blood all over. Somebody fired a shot right through her bedroom window. Shot her, just like Frank."

"Where is she?"

"Emergency . . . they're trying to stabilize her . . . but it's bad."

I ran down the hallway.

Hess called after me. "Pennington . . . why would someone who can shoot like that aim for her stomach . . . make her suffer?"

I kept running. Paid him no attention.

"The question wasn't rhetorical!" he yelled after me. "I thought you might know the answer!"

Lisa was rolled out of the emergency room on a gurney, and then wheeled down the hallway toward the operating room. She was covered with blood below the neck. Tubes and fluids ran in and out of her arms. The doctors and nurses frantically pushing her along were soaked in blood up to their elbows. I caught up with them. "Is she conscious?"

"Unfortunately, yes," said a doctor.

I took Lisa's hand. It, too, was stained in blood. She looked up at me through tear-soaked eyes. Surprisingly, they seemed more tears of sorrow than of pain. "Isn't this funny," she choked out, "I always wanted to have a baby."

"Lisa, you're not having a baby . . . you've been shot."

"I can pretend."

"Talk to me, Lisa . . . tell me what happened."

"I thought it was you calling."

"Somebody called you?"

"A man . . . from a phone booth. I could hear cars."

"What did he say?"

She squeezed my hand so hard I thought it was going to break. Her face contorted in what had to be unbearable pain. "Oh God, it hurts so . . . much . . . why did he do this to me?"

"Lisa, what did the man say?"

"Said go to the window . . . said strip for me. He said he loved me. I thought it was you."

A nurse gave me a look of pure contempt. A doctor shook his head in disgust. Then Lisa let go of my hand as they wheeled her through the double doors. But just as our fingertips parted forever, I heard her cry out, "Who's killing us?"

9 | THE INTERROGATION

It's supposed to rain when those you love are killed. Murdered. The morning after Lisa Prager died, I needed my sunglasses. I had been summoned to the sheriff's office. As I walked across Courthouse Square, I marveled at such beautiful weather at such a terrible time. The luscious five-acre park before the stately courthouse was the envy of small towns everywhere. A point of civic pride in Kickapoo Falls. An informal and friendly gathering spot. Still, I could feel the hostile stares of townspeople as I mounted the steps of the ornate building.

I had always fashioned myself the John F. Kennedy of Kickapoo Falls. Loved by most, but hated intensely by a few. More likely, I was the Richard Nixon of Kickapoo Falls. Admired by half, despised by the other half.

I pushed through the heavy double doors of the courthouse, removed my hat, and made my way through the bustling squad room to the sheriff's office. I thought it was to be a routine meeting to discuss the murder investigation. A briefing. Nothing more. But when I entered, I found Sheriff Zimmer and a detective, unknown to me, standing between the American flag and the Wisconsin state flag. Needless to say, I smelled trouble.

"Close the door," the sheriff told me. Zimmer introduced us. "Deputy Pennington, this is Captain Hargrow from the state police in Madison. I've asked the captain to advise us on the Prager murders."

Hargrow was a thick, round man with thin brown hair that, at his age, should have been turning gray. Gave his hair a dirty look. He had a weather-beaten face. The face of a fisherman. A hunter. A smoker. The hardened face of an experienced cop. A detective, rumpled suit and all.

"Advise us?"

"The second murder complicates things," Zimmer told me.

"How so?" I asked. "They were both killed by the same man."

Hargrow lit a cigarette. "Sit down, Deputy Pennington." He offered me a smoke.

"No, thanks. I quit."

"Yes, but you still bum one now and then."

I took a seat in the hardwood chair in front of the sheriff's desk. "Where did you hear that?"

He didn't answer.

Zimmer dropped into his chair behind the desk. He slipped on his sunglasses and glared at me. Didn't say a word the rest of the meeting. In my entire life I had never seen anybody occupy that chair, that desk, but our Sheriff Fats. I really felt no animosity toward Zimmer, except when I saw him sitting behind that desk, leaning back in that chair, the way Fats used to do. Only when Sheriff Fats sat and glared, it came off as authority. With Zimmer, it seemed more like arrogance.

Hargrow did all of the talking. He remained standing beside the desk. That way he could look down at me. He smoked his cigarette and rifled through a file. I was supposed to believe it was my file. This was no meeting. It was an interrogation. And this is how I remember it:

"Your name, Deputy Pennington, is well known to us down in Madison."

"Really? I've never heard of you."

"So you're convinced one man did both murders. Do you have any suspects?"

"Not at this time."

"Any ideas?"

"I think it's an outsider."

"Why would an outsider come to Kickapoo Falls and assassinate a husband and a wife, five days apart? Isn't it more likely their killer is someone they knew? Or is there something you're not telling us? Come now, Deputy, we're all on the same side."

"Are we? Then why are you here? I mean, why are you really here?"

"I'm here to determine whether you're fit to continue with this investigation . . . and then make a recommendation to Sheriff Zimmer."

"Why would I not be fit to continue?"

"What was your relationship with Lisa Prager?"

"We were friends."

"More than friends?"

"We were friends."

"Did you ever have sexual intercourse with Lisa Prager?"

"No."

"Perhaps I phrased the question wrong. Did you have a sexual relationship with Lisa Prager?"

"I never once had sex with Lisa Prager."

"Would you be willing to take a lie detector test?"

"Yes. In fact, that would be a good idea."

"Would you mind if we examined your rifles?"

"Not at all."

"Would you mind if we searched your house?"

"Go right ahead."

"You own a cabin on Lake Michigan, don't you?"

"Yes."

"Where?"

"Door County . . . out on the island."

"How about if we searched that?"

"Help yourself. I'll leave you the keys. You'll need a boat."

"You're a pretty cool customer, Deputy Pennington."

"I've been interrogated by better than you."

"That's right. You were held by the Germans for a while, weren't you?"

"You have my records."

"Yes, I do. Says here, after the war, you spent a year with Army Intelligence. What did you do for them?"

"That information is classified. I was ordered never to discuss it."

"Fair enough. How about during the war?"

"I served with the Army Rangers. Parachute Battalion."

"And what was your role with the Rangers . . . specifically?"

"I was a driver for high-ranking officers."

"Yes, but weren't these drivers often the company sniper?"

"Sometimes."

"You were in fact a sniper, weren't you, Deputy?"

"That was my role in combat."

"What kind of rifle did you use?"

"A Springfield . . . M1903 A4."

"With a telescope?"

"The army issued snipers a Weaver hunting scope, but I found the Unertl scope used by the Marine Corps to be more accurate. I modified my rifle."

"You had to be different?"

"I had to be accurate."

"How accurate?"

"In the Rangers . . . one hundred percent hits at six hundred fifty yards, and ninety percent hits at eleven hundred yards. One shot, one kill. You don't hit the target . . . you don't get the job."

"And what did you determine was the distance from the boulder in the hills where you found the shell casing . . . to the cab of Frank Prager's locomotive?"

"I put it at six hundred yards."

"That's a difficult shot."

"Not really."

"And this modified sniper rifle of yours fired a 30.06, isn't that correct?"

"Any cop knows that. Quit playing stupid, you're annoying me."

"A 30.06. The same kind of shell found in the hills above the train station."

"What's your point?"

"My point is, you're the only person in town who had a motive to kill both Frank *and* Lisa Prager."

"What was my motive?"

"You were in love with his wife . . . so you shot the husband. Wife found out you killed her husband . . . she threatened to go to the sheriff. You shot the wife. Happens every day."

"It may happen every day down in Madison, but I'm afraid crime in Kickapoo County is never that simple."

"Where were you when Frank Prager was shot?"

"I was on patrol."

"Where exactly?"

"I was coming through the hills."

"And where were you last night . . . about one thirty?"

"Home in bed."

"Any alibi?"

"No . . . I sleep alone."

"So there is no way to prove you didn't do both killings."

"There is no evidence I did. Besides, I wouldn't kill that way. Everybody would know it was me."

"How would you kill, Deputy?"

"I'd toss a grenade through your window . . . then go back to bed. Are we done here?"

10 | THE GUNN CLUB

It was during the Gilded Age that railroad baron Jay Albany Gunn came west and ran his Milwaukee Road right through the heart of Kickapoo Falls, ensuring the small town's survival. The trains from the east barreled out of thick pines, sailed across a tall trestle bridge spanning the Wisconsin River, then traversed a second bridge at the top of Main Street before settling into the depot on the edge of town. A sweet deal for any American community. Mr. Gunn fell in love with the rugged beauty of the area and built a sprawling hunting lodge above the Dells. It was this lodge that became the Kickapoo Gunn Club.

Wisconsin is an Indian word. It means land of dark, rushing waters. Others followed the ambitious railroad baron to the land where, it was said, wave and rock and tall pine meet. Some, like Gunn, came for the investment opportunities. Others came for their health. Even back then, the rolling hills and the dramatic Dells were being touted as God's country. So the genteel families of the East came to the northern woods and drank of its waters. God only knows how healthy they found the bears and the mosquitoes.

German immigrants liked the water and the land of Wisconsin so much, they built their great breweries. The breweries generated great wealth. The railroads generated even greater wealth. It was this incongruous conglomerate of wealthy people, in their rush to opulence, who founded the Kickapoo Gunn Club.

The club became the exclusive domain of the Midwest's social elite, drawing patrons from as far away as Chicago, Milwaukee, and St. Paul. On weekends, they hosted foxhunts and pheasant hunts. They sponsored an annual regatta on Lake Michigan. Several times a year they threw lavish parties, the only time when nonmembers were allowed to enter the opulent club set down on a cliff over the river.

From the very beginning, there were nasty rumors about the Gunn Club. The most persistent rumor was that the members were a fraternity of Freemasons. The initiation ceremony was said to include a secrecy oath that carried the death penalty. That they practiced dark rituals—everything from orgies, the most common rumor, to conspiracies to grab land, fix prices, and even commit murder. In nineteenth-century Wisconsin, nearly every county sheriff was a Mason, as were many judges. It was alleged these public servants valued their Masonic obligations over their oaths of office. This may have been true, since even the lowest-rank Mason faced a gruesome death penalty for violating his oath. As a result, an anti-Mason political movement took root, sweeping all Masons from public office by the dawn of the twentieth century. It was then, the rumor went, that the secret society went underground—changing its name, if not its ways.

The problem with the Freemason theory was twofold. Builders of the great citadels and cathedrals, the Masons were, for the most part, a secretive but noble fraternity. And the only two things a Mason would not tolerate from a brother, the only exceptions to their secrecy oath, were treason and murder. Was it possible that in the state of Wisconsin this secret society had evolved into something its founding fathers would not recognize?

Up until the wheat field killings, I had given little thought to the club. To me, they were just a bunch of rich, midwestern white guys who hunted, played golf, and cheated on their wives. But now, for the second time in two years, I found myself a suspect in double homicides—and like the wheat field case, I was beginning to feel the invisible but heavy hand of the Kickapoo Gunn Club.

After the war, Gunn Club members carved a new golf course out of the big woods by the river. A magnificent Frank Lloyd Wright–inspired clubhouse was built on a hill above the sixteenth green. This clubhouse replaced the old lodge as the center of activity.

Sheriff Fats had been a long-standing member of the private club. In the end, it may have gotten him killed. Webster Sprague, a once powerful congressman, was gone, too—so that it was hard to say who was really calling the shots out at the club. If the rumors were true, and I had no reason to believe they weren't, J. D. Zimmer was also a member of the infamous club. These not-so-secret members, who were supposedly sworn to secrecy, made it known they were not keen on the idea of handing the most powerful position in the county, the office of sheriff, over to a nonmember and an outspoken critic. But would these clowns go as far as murder? Based on what had happened during the wheat field case, I believed the answer to that question to be "yes." Still, wouldn't it have been a lot easier to just kill me? Why kill Frank Prager? And why Lisa?

11 | THE ROAD TO MADISON

It was my day off. Perched behind the wheel of a new Chevy Biscayne with a powerful 409-cubic-inch engine, I skirted the resplendent golf course of the Kickapoo Gunn Club. Sped through the countryside toward the rolling hills. I always did my best thinking on the road. The September sun was keeping me company. As I drove the beguiling back roads, it shined its bright light on some of the richest farmland in North America. I sped past herds of dairy cows grazing before red barns. I passed acres and acres of corn. Wheat, barley, and sunflowers were sky-high, reaching for the heavens. Soon it would be harvest time.

My grandfather, dirt poor, arrived in Kickapoo County from the island of Nantucket. He first tried his hand farming the chocolate-brown earth. But Grandpa failed the land, as they say here, so he traded that land for a parcel of land in town, where he built Pennington Shoes and Boots on Main Street, directly across from Courthouse Square. Though I sold the business after Dad died, the shoe store is still there today. The Pennington name still hangs above the door.

Around a bend in the road, I caught the glimmer of empty beer bottles reflecting the morning light. They had been discarded along the highway. It was something we did well in Wisconsin. We made beer. And we drank it. But by 1962, we still hadn't figured out what to do with the empties. I brought the police cruiser to a stop. Threw it into reverse, and backed up to the litter. It was something Sheriff Fats had taught us. He always kept a bag for trash in the trunk of his squad. Fats was proud of Kickapoo County. Whenever he spotted beer bottles along the side of the road, he'd stop and clean up the mess. We deputies followed suit. There were never orders to pick up trash. No policy. It was just something we did.

I found a half dozen bottles of Schlitz, which, along with Miller and Pabst, was bottled in Milwaukee. I picked up an empty bottle of Old Style, brewed over in La Crosse. And just for good measure, a couple bottles of Leinenkugel's were littered about, which came out of Chippewa Falls. Must have been one hell of a party. I gathered up the bottle caps, tossed them all into a bag in the trunk, and got back on the road.

I left the valley farms behind and drove into the morainal hills at speeds topping seventy miles an hour. The '62 Biscayne offered to police had a 409, 4-barrel package putting out 380 horses with a two-speed Powerglide transmission. It could hit sixty miles an hour in 6.6 seconds. Top speed was 124 miles an hour. I confess, it was not the safest way to navigate the narrow, winding highway leading to Wisconsin's capital, but damn, those speeds had a way of clearing my head.

Were the killings of Frank and Lisa Prager related? They had to be.

Did the man who had called her on the phone kill them both? Probably.

Did this man have anything to do with me?

I was on my way to Madison to see Marilou Stephens, a professor of psychology at the university. Marilou could talk intelligently on almost any subject. The psychology of sex. The psychology of the criminal mind. The psychology of war and football. "Did you know," she once told me during a Badger game at Camp Randall Stadium, "that American football was invented at the East Coast schools by the sons of Civil War veterans? Theory has it, they were trying to emulate the wartime heroics of their fathers."

Interesting. But it was a different theory I wanted to run past the brainy professor. I carried with me to Madison an idea so frightening that I had been unwilling to think about it for years, much less talk about it. It was that same idea that struck me like a sniper's bullet as I stood in the hills that day staring down at the cab of Frank Prager's locomotive. Perhaps, just perhaps, a ghost from my past had returned to haunt me. Or hunt me. If that was the case, it was no wonder I was a suspect. I feared this killer was but a specter of myself.

So I had put my investigation on two different tracks. The Gunn Club was somehow using these killings to get to me before the election. Or somehow, somebody buried deep in my past had been resurrected and slipped into Kickapoo Falls, bringing with him fear, suffering, and death.

The professor and I met at Marco's coffee shop, which had become our favorite hangout. It was strategically located on State Street, halfway between the capitol building and the UW campus. I popped a quarter into the jukebox and sheepishly selected four Patsy Cline numbers, and a song by Roy Orbison. I took a seat in a high-backed booth. White tables. Red plastic seat cushions. The entire place had a collegiate charm. Marilou smiled at me from across the table. Two Cherry Cokes stood between us. I smiled back.

Another thing to know about Marilou Stephens, the woman I called Lou. I considered her a knockout. She was a brunette, with bright brown eyes and a perfectly toothy smile that always disarmed me on sight. I guessed she was older than me by maybe a year or two. In those days, a man didn't ask. It was just something I sensed. She was not married, and I never asked about that, either. We had become friends during the wheat field investigation after she had offered me some bold insights on voyeurism. Profiled my killer. Not all of the psycho mumble jumble she had laid on me during that case came to pass, but enough of it turned out to be dead-on so that I would forever seek out her advice and trust her judgment. Was there something more that I longed for in Marilou Stephens? Looking back, it's really hard to say. I valued her friendship.

"So you're going to church with the President?"

"You heard?"

"It was in the Madison paper," she told me. "The Cathedral of Saint Paul . . . I've heard that's quite a church."

"I'm looking forward to seeing it again."

"Yes, I forgot. You went to seminary school in St. Paul."

"Just one year."

"Father Pennington." She pretended to taste the two words as they rolled off her tongue. "I like it."

"For the sake of the Church, I'm glad I ended up Deputy Pennington."

"And the President?" she asked.

"I'm surprised he remembered me. The last time I saw him, he looked anything but presidential."

I've told this story before, but I tell it again. Mostly because I love it so.

The valley was still sleeping in snow. In fact, it was snowing that morning. March of 1960. The Wisconsin primary was coming up, but nobody was talking about it. Other than the usual small-town gossip, nobody was talking about much of anything. The dying days of winter. I was just coming on duty, about to step into my squad when I saw him standing in the middle of Courthouse Square. He was watching me, as if he wanted to talk. It was seven thirty in the morning. We were the only two people in the square. Saying he looked out of place would be an understatement. He looked like a cross between an athlete and a movie star. He also looked lonely, forlorn, and a little bit lost. I started across the square, if just to say hello. "Good morning," I said to him. "Can I help you with anything?"

His head was bare in the falling snow, giving him something of an angelic look. He wore a black wool coat over a Brooks Brothers suit. Black leather gloves and burgundy scarf. "My name is John Kennedy," he said, extending his hand, "I'm running for President in the primary." I shook his hand. Then he reached into his coat pocket and pulled out a campaign button. Gave it to me.

The young senator from Massachusetts told me he'd driven up from Madison to speak to a civics class at the high school. "Those kids don't vote," I told him.

"No, but their parents do."

I looked around the square. Nobody cared that he was in town. Not even the *Republic.* Personally, I'd been leaning toward Hubert Humphrey in the primary, but only because Humphrey was from neighboring Minnesota.

"Where is the, ah, infamous Gunn Club?" Senator Kennedy wanted to know.

"It's on a golf course . . . out on the river."

"I heard Mr. Nixon has been there."

"Yeah, he spoke at some shindig they had last summer."

"I suspect my, ah, invitation got lost in the mail."

I thought that was funny. In the summertime, I was used to dealing with tourists with that lost look on their faces. So I never forgot his calm and his composure, and his sense of humor, in what must have seemed to the future President a mournful little town. Empty streets. Falling snow. Cold and desolate Kickapoo Falls. I told him he might find some early risers at Lorraine's Café, across from the square. Other than that, I don't remember exactly what else we said that morning. We didn't talk about being veterans, or being Catholic, or anything like that. I do remember watching him walk away toward Lorraine's Café in search of a hand to shake. I never heard from him again, until the White House invitation arrived, asking me to come worship with him in St. Paul.

When I'd finished telling Marilou the story of the deputy and the President, she asked if the recent murders in Kickapoo Falls might affect my plans.

"I'm going to wrap it up before then," I said, a bit too emphatically.

"Seems for women, you're a dangerous man to know, Deputy Pennington."

"Yes. Who would have thought it?"

"That's all right. Women like an element of danger in their men."

"Is that true?"

She smiled. "Maybe." Marilou sipped her Cherry Coke. Eyed me across the table with a sweet touch of concern. "Some of my police friends here in Madison have been following the news from Kickapoo County."

"Yes, I had the pleasure of speaking with one of them. A Captain Hargrow."

"I know him. Anyway, they think you might be too controversial to be elected sheriff."

"What do your police friends suggest I do?"

"You could drop out of the race. That would remove your investigation from politics. It would also lift the political cloud from your trip to St. Paul. You're still young. There will be other elections. Solve this case, add a friend in the White House, you'll be even stronger next time around."

I had run the same scenario through my head on the drive down. So I laid out to Marilou the quandary I'd laid out to myself only an hour before. "The problem is this . . . J. D. Zimmer is relatively young, too. Fats held the sheriff's job for almost forty years. It's not an office with a high turnover. This may be my best and last shot."

"And if you go through life a deputy sheriff, would that be so bad?"

"You're asking a man not to better himself."

"What other options have you?"

I thought long and positive. "Solve these murders. Arrest a killer. Go to St. Paul. Meet the President. Come home and win the election."

She smiled at that. "It's hard to argue with your 'can do' spirit. How can I help?"

"I need some of that psychological insight stuff."

"What's the subject?"

"Evil," I said. "Unmitigated, unapologetic evil."

"Give me an example."

"Nazi Germany."

"Wow. What is it you're looking for?"

"An understanding of the men behind it. What kind of men are they? What makes them tick?"

"You make it sound as if they still walk among us."

"And if they do? We can't catch them if we don't understand them."

"Let me get this straight, Deputy Pennington, you want me to somehow penetrate the conscience of people intimately associated with total evil? I'm not sure they have a conscience."

"How did they outsmart so many people for so many years?"

"Intelligence and morality do not walk hand in hand. They never have. The truth is, intelligence without morality is extremely dangerous. In many ways, the Nazis were brilliant. But that still doesn't mean they have a conscience, as you and I know it. You're searching for a motive for their evil. I'm not sure there is one. There is a theory, generous in spirit, that all children are born good. Somehow society makes them evil."

"Do you believe that?"

"No. I think some people are just born evil. In Germany, these evil people all came together at the same time and at the same place."

"And with the Third Reich in ashes," I asked her, "why would they carry on?"

She sipped her soda pop, thought a minute, and then leaned forward. "If you could crawl into a time tunnel and go back, ten years, twenty years . . . would you make the same bad choices? The same mistakes? No . . . your conscience wouldn't allow it. You know the consequences. But they would. They'd do it all over again. Only next time, no more Mister Nice Guy."

Ignoring her dark sense of humor, I asked, "Monsters? Simple as that?"

The professor gave me the stare of a disapproving mother. A disappointed teacher. "Do you think they're going to apologize? Change their ways? They don't have it in them. The reason there is no treatment for evil, is because evil people don't feel they have a problem. But I'll tell you what they will do, given the chance. They'll kill again. Because that's something they know. That's something they like. When violence becomes pleasure, the worst kind of evil is born."

The dreadful thought that the killings in Kickapoo Falls weren't over had weighed heavily on my mind.

"What do these Nazis have to do with your case?" Marilou wanted to know.

"Maybe nothing," I told her. "I'm just trying to understand the evil that would coldly assassinate two innocent people. One at his job . . . and another in her home."

She sighed, slightly baffled. "You know, ever since I met you, Deputy Pennington, you've seemed to me to be a man in search of a moral compass."

"I've sometimes had a hard time separating the good guys from the bad guys."

"Do you sometimes feel like the bad guy?"

"I think that I've sometimes done some bad things for the greater good . . . and that haunts me."

We sipped our Cokes, exchanged bashful glances, and watched the afternoon sun change the shape of the dark shadows along State Street. That I was in a struggle with my own tortured conscience was obvious to my friend Marilou Stephens. As much as we wanted to move on, the war haunted us all. It was especially haunting to those of us in Kickapoo Falls.

12 | CAMP KICKAPOO: *The Arrival*

From the day he volunteered for the YMCA prisoner's aide job until the day he died, two years after the war's end, my father was called Mr. Pennington. You might interpret this as a sign of respect, but it was quite the opposite. A form of shunning. Suddenly, half of the town stopped using his first name and began coldly addressing him as Mr. Pennington. They couldn't boycott Dad's business. Pennington Shoes and Boots was the only shoe store in town, and during the war years shoes and boots were a valuable commodity. So they voiced their displeasure with him in the only way they knew how:

"Good morning, Mr. Pennington."

"Put that on my account, Mr. Pennington."

"Good day, Mr. Pennington."

This subtle form of shunning continued through my own life, even though I came home from the war a wounded veteran. For years, I was simply called Deputy Pennington. The more malicious folks in town, or the more ignorant, still addressed me as Mr. Pennington, never able to forget that my father had once lent a kind hand to German prisoners of war.

So why would a German prisoner come to Wisconsin and chop trees—help the American war effort? Their incentive was income. Standard POW pay, when working, was eighty cents a day, roughly based on the rate paid to U.S. privates in 1941. Prisoners could not be forced to work more than ten hours a day, six days a week. A savings account was set up for each prisoner, and cigarettes, candy, and sundry items were for sale in the camp canteen.

As the YMCA representative, my father accompanied the army captain in charge of the new camp to the county courthouse, to the office of Sheriff Fats, to meet the big man and brief him on security issues. Or what the army passed off as security.

"Let me get this straight," said the burly sheriff to the young captain. Fats slowly rocked back and forth in the chair behind his desk. "You're going to give a bunch of goddamned Nazis saws and axes and send them into the woods six days a week with only two or three guards . . . in my county?"

"Yes, sir, we are."

"Over my dead body."

Back then, Sheriff Fats may have been the most powerful and most intimidating man in Kickapoo County, but during the war years he was no match for the United States Army. And in the end, he knew it. He looked over at my father. "And you're going give them soccer balls and guitars?"

"And books."

The sheriff shook his head in disbelief. "Well, if this don't beat all. Your son is over there fighting, and you want to help these people?"

"As I understand it, Sheriff, there's a man over in Germany doing the same thing for our boys."

Sheriff Fats, himself a combat veteran of the First World War, wanted to say something about that, but Dad thought out of respect for me, the sheriff held his tongue.

It's important to note here that of all those in town who shunned my father, Sheriff Fats was never one of them, perhaps because of his own war experience. He treated my father with kindness and respect until the day he died. When I came home from Europe, a little bit lost and a little bit broken, Fats hired me as a deputy. Took me under his wing.

With regards to the camp, the biggest fear in town concerned escape. That day at the county courthouse, the army captain tried to assure our skeptical sheriff that most of the German prisoners had demonstrated no desire to flee. For many, life in the camps was far more tolerable than the war in Europe. Above all, there was no place to go. The long train ride to the camps had shown them the size of the United States. No sanctuaries awaited escaped Germans. Fleeing east or west would bring an escapee to the edge of an ocean. To the north lay Canada, to the south, Mexico. Both those countries had pledged to apprehend any escaped POW.

"And if one should happen to escape?" asked the sheriff.

"We'll post army guards in the woods wherever two trails cross," the captain assured him. "According to army policy, if guards spot an escapee they are to shout 'Halt.' If that fails to stop him, they are to fire a warning shot. As a last resort, they are to shoot to wound."

Sheriff Fats called the army policy "shoot-and-scoot." "Since they already have an ax and a free pass," he said, "why don't we pack the little devils a picnic lunch?"

Nevertheless, on a warm spring day in 1943, a train from Camp McCoy pulled into town. It was a train like no other that had ever come through the hills. Armed troops lined the road along the tracks. Townspeople crowded the platform. Stood on car tops for a peek. Hitler's supermen, the desert warriors of Field Marshal Rommel had reached their final destination. Kickapoo Falls, Wisconsin.

"I had expected to see giants," my father told me. "Tall, blond Germans. I thought they would be perfect specimens. But you know what, they were just boys . . . tired and hungry and some of them sick."

The weary prisoners emerged from the coaches, dirty, unshaven, and all looking a little malnourished. Most of them shouldered bundles of personal effects. One even carried a violin. They wore the sun-bleached, shrunken remnants of their gray wool uniforms with visible pride. Many of those uniforms had been exposed to the wet snows and freezing ice storms of the Russian front before the long journey to the blazing heat of North Africa. This was the uniform of the once proud Afrika Korps. Some of the prisoners had fought with Rommel at Tobruk and El Alamein in the days when the Desert Fox stood before the gates of Egypt. Now his men stood before the train station in Kickapoo Falls. The prisoners formed a single-file line with a fair amount of discipline and then began the three-mile hike to the logging camp up in the hills.

13 | THAT DAY IN THE SQUARE

Running for county sheriff was not like running for Congress, or any other elected office. The sole issue was law enforcement. How adept were you at maintaining the peace and catching the bad guys? For forty years in Kickapoo County it was a nonissue. Fats was the sheriff. And Sheriff Fats was the law. Crime was low, and the quality of life was high. For lawbreakers, justice was swift and harsh.

But things began to change after the wheat field case. Not only with the death of Sheriff Fats, but with the realization that evil lived among us in Kickapoo Falls. Yes, there were outside forces at work during that investigation, but many of our troubles were home grown. As early as 1962, there seemed to be a rebellion growing among our young people. The automatic trust that once had come with a badge and a gun was gone. People were rightly suspicious of the sheriff's department. I was being portrayed as the old guard, while J. D. Zimmer was casting himself as a fresh face.

On the grounds of Courthouse Square stood a Civil War cannon that had been dragged through battlefields by Wisconsin's famous Iron Brigade. The cannon was proudly positioned at a slightly erect angle, pointing across Oak Street. The more patriotic folks in town called the cannon the Big Popper. More cynical folks in town called it the Big Penis. Whether it was a symbol of our historic pride, or just another phallic symbol, the old cannon had stood guard over Kickapoo Falls for almost a hundred years. I only mention it because the cannon unofficially became my campaign headquarters. It was on the park benches beneath the cast-iron cannon where I would informally meet with supporters and discuss the politics of the day.

On one clear and outwardly peaceful day I huddled with my fellow deputy, Hess, who was slowly moving my way on the election. He was assisting me on the homicide investigations, and we were ostensibly on our lunch break. We were also being somewhat rebellious. Sheriff Zimmer had let it be known that he did not like to see deputies in full uniform eating their boxed lunches in Courthouse Square. Supposedly it made us look lazy, or something. So as the election neared, a deputy seen openly munching a ham on rye in the middle of the square was something of a political statement. Which is why I was somewhat surprised, and pleased, that Hess had joined me. We dined on sandwiches from Lorraine's Café, sipped our sodas, and talked politics and murder.

"Look," said Hess, "I know you didn't shoot the Pragers. Zimmer knows you didn't shoot the Pragers, and down in Madison they know you didn't shoot the Pragers."

"But?"

"But Zimmer is having it both ways. He's got you doing the legwork on the real investigation, while at the same time he floats it around town that you're a suspect in the shootings. I don't like it. Makes me wonder about our appointed sheriff."

"So what do I do?"

"Well, it would help if somebody took a shot at you."

"That's your idea?"

We were in the final days of summer. The weather was cooling. The leaves on the trees were beginning to blush. Still, the sun was bright and warm, masking the tension in the air. September in the Midwest. The perfect month.

"What did your friend in Madison have to say?"

"About the election?"

"Yeah."

I cleared my throat with a swig of Pepsi. "She thought it might be wiser if I dropped out of the race. It would remove politics from the investigation, and from my trip to St. Paul."

"I don't like getting my politics from women, but she has a point. It's not going to look good if right in the middle of a murder investigation you run off to St. Paul and play footsie with the President."

"It's a church service."

"It's a Catholic Mass. Do you think that's lost on people here? You tie Zimmer to the Gunn Club . . . Zimmer ties you to the Catholic Church. Both of them are seen as rich and secretive organizations with self-serving agendas."

"I haven't sensed any anti-Catholicism."

"Oh, please," said Hess, clearly exasperated. "We could pack every Catholic in Kickapoo County into one pew of the Presbyterian church . . . and still squeeze in the few Democrats."

The thing to know about Courthouse Square was its central location. I mean, the square was smack-dab in the middle of Kickapoo Falls. Main Street ran north of the square. Third Avenue ran south of the square. Oak Street connected the two. The three streets were lined with commerce, two- and three-story buildings, making the square the center of activity. Visible from all corners. That's important, because of what happened that day.

"So who is it?" Hess asked.

"Who is what?"

"I'm a cop too, you know. My gut feeling is that you have a suspect in these shootings, and you're not sharing it. Zimmer thinks so too, and so do the state police down in Madison."

"What else does Zimmer think?"

"Zimmer thinks you're sitting on the killer so that you can make the arrest. An October surprise. Grab the glory. Take all of the credit. Win yourself the sheriff's office."

"What do you think?"

"I don't think you're that smart, and I don't think you're that dumb. So who's our man?"

I still found it difficult to attach words to my thoughts. That's how scared I was.

Hess sensed my hesitation. "Look, Pennington, there's a killer out there. The least that we can do is cover each other's back. I can't cover you if I don't know what I'm looking for."

I took a deep breath. Thought long and hard before I spoke. "Let's say I did some things during the war that I'm not proud of . . ."

"You and a million other GIs."

"Okay, but now let's say somebody from the war wants to get back at me."

"How does killing Frank and Lisa get back at you?"

"From what I can tell so far, Frank and Lisa only have one link to the killer. Me."

"How so?"

"Let's suppose during the war, I killed a train engineer with a high-powered rifle . . ."

"Ah, Christ . . . I hope he was a Nazi."

"Now suppose, years later, our killer shows up in Kickapoo Falls. He learns that not only do I know a train engineer, but that I'm a special friend of the engineer's wife."

"How special?"

"Let's just say 'special.' I'm also a deputy sheriff in charge of homicide investigations, and I'm running for county sheriff, with a fair shot of winning. Tell me, Deputy Hess, if you had a deadly score to settle with me, what would you do?"

Hess munched on his sandwich while chewing on the thought. "First, I'd shoot the train engineer with a high-powered rifle, just like you did. Let you know I'm in town. Then I'd shoot your special friend, just so you'd know it's personal. Of course, eventually, I'd shoot you."

No sooner had Hess spoken those words than the first shot rang out. I heard the ricochet off of the cannon, then the glass bottle of Pepsi in my hand exploded. The second shot also ricocheted off the cast-iron cannon, but this shot hit Hess in the back of his shoulder. Now I was flat on my stomach with my revolver drawn. My left hand was bleeding. I looked back at Hess, who was on the ground, bleeding, but still reaching for his weapon.

"Son of a bitch!" he yelled.

"Are you all right?" I screamed.

"Yes, go!"

I was up and running. Since the Kickapoo National Bank was right across Oak Street, my first thought was of robbery. My second thought was sniper. Cops know gunshots, and the two shots thrown our way were simple .22s. In fact, Hess was up and running behind me, with a small-caliber bullet in his back. People in the square were ducking behind trees for cover. There was a lot of screaming. I could hear children crying. Folks on the street were pointing me toward the roof of the bank building. I sprinted around the back, gun in hand.

The Kickapoo National Bank Building was one of those Greek Revival things built before the Depression. It had a façade of marble pillars and a half-dome roof. In the alley was a metal-rung ladder leading to that roof. It would have been impossible to climb the ladder with a gun in my right hand and my left hand bleeding profusely. So I took my chances. Holstered my revolver and started up the ladder. Hess, in even worse shape, was coming up behind me.

When I reached the roof, I again drew my revolver. I could see sheriff's deputies pouring out of the county courthouse across the square. Like most business districts in small towns, the buildings were all connected. I spotted two suspects moving north across the rooftops, crouching down behind the generators, ventilators, chimneys, and other obstacles that litter commercial rooftops. When I'd made sure Hess had safely reached the roof, I leveled my gun and sent a shot their way.

Back then we holstered .38/.44 heavy-duty revolvers. That's a .38 caliber revolver on a .44 frame. It was designed to shoot a .38 special cartridge. The .44 frame was needed to handle the heavy recoil. The gun could stop a Mack truck. The explosion was deafening. But I confess, my proficiency with a rifle did not carry over to revolvers. I missed the bastards. Now our two suspects were up and running across the rooftops, Hess and I in hot pursuit.

The town was pretty much divided between town kids and farm kids. It had been that way forever. The farm kids were angels, and the town kids were devils. We were chasing a pair of devils. I put their ages at fifteen.

Kickapoo Falls is not New York City. In New York, according to the movies, the bad guys could run across rooftops for miles. In Kickapoo Falls you could only run one block. The two kids were about to escape down a metal ladder when they saw me and Hess leveling our guns at their pimple-faced heads. With that, they dropped their .22 rifle and threw up their hands.

They were dressed in T-shirts and blue jeans. Reeked of cigarettes and beer. The acne on their red faces looked ready to explode. They could see blood dripping from the two deputies before them. They could see the fire in our eyes.

"We didn't mean to hit anybody . . . honest."

"We just thought it would be a hoot to scare you."

"A hoot," screamed Hess. "I've got a bullet in my back, you little shit." With that, the big round deputy grabbed the *hoot* kid by the hair with one hand and by the seat of the pants with the other and with half of the town watching, literally sent him flying from the roof. The kid sailed off of the two-story building like a misfired rocket and landed atop the trash cans in the alley below. He rolled onto the blacktop, groaning in pain. As I've stated before, justice in Kickapoo County was swift and harsh.

Hess started for the other kid, but I held the angry deputy back with my bloody hand. "I've got him," I told him. "It's over." I was mad too, but I got the kid face down on the hot tar roof and put the handcuffs on him.

Other deputies arrived on the scene.

But something else happened to me that day, even before the phone call. I can remember standing on the rooftop and looking out over Courthouse Square. I saw my hometown in a new light. A harsh light. Never before had I realized how vulnerable we all were. How easy it would be to slip into our wonderfully free little world and terrorize the hell out of us. We were easy targets. Sitting ducks. Yes, now more than ever, I feared a monster was loose in Kickapoo Falls. A monster partly of my own making.

14 | A VOICE FROM THE PAST: *First Call*

I had a bungalow at the end of Ash Street, at the bottom of the hill where the tracks followed the river out of town. I went to sleep at night to the singsong of train whistles and steel wheels. The music of people going places. When you live alone, sleep is one of the things you enjoy most. I used to fantasize about sleeping with a woman. In my wilder dreams, I was sleeping with a different woman every night. Sometimes multiple beauties would crawl into bed with me. On those crazy nights, I'd drift off to sleep with my arms wrapped around two pillows, instead of one. Anyway, since Lisa was killed, I'd had a hard time sleeping at all. But the incident in the square had exhausted me. My hand was bandaged. My brain was fried. That night I curled up with a pillow that was just a pillow and drifted into a deep slumber.

I couldn't have been out more than an hour when the phone rang. In fact, I was sleeping so well I at first thought the incessant ringing was in my dreams. I had dozed off in Wolf Pass with a rifle in my arms. A train was coming. An alarm clock was going off, giving away my position. I had to wake and aim. Kill the clock. I shot up in bed.

But the train I heard was just the old Milwaukee Road on the run from Madison to La Crosse. The rifle in my arms was a ratty old pillow. The alarm clock was silent. My phone was ringing. I grabbed at it. "Hello . . ."

"Herr Pennington, I very much enjoyed the show in the square."

"What show?"

"What an entertaining little town you have."

"It's one o'clock in the morning . . . Who is this?"

"Did I wake you?"

"Yes, you woke me . . . Who is this?"

"I suspect you know who this is. I also suspect that you've known for some time that I was coming."

"We have a bad connection. . . . Where are you calling from? . . . I can hear cars."

"That is funny, because that is what Lisa said. What a beautiful woman she was. You should have seen her beauty through a Unertl scope. Did you know that she stripped for me? She came to the window in the moonlight with her red hair, and her fluffy blouse, and her tight pants. Rarely have I seen such beauty in a woman. Tell me, Herr Pennington, did she ever strip for you?"

"What do you want? Why are you here? What are you after?"

"You're awake now. You sound nervous, Herr Pennington. Are you scared?"

"Yes, I'm scared."

"Good. Did you know that your Kickapoo Falls once hosted a prisoner-of-war camp for my countrymen?"

"Yes, my father worked there."

"So I was told. I hope my countrymen enjoyed having a Pennington in their camp as much as I enjoyed having a Pennington in mine. But there is a nasty little rumor in your Kickapoo Falls . . . that you are incapable of satisfying the young women of your town. Is this the truth?"

"Why did you kill those people?"

"Did ever I tell you of Anaka? Sweet Anaka. She worked for me at the

camp, before you arrived. She was the most lovely young woman you could ever imagine. Long brown hair. Big brown eyes. Sharp features . . . her nose, her cheeks. She was tall for a woman, with a figure like a Greek goddess. The Jewish princess, I called her. So pretty, yet so innocent. I felt the need to protect her. Almost like a father. One day, God forgive me for this, but on the last night, before she boarded the train, I made her strip for me. I have weaknesses, you know. I ordered her to take off her dress. She stood before me in only her panties. Trembling. I went to her, but I could not bring myself to touch her. She was just too pretty. Too pure. I was wondering . . . is that how you felt with this Lisa?"

"Don't you ever tire of the killing?"

"I could very well ask the same thing of you, Herr Pennington. You have quite a reputation here in this Wisconsin. They say the young deputy leaves a trail of dead bodies in every case that he works. Are we really so different . . . you and I? We were both soldiers. We are both riflemen. We are both Catholic. Perhaps we even share the same weakness toward women."

"Are you going to kill again?"

"Just once more, Herr Pennington. For old times."

15 | THE JUMP: *1944*

It's only exciting when I look back. At the time, I was nothing but scared. In fact, I was terrified. One of those missions a man would only volunteer for in the exuberance and the ignorance of his youth. And I was young. Barely twenty years old. On a moonless summer night, black as coal, I parachuted out the back of an unmarked airplane over the Bavarian Alps. A rifle was strapped across my chest. It was one hell of a dangerous jump. The plane was at barely twenty thousand feet when it dropped me into a valley. From there I was expected to climb a mountain peak, and then descend on the pass. So I was drifting through the night sky in a strong wind. Dangerous, because if I ran with the wind, I'd come down too fast. Be killed on impact. So I did my best to maneuver into the mountain gusts. But still I hit the trees hard, snapped some heavy branches and fell thirty feet to the ground.

I lay there motionless. My rifle and ammunition pack were pressing down on my chest. Flat on my back, I grabbed hold of the crucifix around my neck and began to count my blessings. And my bones. I was alive. My neck wasn't broken. I could sit up. Could wiggle my toes. I was sore as hell, but I was able to stand. I had my rifle. Had my supplies. I guess you could say it was a successful jump. I found a stand of pines away from my drop point, crawled beneath an umbrella of branches, and rested until daylight. I spent most of the night shivering beneath my parachute. I like to think it was from the cold, but I suspect I was shivering out of fear. I thought of all of the men in all of the armies marching toward Berlin. The kid from Kickapoo Falls had reached Nazi Germany ahead of them all. In the morning, warmed by the sun, I began the slow, treacherous climb to Wolf Pass.

It was summertime and the Alps were covered in green, with brilliant displays of mountain flowers. Only the highest peaks were capped with snow. As I struggled up one beautiful ridge after another, it was hard to believe I was traversing a country at war. But there I was, scaling a 7,300-foot-high mountain, carrying a rifle and a full pack, a ruthless enemy awaiting my arrival. I was in a private's uniform. On my head was a simple green field cap. To be captured out of uniform would have labeled me a spy. Someone to be executed.

I forded a cold mountain stream, then scouted yet another sheet of rock for routes of ascent. Though I tried not to think about it, I could not help but wonder if this was the same route the British commandos had taken. If so, was I climbing into a trap? Never to be heard from again?

I had been scaling the towering sandstone cliffs of the Wisconsin Dells since I was a boy, but the stratified cliffs of the Bavarian Alps were a whole other challenge. The precipitous face contained crevices and gullies, loose rock and mud, and even a few waterfalls. Over and over I used a small hammer to fix pitons to the rock. Then I threaded through the rope. I climbed as fast and as silently as was humanly possible. The only sounds I made were boot against rock and occasionally the soft clink of metal.

So what is it a young soldier thinks about when he is totally alone in an enemy country, scaling a scarred and uneven cliff high atop the Alps? Mostly I thought, Why me? The harsh winters of Wisconsin, the skiing cross-country, and the rock climbing had all combined to make me the ideal candidate. I was the quiet loner type, more ignorant than brave. Those kinds of skills—stealth, patience, and discipline—never go out of style on a battlefield. But most of all, I could shoot with the best of them. I had been born with the killer instinct. So it was I found myself alone, inching toward Wolf Pass with just a Springfield for company. I was determined to stop the trains. The German army and a ruthless SS colonel were equally determined to stop me.

The Rangers had given me a compass and the basics of mountain sense. This way to Germany. This way to Austria. This way to Italy. This way to Switzerland. Close the pass. Back up the trains. Then get the hell out of there. If captured, never reveal the aim of your mission. You were a gunner on a B-17. Your plane was hit. You had orders to bail out. That's your story. Stick to it.

Of course, I was young and invincible. I had no intention of being captured. For me, it was Switzerland or bust.

By the time I reached the pass, the sun was already disappearing behind the west face. I had barely an hour to find a good nest and scope out the train station below—to become one with the environment. To look like nothing. When I found what I thought was the perfect cover of tree and rock, when I was happy with the sight lines, I shouldered my rifle and scouted my targets. If I could hold up train traffic for just forty-eight hours, Allied planes would do the rest.

The depot that was situated in the middle of the narrow pass didn't amount to much. After a slow, hard climb to the top, the trains would stop for fuel and water before passing into Austria. There was a headquarters building up a bluff, and what looked like a barracks for the men. Defensive weapons ringed the pass. Germany's best. The antiaircraft guns were Rheinmetall MG 34/41s—considered by many the finest ever produced. These killing machines could fire nine hundred rounds per minute. In the weapons business, the Rheinmetall was a work of art. It was no wonder so many planes had been lost.

I soon located my worst fear mounted on a train car on a sidetrack. The Big Gun. A cannon the size of a small house. Capable of carving up the mountain. I thought of our old Civil War cannon back in Kickapoo Falls. How tiny it now seemed in comparison. Sooner or later they would turn that gun on me. I had to make sure at all times I was protected by rock and earth. More than that, I had to make keeping men off of the cannon a top priority.

Beyond that, Wolf Pass was a sniper's paradise. I had clear shots. I could see, but not be seen. The terrain was too steep and rocky to rush troops up after me. Still, I had to watch for patrols.

Looking back, I guess it makes sense that the first time I laid eyes on the son of a bitch was through a rifle scope. He marched out of the modest headquarters building in full uniform. Walked down to the tracks. I wasn't all that sure about the markings on German uniforms, but he sure looked to be the man in charge. Colonel Christian Wolfgang Stangl. I followed him with my scope. Laid the crosshairs right across his face. But it was getting dark and shadowy. If I had fired then, they'd have been ready for me in the morning. Before returning to the building, I watched the Nazi colonel inspect the tracks. Search the mountainside. At one point, it almost seemed as if he was staring right up at me. It wasn't possible that I could be seen, but even the idea of it sent shivers up my spine. I lowered my rifle and watched him march back to his headquarters, with no idea our paths would be crossing again and again.

I ate my K rations among the rocks and pines and watched the daylight disappear over Wolf Pass. Suddenly, and without warning, a voice, kin to the voice of God, echoed forever through the canyons. "*Es ist ein guter Tag gewesen. Alle Züge waren rechtzeitig.*"

Startled, I turned to look. Focused my binoculars on the train station. It was almost dark.

"*Es gab keine Ereignisse.*"

It was a loudspeaker. A scratchy public address system. What must have been the booming voice of Colonel Stangl addressed the troops guarding the trains. *"Unsere Arbeit hier ist wichtig. Morgen sind wir ein Tag naeher am Sieg. Heil Hitler."*

"Heil Hitler!"

It took a full minute for the booming voice to fade away through the Bavarian Alps. It would echo through my mind for years to come. I grabbed my canteen and helped myself to a long swig of water. In the morning, with the sun to my back, I would take out the first train.

16 | THE BRIT

The morning after a ghostly voice from the past had reached out and touched me, I made a phone call of my own. To an old friend at Army Intelligence in Washington. I don't know what I expected. Maybe FBI and CIA. Even high-ranking military officers. All of them rushing to Kickapoo Falls. A command post. A manhunt the likes of which Wisconsin had never before seen. But for two days, the silence out of Washington was deafening. Three days after that, I was standing at the depot in Kickapoo Falls waiting for some British detective on the train from Chicago. Guess I shouldn't have been too surprised. You have to understand the times. So many men returned home and wanted to forget the war, that the hunt for Nazi war criminals was never a high priority with our government. When I left Army Intelligence a year after the war's end, interest in hunting down escaped Nazis was already on the wane.

The train arrived ahead of schedule and the passengers began pouring off. Well, they began getting off. There weren't a lot of people pouring into Kickapoo Falls at that time of the year. I checked again the Western Union telegram tucked into my shirt pocket. Sent from London, it was dated September 15.

OFFICE OF SHERIFF KICKAPOO COUNTY
APPREHENSION OF NAZI WOLF STANGL IS OF GREAT
CONCERN TO THIS COUNTRY AND THIS BRANCH
WILL BE JOINING YOU SHORTLY IN HUNT FOR SUSPECT
SIGNED DETECTIVE ALEX LACHAPELLE SCOTLAND YARD

Handing me the telegram, Sheriff Zimmer told me the detective had reached Chicago, and that he was catching the first train to Kickapoo Falls. But there was only one train out of Chicago that passed through Kickapoo Falls. If he missed it, he would have to drive, or wait another twenty-four hours. After a few minutes, with no signs of anybody that resembled Sherlock Holmes, my guess was that the gentleman from London had missed his train.

It was early afternoon. The late-summer sun was spilling warm light over the hilltops. I was standing in the shadows of the depot doorway in full uniform, my Stetson cocked over one eye. Maybe I was trying to look like something out of a Hollywood western to impress my British visitor. Perhaps I was trying to restore some bravado to my shaken psyche. More likely I was paranoid of another sniper attack from the hills. It was just about then that I saw this incredible-looking woman step off of the train. I mean, this woman had the most eye-filling head of chestnut hair I'd ever seen. The beautiful hair surrounded a lively and sharply sculpted face. Almost movie-star looks. A trench coat was draped over her arm, revealing a slender, small-breasted woman in an expensive black dress. Way out of place in Kickapoo Falls. I figured she was headed out to the Gunn Club. Their members had a tendency to stick out.

Now she was walking my way. I stood up straight and fixed my hat. I was sure she needed directions. Hell, I'd have driven her out to the damn Gunn Club myself.

"Deputy Pennington, I presume."

"Yes," I said, somewhat baffled. "Who are you?"

"I'm Detective LaChapelle . . . from Scotland Yard."

"You're kidding."

"No."

"The real Scotland Yard?"

"Yes. The Special Branch."

"I'm sorry, I was expecting a man."

"Disappointed?"

"Surprised. I didn't know Scotland Yard had women cops."

She was pretty from the start. What I mean is, she was almost too pretty to be taken seriously. There weren't a lot of women cops back then. Hell, it had taken me awhile to get used to Marilou Stephens giving me advice on criminal investigations—and I was one of the more progressive cops of my era.

" 'Cops,' " she said. "What a wonderful American term."

"You don't say 'cops' in England?"

"Not as a rule. Some people say 'copper.' 'Cop' is American slang."

"Aren't your police officers called 'bobbies,' or something like that?"

"Yes, sometimes, though 'coppers' is more common. Sir Robert Peel founded the London Metropolitan Police in 1829. As a result, his men were called 'bobbies.' "

"Tell me, why is it called Scotland Yard, if it's in London?"

"The original headquarters stood near buildings formerly used to house kings and queens from Scotland. The area became known as Scotland Yard."

"I didn't know that."

"Yes, in answer to your question, Deputy Pennington, Scotland Yard has women cops . . . coming to a country near you."

"You're not only smart . . . you're a smart aleck, too. I like that."

"That fills me with joy, Deputy. And what is the history of your police here in Wisconsin?"

I had to think for a minute. "Well, way back when, the lumberjacks were getting out of control," I told her, "so some big brutes pinned on some tin stars and began busting heads. Thus was born the illustrious Kickapoo County Sheriff's Department."

"Yes, well, that's fascinating."

Her accent and her speech were what I would call *refined.* That means her voice and attitude were just short of irritating. I grabbed hold of her suitcase and started for the squad. "LaChapelle . . . that doesn't sound very British, to me."

"My grandfather was French," she explained. "In studying a map of Wisconsin, I should feel right at home . . . with villages like Fond du Lac, La Crosse, Eau Claire, and Prairie du Chien. I'm guessing the French got here first."

I shrugged my shoulders. "Considering Wisconsin also has towns named Oconomowoc, Oshkosh, Manitowoc, Sheboygan, Wausau, and Milwaukee, not to mention Kickapoo Falls . . . I'm guessing the French got here a distant second. In the end, your forefathers didn't stay long. Didn't like the food, or something. But then you're British . . . you shouldn't be too hard to feed."

"Is that Wisconsin humor?"

"Yes, it is." I threw her suitcase into the trunk. Watched the young detective standing beside the squad car admiring our scenery. "Well, welcome to Wisconsin," I said, walking up beside her.

"The weather is fabulous."

"The leaves are beginning to turn," I told her. "A few weeks from now, it'll be glorious. Then the bottom will drop out."

"Snow?"

"And cold. The price we pay for living in God's country." We stood in silence for a few minutes as she looked around. Admired the hills. I thought of how much different it must have looked from her native London.

"Is it fair to say this is rugged country?"

"Yes, this can be very rugged country."

"I'm afraid I'll be needing some different shoes. Any suggestions?"

I wanted to make a wisecrack about the first thing a woman does when she arrives in a new town is shop for shoes, but I held the thought. "You might try Pennington Shoes and Boots. It's right there on Main Street, a few doors down from the hotel where you'll be staying."

"Pennington Shoes . . . any relation?"

"My father owned it. My grandfather built it."

"So you're one of the famous shoe Penningtons?"

"Don't get smart." I pointed back to the train station. "We might as well begin your tour right here. Victim number one was a train engineer. He poked his head out the locomotive up there . . . and our man shot him right between the eyes from up in the hills. Then he slipped away . . . like a ghost."

"And you think it was Wolf Stangl?"

"No, Detective . . . I *know* it was Wolf Stangl."

I opened the front door of the squad for her and admired her long legs as she climbed in. Then we headed into town. I enjoyed her curiosity as she stared out the window. "Why are you here?" I asked.

"Excuse me?"

"I mean Scotland Yard . . . why did they send someone?"

"My country has a deep and overriding interest in the apprehension of Wolf Stangl."

"The missing commandos?"

"Yes."

I had wanted to ask her—if the hunt for Stangl was so important, why did Scotland Yard send an obviously low-ranking detective? Of course, I say 'detective' to be polite. I was really wondering why they had sent a young woman.

"And you are absolutely sure it was him?"

"Absolutely," I said. "While I was a guest in his camp, we talked often. When he called the other night, we reminisced about old times not forgotten."

"Have you told your superiors yet about Stangl?"

"No. Actually, I was waiting for the big-shot detective from Scotland Yard to arrive. That way, I figured the sheriff would take me more seriously."

"'Big shot' . . . another American colloquialism. But now with the arrival of a woman instead of the Sherlock Holmes–type you were expecting . . . ?"

"Now . . . I'm probably back on the suspect list . . . if I was ever off."

"Why would you be a suspect?"

"Is this strictly between me and you?"

"If we're going to work with one another, Deputy, we absolutely must be trusting."

She turned those baby-blue eyes on me and I melted like a Hershey bar in the hot summer sun. "I had a very special relationship with the woman that was killed. The wife of the engineer."

"I see."

"It's a small town," I reminded her.

"Well, I'm sure it also happens in big towns."

I turned off Oak and onto Main Street. Pointed out the county courthouse and the park that led up to it. Explained its importance.

"What is this hotel I'm staying at?" she wanted to know.

"It's the Dells Hotel right here on Main Street. It runs full in the summertime. Should be plenty of room now, though."

"The famous Wisconsin Dells?"

"You've heard of the Dells in England . . . or are you just being smart again?"

"I'm being smart . . . I read about them in Chicago. So is that it?"

"Is what it?"

"The Dells Hotel . . . is that the only place to stay?"

"Buckingham Palace is booked for the week, but we might be able to squeeze you into Windsor Castle."

"Buckingham and Windsor being . . . ?"

"A pair of cheap motels flanking a strip club out on Highway Thirty-three. I don't think you'd feel too comfortable out there."

"A motel. Another one of those wonderful American inventions. I should very much like to see one."

What the hell did that mean? The woman wanted to see a cheap motel? I pulled up to the Dells Hotel and unloaded her suitcase. Walked her into the lobby and waited until the gorgeous detective from England was checked in. I'm wondering, looking back, if she possibly could have been that attractive. Or is it only the passing of the years that has made her so beautiful in my mind? I do remember watching her walk away, up the stairs to her room. I found it hard to believe that a real cop could have those kind of legs.

17 | THE DELLS

A mere two hours after safely delivering my new British friend to her hotel, I was cooling my heels on a park bench in Courthouse Square, mad as hell. Detective LaChapelle and I had just met with Sheriff Zimmer and briefed him on our suspect—Wolf Stangl, a Nazi war criminal. A man who murdered as coldly as any man in criminal history. Zimmer chuckled. A mean little chuckle. "Murder has a motive," he declared. "I think we should look to the most obvious rather than to the bizarre."

"This is Wisconsin," I reminded him. "We should be looking for the bizarre."

He all but threw me out of his office. Meanwhile, the brainy beauty from England was invited to remain. The entire episode was humiliating, and I was furious.

Self-pity isn't pretty. Especially in a police uniform. I sat on the park bench feeling sorry for myself, wondering how it was that I got myself into these things. Seemed to me I was constantly paying for a debt I never owed.

From where I was sitting, I could see Dad's shoe store, and the apartment above it where I had grown up. I could see Main Street from almost one end to the other. Over the years, how many parades had I watched pass? I could see the rooftop of the bank building, where a new breed of town kids had fired on us with their .22s. It is amazing how when we are angry, a strange choice of memories comes flooding back.

It was a good hour before the woman from Scotland Yard marched out of the courthouse. Before leaving the hotel, she had slipped into a pair of slacks and a khaki jacket, crisply tailored but too warm for the glorious weather we'd been enjoying. A comfortable pair of Pennington shoes now adorned her feet. Her hair had been pinned back, revealing even more of her sharp face. To show her the depth of my anger, and my humiliation, I didn't bother to stand.

She stared down at me, like the sleek and shrewd cat that had just swallowed the proverbial canary. "I should like to see the Dells," she said, with her irritating accent.

I glanced up at that smug face of European beauty. Something in those steely blue eyes convinced me she was still on my side. Too bad she couldn't vote. I gazed into the fading sky. Fought to control the anger in my voice. "I'll run you up there now. Be sunset soon."

We talked very little on the short drive north. Well, she talked some. Mostly I listened. Finally, she announced, "I was led to believe that you were the chief investigator. But it now appears there is a second investigation underway."

"Captain Hargrow," I told her. "He's with the state police in Madison."

"Yes," she said. "They seem to be seriously concerned about you."

"I've been down this ugly road before. And Wolf Stangl?"

"Apparently, your little ploy to throw them off. Why didn't you tell me you were running for sheriff?"

"The upcoming election, Detective, has nothing to do with this investigation. What else did Zimmer tell you?"

"That you, Deputy Pennington, are a very dangerous man for a woman to be associating with."

"Well hell, I can't argue with that."

We parked in a dirt lot back of the Lower Dells. My timing was perfect. The sun was just beginning to dip into the western woods. The detective and I followed an old stagecoach trail through the trees to the rocks. Whitetail deer and flocks of wild turkeys scattered before us. Back in those days the surrounding woods were teeming with game. The British detective pretended it was just another walk in the woods, but I could tell she was awed.

At the top of the trail we scaled a cliff known as Hawk's Bill. I've written of it before. In fact, I once took a flying leap from Hawk's Bill. At the peak of the cliff, the rocks formed what appeared to be the bill of a hawk, its mouth wide open as if screaming defiance. We strolled to the edge of the cliff, tall pines jutting right out of the rocks. Only a few layers of porous sandstone separated us from the swirling eddies of the Wisconsin River below.

In the heart of Wisconsin live a million Indian legends. I shared with our visitor my favorite. "The Hawk Indians would drag their own people up here if they were accused of a crime," I explained. "If a hawk flew over, it meant the accused party was guilty. Then the accused was weighted with rocks and thrown into the river below. They did the same with their captives. The water is about sixty feet deep at this point. About as deep as the Wisconsin gets."

She smiled at the story. An ironic smile. A smile I hadn't seen all day. She looked exotic out on the cliff. Mysterious. As if she belonged in another place and time. A woman from another world.

Now the sun was setting fast, and stretching out before us was nearly a mile of riverfront. Painted rocks of ever-changing hues shot right out of the water, creating eerie cliffs of fantastic shapes and colors, with lacy pines hanging spooklike over the waves.

"Some call this God's country," I explained. "Others claim it's a pagan land . . . teeming with evil spirits."

The setting sun reflecting off the water was near blinding. A thousand golden stars were dancing over the waves. I was wearing my shades, but Alex LaChapelle was forced to shield her eyes from the reflection. "There is a haunting beauty to it all," she finally admitted.

"I fear it's all doomed. Come back in twenty years," I said, "and you'll have to squint just to see a tree."

"Why?" she wanted to know.

"Too many people," I told her. "Rather, too many of the wrong people. Oh, the rocks and the water will still be here, but at the present rate . . . they'll be flanked by a tasteless carnival that stretches the entire length of the Dells."

Every now and then came a break in the sandstone cliffs where a sandy beach appeared as inviting as a summer day. Out in the middle of the wide river was a rocky island. One of several on the Lower Dells. Ten thousand years of erosion had carved small caves into the island cliffs. It was near the island, as we both stared that way, that we witnessed the rarest of sights. A giant sturgeon shot spinning out of the water, like a living, breathing spear. The great fish spun in what seemed like slow motion. We could see its huge gray flanks, and the setting sun reflecting off its white belly. It came down hard on its side, where it made an incredibly loud splash, a splash that could be heard for a mile. Then the legendary fish was gone, leaving only the echoes of its splash and the water circles where it had reentered the river.

"Wow!"

I can't remember which one of us muttered the word, but "wow" was the only word to describe an airborne sturgeon.

"It really is a rare sight," I told her. "They usually jump at dawn and dusk. For years the state tourism board offered a cash prize for anybody who could snap a photograph of a leaping sturgeon. Nobody ever claimed the prize."

"Is it a rare fish?"

"Unfortunately, sturgeons are the source of some of the world's finest caviar. Because of the price on their heads, they're being over-fished, and poached. It's a whiskered bottom-dweller. In the Wisconsin River, they can get six feet long and weigh over a hundred pounds. Been around since the days of the dinosaurs. But I'm afraid the sturgeon is like the Dells . . . in danger of disappearing."

"Tell me more."

I pointed across the water. "In the old days, Indians would row their canoes into those caves in the island with torches. The light of the fire would attract the insects, and the insects would attract the sturgeon. Then the Indians would spear them. Must have been some huge fish." I paused to reflect on what I had just said. "My old sheriff first told me that story."

"Sheriff Fritz Galatowich?" she asked.

"He was just Fats to us. I suppose you read of him, too."

"I did. I was especially sad to read of his demise. It must have been hard on you."

"It was."

She turned to me, her back to the river. Cut off my view of the cliffs on the far shore. "Tell me, Deputy Pennington, how is it you want to handle this case?"

Sheriff Zimmer had obviously told the woman every negative thing ever whispered about me. Still, there was something in those beautiful blue eyes of hers that convinced me I could trust her. That she believed we were in fact dealing with the former SS officer. I took off my sunglasses in the hopes that she could read the sincerity in my own eyes. "When he called me on the phone the other night . . ."

"Stangl . . . ?"

"Yes . . . he knew certain things about me that were never discussed while he had me locked up during the war."

"Such as?"

"He knew my father had worked at the German POW camp that was here in Kickapoo Falls."

"Yes, tell me of the camp."

"It was just a small logging camp up in the hills. It held, maybe, two or three hundred men. The main camp was at Camp McCoy."

"What else did he know about you . . . that he shouldn't have?"

"Let's just say he knew about a medical condition that I may, or may not, have."

"What kind of medical condition?"

I was embarrassed. The angry kind of embarrassed. I may have raised my voice to make a point. "The kind of medical condition a man doesn't like to talk about . . . especially with a woman. In fact, I've been told the problem may only exist in my head."

"I think I get the picture."

"Do you?"

"So then . . . how is it you carried on this *special relationship* with Lisa Prager?"

It was the first time I'd heard her use Lisa's name, and it sounded odd coming from this detective from so far away. "The details of my relationship with Lisa are not important . . . other than to know our relationship was *unique* and *special*."

"Still, as a detective, I'm curious. And as a woman."

I didn't answer her.

She went on. "If Wolf Stangl knows these things, then obviously he's been rummaging through your village for some time. How is that possible without your detection?"

"It's not."

"Then how?" she asked.

"Somebody in town has been feeding him information."

"I see."

I put my sunglasses back on, even though it was near dark now. She turned away from me and we looked out to the blackened water where the sturgeon had leaped for our attention. Yes, there were things I was not telling her. But you know, standing there on Hawk's Bill, the feeling suddenly washed over me that there were some things the lovely detective from England was not telling me. Like why she was hunting a Nazi war criminal in the heart of Wisconsin. I glanced up at the evening sky, but it was too dark to see if any hawks were flying overhead.

18 | A LITTLE VOYEURISM

It was late. I was tired. I wrapped up some paperwork then flicked off the desk lamp. Stood to leave. Sheriff Zimmer was still in his office. Just sitting at his desk. He had his damn sunglasses on, but I could see him eyeing me through the glass partition. I didn't bother to nod goodnight. I left the squad room and cut through the darkened courthouse. Exited out the front doors and down the wide stone steps. I mention this because my car was actually parked at the back of the building.

It was a weeknight. Street lamps decorated Courthouse Square, but the square itself was void of people. The town was in bed. I stood in the middle of the park. Moved into the shadow of a tall elm. Stared across Main Street at the Dells Hotel.

Her room was on the second floor, overlooking the street and the square. A lamplight was on. The heavy curtain that ensures privacy had yet to be drawn. Hanging over the window was only a sheer white curtain, so delicate and thin it gave the room a heavenly glow.

I stood there watching for maybe five minutes, thinking about the day we'd spent together. I was just about to pack it in and go home when I saw her, emerging from the bathroom. She was wearing something white. She walked around the bed. Paused at a dresser. Then she edged over to the window. The woman moved like an athlete. A dancer. Strong, but graceful. I stepped back a foot, deeper into the shadow of the tree. She parted the flimsy white curtain with the back of her hand. Stared out at the night.

It's hard to describe what she looked like in the window that night. Apprehensive, perhaps. Maybe lonely. Hovering above the glow of the street lamps, she was certainly mysterious. If our story were a Hollywood movie, I'd be wondering if she were some kind of spy. A double agent. Gorgeous, but lethal. Alex LaChapelle had come a long way on a tip from a small-town deputy sheriff.

I saw her glance up at the moon. It was a crescent moon that night. Indians called it the moon of the silver canoe. I don't know what they called it in England, but it was probably the only thing in Kickapoo Falls that was familiar to her. I'll bet she found it comforting. I swore I could see a rueful smile slip across her face.

If you throw all of your love at a woman who gives you little in return, is it really love? Or is it just an infatuation? Or an obsession? I always argued it was love. Friends argued it wasn't. My psychologist friend, Marilou Stephens, believed that if a woman had ever given herself to me, heart and soul, I'd have turned and run like a frightened deer in the autumn woods. She said I only loved women I couldn't have.

The British detective fixed her gaze on Courthouse Square, and that embarrassing feeling washed over me that I had been spotted. Found out. But that was not possible. I'd spent too many years lurking in the shadows to get caught. I held my ground.

Finally, the British beauty let the white curtain fall. I could see her silhouette behind the translucent cloth. She stood perfectly still, like a statue of a Greek goddess, as if waiting for me to make the next move. At last, she drew the heavy curtains. And I waited in the dark until the light went out.

19 | CAMP KICKAPOO: *Up and Running*

Having a POW camp in the heart of Kickapoo County proved to be a challenge from the start. Half the folks in the county came from strong German stock. In fact, many of them still spoke German. Had relatives in the old country. Needless to say, this provided them with a sympathetic connection to the prisoners. Women particularly felt sorry for them. Old ladies sent baskets of food up to the camp, and young girls were constantly driving by the stockade and flirting with the POWs through the barbed-wire fence. The reverend of the Lutheran church offered to give services every Wednesday in German. A Catholic Mass, in German, was held on Sundays. All this had the effect of dividing the town of Kickapoo Falls into two warring camps of its own—five thousand people who hated the thought of Nazis living in their midst, and five thousand people with German blood in them who felt sorry for young soldiers half a continent and an ocean away from home.

My father was the odd man out. Dad didn't have a single drop of German blood in his veins, but he was doing more to aid the prisoners than anybody in town. Still, this aspect of the story isn't really about my father. It's about the prisoners he encountered. Two prisoners, in particular.

From what my father could decipher among the prisoners, a *soldat* was a private. An *obergereiter* was a corporal, and an *unteroffizer* was a sergeant. The army figured only fifteen percent of the prisoners were true Nazis. Most of them officers. So the officers and the enlisted men were segregated. They were kept at different camps because trouble had developed whenever the two were mixed. The swaggering, insolent, died-in-the-wool Nazis, it was believed, had pretty well been weeded out. But it was rumored at the time that the prisoner-of-war camps for enlisted men held a sprinkling of high-ranking Wehrmacht officers disguised as noncoms. At Camp Kickapoo one of them was undoubtedly *Unteroffizier* Frick.

The camp commander apparently did not realize his small camp for enlisted men held a man from the SS because nobody thought to check the prisoners for the telltale arm tattoo. But the German prisoners quickly learned the identity of SS man Frick. Still, out of fear and perhaps a sense of loyalty, they kept their mouths shut. Anyway, Dad had more access to the prisoners than the camp commander and the guards combined, and he swore Frick was a rabid Nazi. In fact, that's what dad called him. Nazi Frick.

My father told me Frick was older than the other boys. He had penetrating dark eyes and an arresting manner that hinted at leadership qualities beyond those of the ordinary *unteroffizer*. Frick also spoke fluent English. At times, flawless. No sooner had the prisoners arrived than Frick established himself as the spokesman for the new camp.

Not all of the prisoners worked in the woods chopping trees. Some worked on maintenance crews as mechanics, plumbers, carpenters, and such. Others were tailors, cobblers, barbers, and cooks. Each prisoner was issued blue work clothing with "PW" in white on the back of the shirt and coat. They were given two pairs of cotton trousers, a wool shirt, an overcoat, a pair of shoes, socks, gloves, underwear, and a raincoat. Their German uniforms, what remained of them, could be worn during leisure hours.

Ironically, my father told me, most of the big donations for the prison camp came from the Kickapoo Gunn Club. Not really surprising, since they controlled most of the money in the valley. And maybe not so surprising because some in the valley had always believed the oh-so-private club was just a pack of Nazis hiding behind the American flag.

The second prisoner my father told me so much about didn't arrive with the others. Apparently, he had escaped from Camp McCoy. Several weeks later he was arrested in Madison while enjoying a baseball game—a hot dog in his mouth and a girl on his arm. The sheriff down in Dane County said he'd been doing a pretty good job of blending in. That prisoner's last name also turned out to be Stangl. Paul Friedrich Stangl. It was a coincidence my father and I marveled at till the day he died. The young Stangl was a *soldat*. A private. He would eventually become the most popular prisoner in the camp. On both sides of the fence. A legend in the valley. So well known, in fact, that everybody in town took to calling him Pauly. He also spoke English. Or rather a charming form of broken English. Though fleet-of-foot, everybody was assured the handsome young man from Germany was harmless.

Fats, too, was always telling me Pauly stories. Like the first time the little *soldat* escaped from Camp Kickapoo. He had everybody in the county good and pissed. Literally. To discourage escape attempts, the guards had spread tall tales of the wolves, bears, and witches that inhabited the forest. They told the prisoners there were wild Indians in the neighborhood. In fact, Fats paid a couple of Ho-Chunk to ride up to the camp one day on horseback in full regalia. "Wave those tomahawks around," he said, "and scream a lot."

But none of the theatrics could discourage *Soldat* Stangl. While out chopping his quota of trees, Pauly walked into the woods to relieve himself. Apparently, he just kept on walking. Next day, Sheriff Fats picked him up hitchhiking on the edge of town. While returning him to the camp in the front seat of the squad car, the handsome young German regaled the sheriff with the tale of his sexual exploits the night before—with the proverbial farmer's daughter, no less. A sexual encounter so detailed and erotic the sheriff found himself mesmerized.

"Okay, now let me get this straight . . . she was actually on her knees while you were doing this?"

"Yes, Sheriff . . . and I was on *mien* back."

"And all of this was in the cow barn?"

It was the first of many such stories. To this day it is believed that more than a handful of people in Kickapoo County are direct descendants of one *Soldat* Paul Friedrich Stangl of the German Afrika Korps.

20 | A WALK IN THE WOODS

I sometimes dream of ending my life a dirty old man. What would it matter? Everybody I loved is long dead and gone. Hell, just about everybody I knew in my old hometown has been laid to rest. I outlived them all. In fact, I seldom return to Kickapoo County. Not because of my age, but because around every bend in the road lies a haunting memory.

Then a cold gale off the water snaps me out of it, and I am again a frail and lonely old man on the rocky shores of a great lake, scribbling the chapters of my life onto a yellow legal pad. It is at these times I almost envy the Alzheimer's patients. Their minds go before their bodies. Old age is cruel. Nothing good can be said of it. We so-called healthy ones know the pain and frustration of having the wants and desires of a still-sharp mind trapped inside an eggshell of a body that is rotting to death, inside and out.

My trip to St. Paul was two weeks off. I was expected to attend Mass with the President of the United States. A Nazi war criminal was loose in Kickapoo County, freely assassinating my friends. I was in the middle of a tight election with the acting sheriff, who I now believed was subtly trying to pin the murders on me. And now a fresh hell was waiting for me. Once again I found myself falling in love. Oh, yes, head-over-fucking-heels in love. I wish I could explain it. I swear, I didn't set out to fall in love with these women. Maggie Butler and I grew up together. I don't remember a time when I didn't love her. Lisa and I just stumbled onto one another. As for Alex LaChapelle—she flew halfway around the world to land in my backyard.

So, would I fall in love with any woman? Did I just need an obsession to replace Maggie and Lisa after their deaths? Did Alex just happen to fit the bill? No, I don't think so. Time hasn't clouded my memory all that much. Alex LaChapelle was incredibly beautiful. And she was smart. And she was fun. And she liked me. In the end, I think that's what hurt the most.

The brainy British detective and I had been working closely together for a week. Exchanging information. Again familiarizing ourselves with Wolf Stangl. At the time, I thought it was harder for me. I had tried my best to bury the war. Put it in the past. Still, Alex kept inquiring about my experiences with Stangl during my imprisonment. Instead, what I gave her that first week were simply the facts we had gathered at Army Intelligence in the year after Germany's surrender.

Christian Wolfgang Stangl was born in a small town in Austria in 1901. He became a policeman in 1923, serving in the Austrian town of Linz. But we believed as early as 1932, the Nazis had been planting police in Austria. We suspected Stangl was already a Nazi when he began his police training. Eventually he became a respected *Kriminalbeamte*. A homicide investigator. The man was also an avid hunter. An expert with a rifle. Then, in July of 1934, the Austrian Chancellor, Engelbert Dollfus, a devout Catholic, was assassinated. Everybody knew the Nazis had killed him. Stangl, also Catholic, was tops on the list of suspects. After the *Anschluss*, which was the welcomed annexation of Austria by Germany in March of 1938, Wolf Stangl, as we knew him, officially joined the SS, while at the same time many of his fellow Austrian *Kriminalbeamten* were being summarily executed. Not surprisingly, the new man rose fast in the ranks. Ultimately, he was put in charge of the border region of Germany and Austria. Including, and especially, Wolf Pass.

Stangl had a wife, and two children. His young son was taken prisoner in North Africa. Shipped off to America. It was said his wife was killed in Allied bombing. We lost track of the daughter. Stangl escaped to Syria at the end of the war. Last I had heard, he was believed to be hiding in Brazil. Besides America and Great Britain, both Germany and his homeland of Austria had criminal warrants out for his arrest.

The thing of it was, Alex knew all of this. She could recite Stangl's dossier backwards.

Not completely trusting Sheriff Zimmer, the British detective and I did most of our work outside the squad room. Away from the courthouse. In a small town like Kickapoo Falls, this led to juicy rumors about Deputy Pennington and his new female friend from England. On this particular day, I took her for a long walk in the deep woods that led north toward the Upper Dells. It was a natural path we strolled, probably carved by animals.

We were past the luxury of summer's long light. There was an autumn flavor in the air. The days were growing shorter. Cooler. The late afternoon air was crisp and dry. The pale blue sky was cloudless. Sunlight filtered through the treetops, mostly black ash and white birch. Alex kicked at crackling leaves beneath our feet. Watched them scatter.

"I don't know what else I can tell you."

"I don't need facts and dates from you, Deputy. What I need from you is the essence of the man. Who is he? What makes him tick? That's how we'll capture him."

"If that were the case, I'd have him by now. Wisconsin has strong German roots. He has help here."

"Americans helping Nazis?"

"German-Americans helping Germans."

"After the war . . . how did he escape?"

"In Austria," I told her, "Stangl is a fairly common name. It wouldn't have taken much to alter his papers. There were a lot of forged documents floating around at the end of the war. Often the dead were literally stripped of their identification. Anyway, he crossed the mountains into Italy, probably on foot. He's a good climber. He knew the mountains well. We know he used false papers and took a train from Florence to Rome, where he made his way to the Vatican. Then he disappeared."

"So those stories are true?"

"You mean the stories about the Vatican helping Nazi war criminals escape prosecution? Yes, I'm afraid they're true."

She put a hand on my shoulder. "Does that hurt you . . . being a Catholic . . . being invited to St. Paul?"

We paused in the woods. "Yes, it hurts."

A white wind sailed through the trees. The leaves were tinged with yellow, and specks of orange. Every once in a while, a bright ripe leaf broke free of its branch and floated to the ground, like a silent melody. The fall season with its ephemeral beauty always left me with a touch of sadness. The green summer past. The golden harvest. The shedding of the fire-colored leaves. And on this walk, the realization that my time with Alex LaChapelle would be as short as the autumn months.

Can a man really fall in love in only a week? Hell, with a woman like Alex, I might have been in love in less than an hour. In fact, all my life I was a strong believer in love at first sight. I had to believe in it, because I went through life telling myself *she* was out there, I just hadn't met her yet. Right up to my solitary retirement, to the day I retreated to this island, I still believed *she* was out there.

The fragrance of her perfume mixed with the woodsy redolence of early autumn and made Alex irresistible. The perfect woman. Plus, she had this nifty trick of putting her hands on me. I never believed for a second it was natural. Or innocent. She was brainy and beautiful, and she knew how to use those qualities to her advantage. Every so often during a conversation, whether it was in the squad room or on a walk in the woods, she would reach over and touch me. On the arm. On the shoulder. On the back of my hand. It was disarming, and she knew it. These were not gestures I could return. If I had reached out and put my hand on her arm, it would have taken all of the strength in my body. And it would have been awkward as hell.

We continued meandering down the path. We could hear the sounds of squirrels at work, packing up for the long winter ahead. Small birds flitted about, enjoying the day. A tree branch broke in the woods behind us. Fell to the ground. It didn't really startle us, but we turned to look.

"Are there bears in here?" Alex wanted to know.

"Black bears," I told her, "probably more scared of us."

"And Indians?"

I chuckled at that. Typical European. "We might run into a Ho-Chunk, but he'd be just like us . . . out for a stroll."

We came to a bluff above the dam. It was cool and damp. Heavy ferns sprouted from the walls. "What is above the dam?" she asked, pointing upriver.

"You mean the Upper Dells?"

"Yes, what's up there?"

"It's called the Narrows. Water moves pretty fast through there. It takes in Black Hawk Island. Witches Gulch. Chapel Gorge. Demon's Canyon, and Suicide Cliff."

"Dear God . . . it sounds dreadful. I should very much like to see it."

"We'll get a boat, and I'll take you up there one day."

"Why not tonight?"

"You don't go up there at nighttime."

"Ghosts?"

"They say only the devil himself would visit the Narrows after dark."

I thought she was going to laugh at our local superstitions, but she seemed to give it serious thought. We listened to the river spilling over the dam, and watched the dark swirling eddies as they sucked everything into their vortex.

"Do you believe in evil spirits, Deputy Pennington?"

"I believe in evil, Detective, and I don't believe in tempting fate."

"So then . . . if a couple wanted to be truly alone in Kickapoo Falls . . . they should take a boat up the Narrows after dark?"

"Yes . . . to the southern tip of Black Hawk Island, across from Chapel Gorge. But they wouldn't be alone."

"The evil spirits?"

"There was a house on the southern tip," I told her, "where the lumbermen stayed. It offered liquor, lodging, and women. Drinking, fighting, and whoring. There were more than a few murders out there . . . and that doesn't count the men who drowned trying to run timber through the Narrows. Anyway, townspeople finally burned the place to the ground. But its spirit still remains."

Atop the bluff where we stood was a stand of pines. The wind through the trees is one thing, but a wind singing through the pines is magical. We listened for a minute. I couldn't keep my eyes off of her. I could see that her mind was at work. I wanted to believe it was working on me. But as it turned out, it was another man who dominated her thoughts on that walk in the woods.

21 | A VOICE FROM THE PAST: *Second Call*

I didn't watch much television, but I was having a hard time sleeping, and there was an old movie on the late channel. I loved the old black and whites. That night it was *Svengali,* with John Barrymore as the sinister musician who casts a hypnotic spell over beautiful, blue-eyed little Trilby—willing her by sheer hypnotic force into a great singer. But as the evil Svengali's influence wanes, Trilby's haunting voice begins to fail her, while at the same time, the natural beauty of her personality returns. The melodrama was nearing the climax when the phone rang. I got up and turned down the sound on the set. "Hello."

"Herr Pennington, did I wake you?"

"No, I'm up."

It was near midnight. I remember because I'd just heard the whistle of the old 11:45 as it passed through Kickapoo Falls. Again he was calling from outside. The connection was bad. I could hear cars rolling by in the background, but not as many. In fact, very few. He seemed to be at a different location. Not a highway. Perhaps he was in town. Remember, the year was 1962. Back then, telephone calls were virtually anonymous. We had done away with small-town operators, but we had also done away with any hope of tracing a call.

"Are you having trouble sleeping?"

"I'm fine. Thank you for your concern."

"Your troubles come from sleeping alone."

"Or maybe they come from once sleeping in a prison camp."

"Or a sniper's nest."

"What do you want?"

"Tell me, Herr Pennington, have you ever slept with a woman? I do not mean only the sex. I mean, have you ever lain down with a woman and gone to sleep beside her? Woke with her in the morning?"

"Do you think you can just show up in my hometown and kill my friends? Taunt me? I know the word 'consequences' is not the kind of word a Nazi would be familiar with . . . but there are going to be consequences."

"And how will you deliver to me these consequences?"

"I want to meet with you. Face to face. No guns. No weapons at all."

"I do not trust you on that level."

"Why?"

"You have survived, Herr Pennington, by people underestimating you. I shall not make that mistake again."

"I want to stop the killings in Kickapoo County."

"Two dead. Hardly comparable to the trail of dead bodies you have left across Wisconsin."

"You pretend to know a lot about my state . . . about me."

"I do not pretend. As a matter of fact, I heard a story recently . . . a good Wisconsin story. It is a fable worthy of the Brothers Grimm. It happened some ten years ago, as it was told to me. A very wicked old farmer and his pretty young wife lived far out in the country, off the old Portage Road in Kickapoo County. Seems after a hard day working in his fields, the wicked man would come home and beat his pretty wife."

"Who told you this story?"

"So young was she, and he would beat her senseless. Then, when she was totally submissive to him, he would do unspeakable things to her. Sexual things. And he would do these things in the bedroom, with all of the lights on. Almost in the window, as if he were proud of it. A picture show, of sorts. One fine autumn day, this very wicked old farmer was driving his tractor home from a hard day in the fields when a shot rang out from the distant woods. Ah, mein Gotte, *mean farmer was now dead farmer. A bullet had passed right through his head. Well, now, the fat Sheriff—"*

"Sheriff Fats."

"Yes, sorry . . . Sheriff Fats went out to investigate the mysterious slaying. He of course suspected the pretty wife. But the shot, they say, was fired from so far away, and was so deadly accurate, it was not possible that she could have been the killer. It was deer-hunting season, you know, and as often happens in your Wisconsin, all too conveniently, the whole thing was written off as some kind of hunting accident. The young pretty wife then sold the farm and moved to a big city, where she lived happily ever after. Had you heard this story before?"

"Yes . . . only you got part of it wrong. She wasn't his wife. She was his daughter."

"Ah, the plot thickens, as they say. Tell me, Herr Pennington, how did our killer know what was going on in their bedroom?"

"There was a report."

"Written by a young deputy?"

"As Fats once said . . . some people need to be shot."

"I agree. Funny how we are so much alike, you and I."

"I am not like you."

"I heard Alex is in town."

"You talk as if you know her."

"Did she tell you about her father?"

"What about her father?"

"Are you not curious as to why the British would send a woman like her to hunt a man like me?"

"Yes, I'm curious."

"Her father was Captain LaChapelle. A British commando."

"What happened to him?"

"He died at the pass."

"How did he die?"

"Some other night . . ."

"How did he die?"

"She is quite beautiful, is she not?"

"She is . . ."

"Her hotel room . . . do you think it is comfortable?"

"Why do you ask?"

"She's just turned on the light."

I dropped the phone and ran. Grabbed my Springfield on the way out the door. I had at least three shells in it. I sprinted up Ash Street to Oak, then cut across Courthouse Square. For the second time in as many weeks, I found myself sprinting through my own hometown with a gun at the ready. I was scared. The air filling my lungs was cool and crisp, but I was sweating. Did he have her window in his crosshairs? Was he waiting for her to walk across the room? Or was he just luring me to a location where he'd at last have me in his sights? I ran by the light of the moon. The light of the stars. It wasn't until I reached Courthouse Square that the street lamps were plenty enough to see down the block. But as I knew all too well, the lights threw deep shadows.

The square was deserted. The courthouse was dark. I could see the outline of the Civil War cannon, forever standing guard. Across the street, I could see a light in her second-floor room, but she was not near the window. All appeared quiet. I backpedaled across Main Street, my back to the Dells Hotel, my rifle at the ready. I saw shadows floating about Courthouse Square, but I had learned long ago never to shoot at shadows.

I burst through the hotel lobby and raced up the stairs, two at a time. I pounded on her door. I was just about to kick it in, when Alex opened up.

"What are you doing here . . . and why a rifle?"

I pushed past her and quickly turned off the lights. Took her hand and pulled her away from the window. "When did you get in?" I asked, out of breath.

"Just a few minutes ago," she said, a bit of anger in her voice. Again she motioned to the rifle. "What are you doing with that?"

"He called."

"Stangl?"

"Yes."

Suddenly she was as alert as I was. "What did he say?"

I caught my breath. "He said he had once underestimated me . . . that he'd never make that mistake again."

"Just the other night," she said, "I had the feeling I was being watched."

I swallowed hard. "Did you see anything?"

"No. Just evening shadows."

Our backs were now hard against the wall. We stood in stony silence for a minute, staring at the light from Courthouse Square spilling through the window. She was wearing a white bathrobe. Her rich hair was down over her shoulders. Her perfume was faint, but intoxicating. I reached down and held her hand. I'm not sure if it was for her benefit, or mine.

Finally, she said, "He's not out there . . . or he's not out there anymore. This is just part of his game. Cat and mouse."

She was right, of course. Though my heart was beating fast, she was right. Back then, there were no phone booths in our town. Lorraine's Café had a public phone, but Lorraine's was closed. "You can't stay here," I told her.

"He's a sniper, for God's sake. Where would we be safe?"

"I'll find a place."

"You're being rather overdramatic, I think."

"Those have been rather dramatic phone calls I've been getting." Again we stood in silence, the lights of the street our only illumination. At last, I ducked across the room and pulled the heavy curtain closed.

Now we were in near-total darkness. I could barely see Alex's ghostly figure across the room. Then her voice came out of the black. "Tell me how it was he underestimated you."

"That's not important."

"But it is important. What was it he said about killing again?"

"Tonight?"

"No, the first time he called."

I thought back. "He said he was going to kill once more. For old times."

"Did he mean 'again'? Or did he mean, 'just once more'?"

"His exact words were, *'Just once more, Herr Pennington. For old times.'*"

Standing there in the dark, I suddenly saw those words in a new light. There was a long quiet. When I finally spoke, my voice had an ominous ring to it. Almost trembling. I barely recognized it. "My God . . . that's what this is all about."

"What is it?" she asked.

"My trip to St. Paul," I whispered. "He's going to shoot the President."

22 | THE TRAINS: *Day One, 1944*

While the shortest distance between two points is a straight line, bullets actually fly in a shallow curve. They rise above the line at the beginning of the shot, and then drop below the line as they near the target. This is called the 'trajectory.' Even in the best of weather conditions, corrections have to be made to account for the rise and drop. Just as he does when using his scope to judge the distance, an expert rifleman can pretty much figure his trajectory in his head—up to five hundred yards. After that, it's all instinct. Guys like me never bothered with the math. I took aim. I made the corrections. And I fired.

I clutched the crucifix around my neck. I was blessed with a near-perfect day. Dawn broke on clear skies. I had slept little in the past two nights. Still, my adrenalin was sky-high. Blood was racing through my veins the way a stream races down the mountainside. I felt as sharp that morning as I had ever felt in my life. In fact, never again would I know the thrilling intensity of that feeling. Some of it was the mission. Some of it was ambition. Maybe even the altitude was a part of it. But I suspect most of what I felt that first morning was just the exuberance and wonderful ignorance of my youth. When my forty-eight hours on Wolf Pass were up, I would never be young again.

The sun was rising just over my shoulder. I removed the cotton cloth from my rifle. Checked my scope for dust. I snapped in a five-round box magazine, slid the bolt home, and then shouldered my Springfield '03. The rifle was forty-three inches long. Just under nine pounds. The weapon's ideal weight and length provided excellent balance. For all of the state-of-the-art weapons the Germans possessed in Wolf Pass, as long as I shouldered my Springfield, I felt it was a fair fight.

It was still early. No trains were in sight. So I went through the motions. Sweep the pass, north to south. Shoot a railroad worker. Shoot an officer. Cover the Big Gun. If I could hit the engineer while his engine was still idling, the noise of the train would mask the gunshot. It would give me another minute. Another shot or two before everybody scrambled. Before all hell broke loose.

Mountain air is cold in the morning. Near freezing, even in the summer. I tried to stay warm. Tried to relax. I ate my breakfast from a tin can. Swigged some water from a canteen. I trained a pair of binoculars on the tracks. The German soldiers guarding the trains were from the elite L1 Mountain Corps. That's how much importance the Nazis placed on Wolf Pass. Hell, it was their escape route. It was their gold. These highly trained soldiers were just beginning to stir when I heard the slow chug of the morning train and the long shriek of its whistle.

Growing up, I had been delighted with the sound of the steam whistle. I had watched with joy as the old Milwaukee Road roared over the bridge at the top of Main Street then into the station at Kickapoo Falls. But this was the top of a mountain. The trains did not roar into this station. After an uphill fight, they limped in on their last breath, looking only to replenish their fifty thousand gallons of water. In fact, the slow-motion entrance surprised me. The locomotive crept to a halt about halfway through the pass, leaving the other half of the station greatly exposed. Good for me. Bad for them.

With my heart racing fast, I put the crosshairs on the face of the engineer as he stuck his head out the window and looked down his train. Then I steadied myself. Breathed deep. Let it out. *"Shoot with purpose. Shoot with moral indignation."* I squeezed the trigger and sent a 30.06 missile screaming across the pass at two thousand feet per second. The engineer disappeared into the cab. His cap toppled down to the track. One minute he was there. Literally one second later he was dead. What did I feel for him? God forgive me, I felt nothing for him.

His fireman was in shock. Stood perfectly still before the boiler. I edged the rifle to my left and took him out. Then I swept the pass. The Big Gun was unmanned. The soldiers had heard nothing above the noise of the train. On an elevated platform, a railroad worker was maneuvering a waterspout over the engine. He was my last freebie. I sent him flying from the top of the platform, a hole in his chest. Now the war was on.

Soldiers rushed to the worker on the ground, then turned their attention toward the mountain. I waited a second to see who was giving orders. Then I let him have it. I was now four for four, and less than two minutes had passed.

I swept my sights back to the Big Gun. Watched as the first soldier tried to climb aboard and man the gun. Soon I was five for five, and it was time to reload.

What followed next was my first shot at Wolf Stangl. I saw him rush from the headquarters, throwing on his SS jacket as he ran down the hill to the tracks. Soldiers were scattering like cockroaches. He moved with no fear of a sniper. My thinking was that he hadn't yet realized what was happening. It was a difficult shot. He was on the move. He passed one obstacle after another. As he neared the still idling engine, I fired. He grabbed at his face and fell to the ground. For a second, I thought I'd gotten him. But then he was up and scrambling for cover. My bullet had splintered a wooden post. Exploded it in his face. Close, but no cigar.

I had to keep soldiers off the Big Gun. Two more went down that way. Then the Rheinmetall machine guns opened up on me. But they were shooting blindly. Rocks and trees were disintegrating beneath my position. I leveled my crosshairs on the machine gun nest to the north. One shot, and it fell silent. I swept back across the pass to the nest on the south. It, too, went quiet. I refocused on the Big Gun, but with three soldiers lying dead beside it, nobody was moving in that direction.

Then came that moment in a sniper attack when all of the guns fall silent. It is an eerie quiet. The calm after the initial storm. Everybody was dug in now. The waiting game began. A deadly game of chess. Colonel Stangl would have to admit—game one had certainly gone to me.

Americans have never taken kindly to snipers. No matter the uniform. No matter the cause. They find something distasteful about the business. Almost like shooting somebody in the back. Or shooting somebody who is unarmed. If John Wayne wouldn't do it, perhaps it shouldn't be done. We didn't get the glamorous medals, or the big promotions. We just got the dirty job done.

The rest of that first day went by in a blur. For hours, we played cat and mouse. Soldiers and railroad men had taken refuge beneath the train. They were hiding back of buildings. Or crouched behind trees, making themselves as skinny as possible. I think I only got two more by nightfall. One worker. One soldier. But nothing in Wolf Pass moved. Late in the morning, I had seen a second train backed up down the track. By late in the afternoon, I heard the lead engine go dead. Sputter and hiss, out of water.

With the sunset, the strain on my eyes was beginning to show. It was hard to tell people from shadows. That first day, I had had the element of surprise. When the sun came up on the second day, it would be a whole different chapter. God only knew what the Nazi colonel was planning for me in the cover of dark.

23 | THE TRAINS: *Day Two, 1944*

If the notorious Colonel Stangl had concocted a plan overnight—so had I. I would seduce them with another bright sunny day. Make them believe that I had departed in the dead of night. Coax them from their hiding places. Send them back to work. I would lie as still as the rocks around me. Melt into the mountain. I would become the invisible man. Avoiding detection at all cost. What I wouldn't do is take another shot at them. Not soon, anyway.

I swept Wolf Pass with the binoculars. The Big Gun was now manned behind heavy armor. Reinforced overnight. There were teams of three soldiers at each machine gun. I knew patrols would be in the mountains. And there was one other interesting development. Almost brought a smile of admiration to my face. From the wide-open window of the headquarters building, a rifle with a Unertl scope was sweeping the mountainside. I had no doubts about who was behind that rifle. But the headquarters building was up a hill. Within my range, but just barely. A shot and kill would be beautiful. A shot and a miss would give me away. Maybe do me in. Free the trains. So I waited.

I lay down in silence for nearly four hours. They didn't fire on me, and I didn't fire on them. I was hungry and cold. I lay there watching as they began to stir. Watched as they crept from their hiding places, probably on orders of death. And though there certainly wasn't anything sexual about the experience at the time, there was something I found terribly exciting about watching people from a secret vantage point. Something stirred deep inside of me. I never enjoyed the killing. But God help me, I did enjoy the waiting and the watching.

Eventually, an engineer, probably from the second train, climbed into the cab of the first train. I couldn't afford to let him get that engine fired up. Another fireman began shoveling coal. It would have been nice if they'd have been wearing Nazi uniforms, but I had little choice. So just when everybody in Wolf Pass believed that I had left in the night, that the mountain was clear, I squeezed off another shot. Killed another engineer. My second shot barely missed another fireman as he jumped for cover. Then ten kinds of hell broke loose. The sound of their cannons was deafening.

I took cover behind the rocks. The first stones hit me in the head. I tried to pull my cap down over my ears. Then a good-sized stone struck me in the back. I spun around in pain. Reached for my kidneys. When I looked up, I was witness to an explosion and an avalanche of rock and earth. I tried to jump out of the way, but there was no time.

It's hard to describe what it feels like to have a mountain dropped in your lap. It was even harder to determine exactly what my injuries were. When all was quiet again, I spit the earth from my mouth and crawled halfway out of the rubble. I was sure a bone in my thigh was broken. Other than that, all I knew was that I had the rupture from hell. I actually laughed. I still had to hike to Switzerland.

I pushed the mountain off of me, one rock at a time. Crawled out from beneath the boulders. Tore my feet free. I was in a hell of a lot of pain. The war-is-over-for-you kind of pain. My left leg hurt so bad it was almost numb. I had the stomachache to end all stomachaches. My eardrums were ringing from the explosions. I located my rifle and a canteen. I had three shots left, and one day of water.

They followed up with another sustained burst of fire. But this time their target was farther down the mountain. Threw only debris my way. I was actually happy about that second round. It meant they didn't know where I was. Colonel Stangl, no doubt, would level the mountain to kill me.

There was no more firing the rest of the morning. I lay there in agony. The only medical help was in Wolf Pass. But surrender wasn't yet an option. I certainly couldn't surrender to Stangl. Several times during those morning hours, I could hear boots trampling above me. But with the damage to my ears, it was hard to detect where exactly they were. Sometimes it seemed as if an entire brigade was right on top of me. I could discern voices. German voices. I listened to the static of their radios. Then all of the hostile sounds would drift away in echoes.

Perhaps it had been a suicide mission all along. They had found a kid ignorant enough and talented enough to pull it off. A skinny little Wisconsin kid. Just one more of the Dairy State's sacrifices to the war. I thought of my dad back in Kickapoo Falls. Dad was one of those volunteer types. What kind of patriotic things was he signing up for to help the effort? I figured with the war on, he was probably the most popular guy in town. When was the next time I would get to write? Where was the next letter I would get to read? That's one of those little things I remember most about the war. The letters. News from home.

As the hours passed, my hearing began to return, even though most sounds remained distorted. Still, I was able to hear the rumble of the planes in the afternoon. They flew above Wolf Pass. Not through the pass. Not at it. They were like soaring eagles. I listened to the din of the Big Gun and the rattle of the machine guns. Flying dirt and debris rained over me. But the Germans weren't shooting at me. They thought I was dead. With the sun in my bloodshot eyes, I guessed the planes overhead were British. Then I heard the bombs, falling down the mountain. The explosions grew louder and louder as they worked their way up to the pass. Payback for the missing commandos. It would be months before I knew how much damage they had inflicted, but from the glorious sound of the exploding bombs, the destruction had to be significant. In my mind, I saw flying railroad cars and twisted tracks all the way down the mountainside, in the same way that I had smashed my toy trains when I was a boy. Then, all too soon, the echoes of the friendly fire faded to silence, and I listened to the planes as they flew away, over the Alps.

At long last the sun began to sink behind the pass. It was near dark. I had been lying on my back, cradling my rifle since morning. Then I had a thought. A devil of a thought. I would take one last shot. Like a signature.

With all of the strength that I could muster, I rolled to my stomach and shouldered my weapon. Swallowed my aches and pains. I swept the pass, north to south. I was looking for a uniform. A Nazi uniform. The soldiers were milling about, alert, but out in the open. Night was falling. My timing had to be perfect. Light enough to see, but dark enough to avoid becoming a target myself. When the hour of the dark shadows was at hand, I located my man. He was tall, like Stangl. He was in uniform. One second later, he was dead. I was still alive. And my forty-eight hours on Wolf Pass were up.

24 | A WOMAN IN THE HOUSE

I sent off a strongly worded warning to the United States Secret Service in Washington, expressing my fears of Colonel Stangl. I used official stationery from the Kickapoo County Sheriff's Department, and I listed personal references at Army Intelligence. I knew how many threats were made every day against the American President. Especially that President. People today remember John F. Kennedy as this mythic young President, handsome and healthy in appearance, who served in a time of peace and prosperity. What they don't remember is that a lot of Americans hated his guts—and the people who hated him did so with a frightening intensity. Protesters followed him around the country. He was Catholic. He was a Democrat. He was a liberal. He was soft on Communism. He was in Vietnam. He was out of Cuba. He was for this, and he was against that. So in my letter, I also offered to decline my invitation to worship with the President in St. Paul. For security reasons, I would find a way to quietly back out.

I put out an alert around Kickapoo County. Well, actually, it was more of a whisper campaign among the deputies. Watch for strangers using public phones along the highways during the nighttime hours. I gave them a detailed description of Wolf Stangl. I shared with them his Nazi photograph. He would be older, of course. Past sixty. Catching him in a phone booth along the highway was a long shot, but I was doing my best to make sure all of my bases were covered.

As for Sheriff Zimmer, my boss and political rival, I didn't tell him shit. Left him hanging. Our working relationship was growing frosty. At the time, I thought it was just the natural stress of two determined men in an upcoming election. Deputy Hess, however, was growing suspicious. What if Zimmer wasn't everything he said he was? He would put a tail on his own sheriff. See where it leads. I didn't like the idea, but to my everlasting regret, I did nothing to stop him.

Detective Alex LaChapelle of Scotland Yard continued to stay at the Dells Hotel. Still, I had convinced her to at least spend a part of every evening with me. Sometimes we'd cruise the hills. We'd drive to restaurants out of town, where I'd pull up to a shack beneath a Leinenkugel's beer sign. Then I'd treat her to Norwegian meatballs made of pork and veal, in a sour cream sauce flavored with cardamom.

I showed her some of my favorite spots along the Wisconsin River. I tried to keep us moving, making sure we were never followed. My feelings of love and hate for her grew with every irritating hour. I loved spending time with her. I hated the idea of her leaving.

I was also expecting another call from our Nazi madman. He would phone in the evening, of that I was sure. It would be late, and I wanted Alex there when he called. I had an extension phone installed for the occasion. Hooked up a tape recorder. Back in those days, having two phones in your home was considered decadent. But, what the hell, it wasn't the first or the last time folks in Kickapoo Falls would accuse me of decadence.

"He'll call tonight," I told her.

She stared at me with that you're-an-idiot British smirk. "But isn't that what you said last night?"

"Well, you weren't here last night."

I took a seat on the couch, next to the newly installed phone. My old phone was in the bedroom. Alex sat in an overstuffed chair across from me. I'd just served up two cups of lukewarm coffee. I wanted us wide-awake when the son of a bitch called. The night was warm. The air inside was a bit muggy.

She glanced about the living room. "This is a rather charming little cottage . . . in its own way." To me, her accent was still fingernails on a chalkboard. Smug, no matter what she said.

"It's not a cottage," I told her. "It's a house." In saying that, I suddenly realized that she was the first woman who'd ever been inside of my house. Hell, few men had ever been in my house.

"Rather small for a house, don't you think?"

"It's clean and comfortable . . . that's all I need."

"Ah, yes. Isn't that what's known as midwestern sensibility?"

"Yeah, that's us. We've got sense and sensibility coming out our ears."

"Was that a pun?"

"How so?"

She smiled and sipped her coffee. "Tell me, Deputy, was your Maggie ever here?"

"She wasn't *my* Maggie . . . and no, she was never here."

"Did you ever kiss Maggie?"

"No."

"But you say you were in love with her."

"All my life."

"Did you ever kiss Lisa?"

"Kiss? No."

"But you had a sexual relationship with her?"

"Yes."

"How?"

"You know, Detective, I really don't feel comfortable discussing the sex lives of dead women. Especially women I may have loved."

"I'm not inquiring about their sex lives . . . I'm inquiring about yours."

"I thought you British were supposed to be reserved."

"That's a myth we perpetuate."

Before she could get back to me, I tried to turn the tables on her. "How about you, Detective LaChapelle? I mean, you're near thirty. You're still not married. You have no children. What's your problem? And don't you dare tell me that you don't have one."

"If you must know, there's a man in my life," she said, as she set her coffee aside.

"Really? Have you ever had sex with him?"

She thought about that question long and hard. In fact, her thinking seemed almost painful. "Yes, Deputy, on several occasions."

The boldness of her answer surprised me. Again, this was small-town America in 1962. I thought about what she had just said. Tried to picture her in bed with some anonymous Brit. "He's a lucky man," I finally muttered, with a touch too much envy.

"Thank you . . . I think." She stood, arms crossed, and strolled around the room. She was wearing those tight black slacks that were so popular back then, and a white sweater with a thin gold chain draped over it. Her hair was pulled back that night, not flowing free, the way I liked it best. She carefully examined my things. I had a stone fireplace, and on the oaken mantel were some pictures of my late father. Just the two of us, sailing on Lake Michigan. A small gilded frame held a picture of my mother, a crucifix around her neck. She died when I was a little boy. Plus, there was an old photograph of the Kickapoo Falls High School football team of 1941. "I've been asking around town about you, Deputy Pennington. You've achieved almost legendary status."

I chuckled at that. "Hardly the case," I assured her. "Now Sheriff Fats . . . there was a legend."

"A corrupt legend . . . if I understand correctly."

"We're all a little corrupt, in our own way."

She lifted the team portrait off the mantel. "I don't understand much about American football . . . but they say you made the longest touchdown run in the history of Wisconsin."

"Actually, it was the longest touchdown run in the history of the game."

"You don't say. How far did you run?"

"A couple of reporters stepped it off at two point one miles."

She turned to me, a bit baffled. "Correct me if I'm wrong, but the playing field is only one hundred meters . . ."

"One hundred yards."

"Yes, one hundred yards." She smiled at the thought. "So, let me see if I have all of this straight. You were able to run two point one miles on a field only one hundred yards in length . . . while all of your life you were madly in love with a woman you never touched, much less kissed . . . and later, you were able to carry on a sexual relationship with a married woman when, by your own admission, the length of your . . ."

I cut her off. "All right, that's enough."

"My, my, Deputy Pennington . . . I'd say your legendary reputation is well deserved."

"You know, you're starting to piss me off."

"*Piss me off*," she echoed. "I believe I shall leave Wisconsin with an entirely new vocabulary. Why do I *piss you off*, Deputy?"

"Because you talk funny."

A cool breeze shot through the room. I heard the whistle of the night train. I could feel the rumble of the steel wheels. Then the phone rang.

25 | A VOICE FROM THE PAST: *Third Call*

The fun, if we were having fun, drained from our faces with the ringing of the phones. I nodded to Alex, and she walked off toward my bedroom. "Don't mention anything about St. Paul," she said, as she disappeared around the corner.

Funny as this sounds, even in the middle of the incessant ringing, I was thinking that wonderfully beautiful Alex was walking into my bedroom.

I turned on the tape recorder. Let the phone ring one more time. Then I picked up the receiver. "Hello."

"Herr Pennington, I was growing impatient. How are you this fine, warm evening?"

"I'm okay . . . and where exactly are you this fine, warm evening?"

"That is good. Yes, that is good. Tell me, Herr Pennington, is the weather always this pleasant here in Wisconsin?"

"It looks like we're in for a rich autumn."

"I should very much like to stay."

"Yes, and we'd like you to stay, Colonel . . . for twenty to life."

Besides the static, I could hear cars in the background. They were passing at high speed. He was calling from the edge of a highway.

"You are in fine spirits tonight."

There was a break in the traffic. I heard a diesel engine. It was accelerating through first gear. Pulling onto the highway. He was at a truck stop. Or maybe one of those fancy rest stops out on the new interstate.

"Speaking of spirits, you said you were going to kill one more time. Whom do you have in mind?"

"And ruin the surprise?"

"Is it me?"

"Have I reason to kill you, Herr Pennington?"

"I've given you plenty of reasons to kill me."

"Is Alex there?"

I turned quickly to the windows. All of the curtains were drawn. The doors were locked. I looked in the direction of the bedroom. Nothing but silence. "No," I said.

"Should I tell you about her father?"

"Some other night."

"Captain LaChapelle was a very brave man."

"Some other night."

"He sacrificed his life for that of his men."

"Then what became of his men?"

"You see, the captain came to the pass to stop the trains."

"So did I."

"Yes, but he was captured."

"So?"

"So . . . I gave him the chance to stop a train."

"Let's talk about something else."

"Did you ever watch those Hollywood movies . . . the wonderful old movies with no sound?"

"Silent pictures."

"Yes, silent pictures. My favorite, you see, was the one where the villain would tie the frightened young woman to the railroad tracks . . . and then, at the last minute, with a train barreling down on her, a handsome young ranger would ride to her rescue. Well, the good captain found himself in a similar bind . . . but his hero ranger arrived much too late. It did not really matter, for as it turned out, Captain LaChapelle could not stop a train, after all."

"That sounds a little melodramatic, Colonel, even for you."

"It happened on a rather steep slope of track, at a bend in the mountain on the way into Austria. The poor engineer couldn't possibly have seen him until the final seconds, if he saw him at all. Think of the captain's final minutes. The sound of the oncoming locomotive roaring down the mountain. The rumble of the steel wheels. What does a man think about in what he knows to be the last minutes of his life? His wife and daughter, no doubt."

I could not picture the British captain literally tied to a railroad track, but I could see him in the small headquarters building in Wolf Pass, under arrest, and standing before Colonel Stangl. "Do whatever you want to me," he might have said, "but see that my men are treated fairly."

"Your men," Stangl would have told him, "are to be taken to a prison camp in Germany."

But they never made it to any camp. "Did you kill his men that way, or did they die like those GIs in your camp that morning?"

"Commandos . . . I never cared for their type of warfare. It's not clean. Not like what you and I do, Herr Pennington. Snipers don't get their hands dirty."

What happened next was frightening and confusing. A cop's worst nightmare. There was a tapping noise on the other end of the line. Then came a muffled voice. *"Can I talk to you, pal?"*

Stangl turning away from the phone. *"One moment, Officer."* A second later, he was back to me. *"I have to go now . . . a friend of yours has surprised me. Now I shall surprise him."*

I could hear the phone drop. There was a shot. A pistol shot. Loud. Maybe 9mm. Somebody yelled in pain.

The Nazi war criminal was back on the phone. *"Goodnight, Herr Pennington."* For good measure, he added, *"Goodnight, Fräulein Alex."*

Then the line went dead.

26 | THE TRUCK STOP

Alex and I were in my squad, racing out of town. I was behind the wheel. She sat in stony silence beside me. I radioed in a possible shooting. Asked for the location of all our deputies. The dispatcher informed me that Deputy Hess in car three was last heard from at a truck stop on Highway 33, just past the old stadium. He wasn't responding to the roll call. I requested an ambulance and backup for that location.

A wafer of a moon was peeking through cloudy skies. The air was warm. The roads were dry, but the breeze was redolent of an early autumn storm. I floored the accelerator of the Chevy Biscayne. We raced by the Kickapoo Falls Stadium, where years ago I had played my football games. Where I had made my infamous run. Its lights were dark. The bleachers were broken. Highway expansion had doomed the place. A new high school with new athletic fields was being built on the edge of town.

Then this came over the radio: *"All cars, sheriff needs help . . . truck stop on Thirty-three."*

There is only one way to describe the county highways at night as they stretched toward the hills out of town. Black. Pitch black. There were no street lamps. No homes. No businesses. My high beam headlights and the flashing red light atop the roof were all that lit the way, until I saw a flash of lightning in my rearview mirror. A rumble of thunder followed. I was pushing sixty miles per hour around tight two-lane curves. If Alex objected to my manic driving, she didn't say anything.

I think back now on all of the years and all of the accident sites at which I arrived, lights flashing, sirens wailing. At many sites the tires would still be spinning, the smell of burnt rubber permeating the air. Gasoline would be mixing with blood. And the bodies, often thrown from the car, could be anywhere within a quarter mile. Contrary to what you might think, there was never a lot of screaming. The human sounds, when there were sounds, were often sickly and faint. Those not killed in the initial impact were usually in shock. Which is why the site I arrived at that night was so unusual.

There was no crash. No suspect vehicle. Car one, the sheriff's car, was pulled to the side of a phone booth, lights flashing. Car three, another Biscayne, was right in front of him. Lights flashing. Engine running. But the driver's side door was wide open.

I pulled right up to the phone booth where I suspected the call to my house had been made. The door was open. The booth was dark.

I jumped from my squad. Approached Sheriff Zimmer, who was frozen in my headlights. That's when I saw him. Deputy Hess, for seven years my colleague and my friend, was lying facedown on the blacktop. The back of his head was open, as if shot at close range.

The sheriff was standing over him. "Looks like he got one to the stomach, and then one to the head as he crawled to his car."

I was saddened. I was furious. "He must have come across the son of a bitch talking on the phone."

"Who?" Zimmer asked. "Who did he happen on?"

Alex spoke up, walking up behind us. "He undoubtedly confronted Wolf Stangl, the Nazi war criminal we told you about. We have Stangl's voice on tape."

"Do you believe us now?" I asked.

For the first time since I'd known him, Zimmer actually showed some personality. Pure anger. "You two could have been a little more cooperative . . . and a little more forthcoming."

Lightning flashed over the hills, in the direction of Kickapoo Falls. The thunder rumbled closer as the three of us stood in angry silence over the fallen body of Deputy Hess.

It was Zimmer who finally broke the spell. "All right. I'm going to get this son of a bitch . . . whoever he is. Nobody comes into my county and kills my men." He looked me dead in the eye. Thumped his chest with his thumb. "It's my investigation now," he said. "Let's see if this ghost of yours really exists."

27 | AFTER THE FALL

We left the shooting scene late—after the coroner from Madison arrived and carted away the young deputy. It wasn't until we were alone together, driving back to Kickapoo Falls, that I thought of Alex LaChapelle and the emotions she must have been wrestling with. I had been so wrapped up in trying to get to Hess, I hadn't had time to think about the things she had heard during that telephone conversation. Was that really the way her father was killed? Or was Colonel Stangl only engaging in psychological warfare? "I didn't believe him," I said to her.

"You didn't believe who?"

"Stangl . . . about your father. Why . . . who did you think I meant?"

"I believed him."

"Those things he said about your father . . . I don't think they're true. He knew you were listening."

"They're true."

"The man plays games with people's minds . . . using other people's lives. He'll kill the man next to you, and make you believe that somehow you could have prevented it. I've seen him do it. He's the devil on earth. He's the very definition of evil."

She was listening to me, but she wasn't looking at me. Kept her face to the passenger-side window. The lightning beyond the glass was constant. The thunder rumbled closer and closer, but the rain never really came. The storm seemed to be moving north of us. We drove on in silence, both of us engaged in our own dark thoughts.

"I'm sorry about your friend," she finally said, disturbing the quiet.

"It doesn't make sense."

"No, it doesn't."

I tried again to control my anger. "How does a cop approach a murder suspect, and then get shot in the back of the head . . . at close range?"

"His weapon was still holstered."

"Exactly."

"We're talking about Wolf Stangl."

"He's a madman," I told her, "and Hess knew that."

We at last came down out of the hills. Could see the lights of Kickapoo Falls. I pulled up to the stop sign on Highway 33. It was near two in the morning. The highway was deserted. I stared at the white lines dividing the blacktop. Thought about the years and the miles Deputy Hess and I had spent together. A camaraderie exists among cops that simply can't be explained. An even more inexplicable camaraderie exists among men who have been to war.

Hess was a farm kid. Unfortunately, the farm went to his oldest brother. So with few prospects, the kid enlisted. Went to Korea with the United States Marine Corps. A nineteen-year-old machine gunner who became a stoic survivor of the Frozen Chosin.

MacArthur had told the boys they'd be home by Christmas. Instead, Hess and the First Marine Division found themselves surrounded by the Chinese army at the Chosin Reservoir, seventy-eight mountain miles from the Sea of Japan. The only way out was to fight their way back to the sea. As fate would have it, it also turned into one of the coldest winters ever recorded along the North Korean–Manchurian border.

Like a lot of combat veterans, Hess never talked much about his war days. It was only during a sub zero winter evening, with a few beers in him, that he opened up to me. Maybe because he knew I was haunted by my own war.

"The nighttime temperatures hit twenty-four degrees below zero," he told me, as we sat alone in a roadside bar. "And there was this constant, blinding snow. The Chinese were just shadows in a storm. A lot of them were from the southern provinces, and when the skies cleared, we found them frozen in their shooting positions. No wounds. No signs of struggle. They just froze in place."

Through weeks of heavy fighting and heavy losses, the Marines slogged their way back to the sea. The wind, howling out of Siberia, never stopped. Nor did the shooting. Hess always believed it was his strong Wisconsin roots that had saved him. If he was to die in the snow and cold, it would be in the snow and cold of Kickapoo County. He was going home, goddamn it, and the entire Chinese army would not stop him.

According to military historians, the Marine breakout from the Chosin Reservoir was a great success. A classic retreat strategy. But the battle itself was a huge defeat. On a long and winding mountain road, buried in snow and ice, another kid from Kickapoo Falls had journeyed from boyhood to manhood the hard way. "When it was all over," Hess had said to me that night, "we were afraid we would never again be fit for polite society."

As was his way, Sheriff Fats closely followed the exploits of our hometown boys fighting overseas. No sooner had Hess stepped out of his Marine Corps blues, than Fats offered him a deputy sheriff's uniform. Hess, afraid of civilian life, jumped at the chance.

"There is one other possibility," Alex said, bringing me out of my stupor.

I turned off of the highway, toward town. "Yes, I know."

"Shall I give it a voice?"

"Not tonight. I want to sleep on it."

28 | CAMP KICKAPOO: *The Holy Ghost*

It's hard to describe Patty Best. Rather, it's hard to describe what a girl like Patty meant to a school full of sixteen- and seventeen-year-old boys. I was a senior at Kickapoo Falls High when she fully blossomed. Patty was a year behind me. She would have been in the Class of '43.

The girl was perfectly rounded in all of the right places. To this day, I've never seen a woman with a figure quite like hers. Let's start with that face. It was a round, cheeky face without appearing fat. I mean, cheeks like ruby-red apples. Above the cheekbones sat a pair of big round, bedroom eyes. Her dark brown hair flowed around her soft face like a falls. Fell to her shoulders in waves. Moving on down—this girl had the biggest, most perfectly rounded breasts ever seen on a sixteen-year-old. We boys never actually saw bare nipples, but these were not the kind of tits that could be faked, or hidden. Even back in those more conservative times, Patty knew how to dress to show off her tits. Lower still, her hips had the kind of curves of which architects dream. Her ass was a prize. Nothing short of sculptured. Holding up this work of godlike art were two of the most gorgeous legs ever to walk the rich dark soil of Wisconsin. In those prewar days, I doubt there was a boy at Kickapoo Falls High School who didn't go to sleep every night whacking off to the devilish image of Patty Best.

She was not a cheerleader. Not a troublemaker. Not a snob. Patty just liked to have a good time. I guess you could have called her a party girl. She certainly knew she was sexy, but she kept her reputation short of slutty.

Even though it was a small town, I didn't know Patty all that well. Remember, back then I was partly blinded by my love for Maggie Butler. Still, Patty Best was the kind of girl whose picture you stuffed into your wallet when you went off to war. Then at just the right lonely moment, you'd whip it out and show the men what was waiting for you back home. Of course, it was all bullshit. But, then, that was the army.

I don't write of Patty Best because of anything that happened in high school. It was the trouble she got herself into after high school, while I was away, that set in motion a string of deadly events that would have national and international repercussions. Sounds funny that a small-town girl from Wisconsin could set nations at war to arguing over moral justice, but our beautiful and well-endowed Patty managed to pull it off.

My father had a lot of euphemisms for sex. In fact, sometimes it was hard to tell what the hell he was talking about. So for the sexual escapades of German prisoner Paul Friedrich Stangl, I had to rely on Sheriff Fats, who was always more than happy to retell these stories in all of their erotic glory.

You see, Patty Best was one of the town girls who liked to drive by the barbed-wire fence and flirt with the prisoners. It's not exactly clear when she and *Soldat* Stangl first met, or how they arranged his escapes, but he was usually out at nightfall, and in by dawn. Sometimes when her Pauly needed an entire weekend, Sheriff Fats would be hauling his German ass back to the POW camp on a Monday morning. It was during these morning drive times that Fats, perhaps out of some sense of patriotic duty, would pump the escaped prisoner for vital war-related information.

"Are those tits of hers real?"

"Oh—mein Gott! You would not believe them. So real. And so soft. I suck on them like I am the little child."

"You've actually sucked on them?"

"Ja, ich mochte mich verschulden, sie habe meinen Mund . . ."

"In English! In English!"

"Yes, yes. I want to choke, they have filled my mouth with so much pleasure."

"Okay, then what?"

"We are in a field in the grass by the big river with a full moon sailing across the sky. I have this big teats in my mouth, and I slip my hand down her pants until my fingers go to the inside of her."

"You're shitting me, right?"

"No, Sheriff. No shitting you. But this is as far as she lets me go . . . for now."

"But you actually sucked on those tits? Both of them?"

"*Ja,* Sheriff. I actually sucked on them. Both."

"Goddamn. I'm going to have to rethink this war, because you are one hell of a soldier."

In fact, it was being that kind of soldier that may have led to *Soldat* Stangl's problems at Camp Kickapoo with *Unteroffizier* Frick. It is not easy to say where the hostility began between the two men. My father thought their mutual animosity and distrust started long before the two soldiers were taken prisoner. For if Frick was indeed a rabid Nazi, the young Stangl may have been the anti-Nazi.

It was a known fact that some of the prisoners at Camp Kickapoo had come from a motley group of soldiers branded the 999 Penal Division. As the war sapped Germany of its young men, Hitler's army turned to Germany's prisons for fresh bodies. Though some of the men of the 999 were probably robbers, rapists, and murderers, most of them had been arrested simply for their politics—usually Social Democrats or Communists. Paul Friedrich Stangl, it turned out, had two strikes against him. He was a petty thief, and the son of an SS officer who thought a little jail time might do his wayward kid some good. During the fighting in North Africa, it was these thieves and political prisoners who surrendered the first chance they had, rightly believing they had more in common with the Americans than they did with the Third Reich.

At Camp Kickapoo, the German prisoner everybody liked to call Pauly didn't seem all that political. In fact, he didn't seem to give a damn one way or the other. This alone could have led Frick to hate him. Curse him. Beat him. Even if a prisoner couldn't embrace the Nazi cause, he had better not show indifference, which in Germany was the biggest sin of all. Frick, my father said, came to believe that Pauly was a threat to discipline in the camp. So the rabid Nazi called on the *Heilige Geist*. The Holy Ghost.

Back to the days of Bismarck, the Holy Ghost was a secret society operating among Germany's enlisted men. An avenging spirit bent on maintaining discipline and fear among the troops. Their most common tactic was to throw a blanket over a soldier's head and then beat him senseless. This way, blood was kept to a minimum, and the victim never saw his attackers—the way one never saw the Holy Ghost.

When my father came across young Stangl after his first beating, he hardly recognized him, his face was so badly swollen. After fetching him the American doctor, Dad tried to determine what had happened. The only words he could get from the usually gregarious Pauly were, *"Heilige Geist."*

As the war years drifted by and 1943 quickly became 1944, and then 1945, prisoner Paul Friedrich Stangl underwent a marked change. For one thing, he stopped escaping. Or he stopped getting caught escaping. Where he was once loud and funny, he was now quiet and sullen. Some of his fellow prisoners joked that he was in love. And, indeed, there were rumors in the camp of an American girl. But some muttered *"Heilige Geist"* under their breath. Others just muttered *"Frick."* Those who had mastered the subtleties of American English muttered *"fucking Frick."*

If Sheriff Fats jokingly believed young Stangl was one hell of a soldier, he most certainly believed Patty Best was one hell of a girl. In a strange way, we were all proud of her—that little old Kickapoo Falls could produce a spirit that striking, that sexy. It's hard to say what kind of woman she would have become. I believe that eventually she would have left Wisconsin. Would have had to. The girl simply had too much going for her. New York, or maybe California, would have been more her style. I like to think of her in the movies. Or maybe strutting across a Broadway stage with the conceit of a Mae West. But, tragically, none of that was to be.

Not long after the Holy Ghost paid another call on prisoner Stangl, Patty's young and adventurous life came to a violent end in the Kickapoo Hills. Her once beautiful body was found lying faceup in the woods, off an old logging road. Her throat had been severed with an ax. Her breasts had been chopped off. Fats said the scene was a bloody mess.

The murder weapon was found poorly hidden in the woods, not far from the body. Every ax and saw in the prison camp was numbered. This bloody ax was registered to POW P. F. Stangl.

Back at Camp Kickapoo, prisoner Stangl was missing. It would be his last escape. The hunt was on. A small-town girl in the heart of Wisconsin was presumed murdered by a German prisoner of war. A goddamned Nazi. If not captured quickly, all hell would break loose.

29 | ANOTHER FUNERAL

When I get mad, I pick up my rifle. I always have. Growing up above the Dells, a lot of Wisconsin deer paid with their lives for my adolescent anger. I gave up hunting after the war. Tried to confine my shooting to target practice. Yes, I was still an angry young man, but my anger took on a deeper meaning. So it was that after the funeral of Deputy Hess, I found myself at the firing range in the big woods above the Kickapoo Gunn Club, squeezing off one round after another. The dark outline of a man six hundred yards away was riddled with 30.06 hits. His head was in shreds. His heart was missing.

"I think you got him," Alex said.

We'd had our first frost. After the murder of Deputy Hess, the nighttime temperature plunged to 31 degrees. But the days rebounded nicely. Autumn was in full bloom. The sun was high in the afternoon sky. The lakes and ponds of Kickapoo County were the color of gunmetal, reflecting a thousand different colors on a thousand different trees. Once again, the bright weather of the fall season was not in sync with the dark mood of the day.

I think the most impressive funerals in the world are the funerals for

American cops killed in the line of duty. The squad cars come from miles around. Nobody plans it. Nobody asks them to come. They just start showing up. On the day we buried Hess, the freshly washed and waxed squad cars began streaming into Kickapoo Falls at dawn, glistening in the morning sun. They double-parked in circles around Courthouse Square. There were sheriff's cars there from every county in Wisconsin, and some from Minnesota. Minneapolis, St. Paul, Milwaukee, Green Bay, and even the Chicago police department sent squads up to the funeral. Hundreds of cars, making for a funeral procession miles in length. No horns. No sirens. Just flashing red lights as far as the eye could see. Townspeople, tears in their eyes, lined Main Street as the hearse rolled by. At the cemetery, a kid from the high school played taps. Veterans of the First World War fired off a twenty-one-gun salute. Two Marines stood honor guard. The flag was folded and presented. A simple payer was said. That was the way we buried our own.

Sheriff Zimmer had spoken eloquently at the service. "Today," he intoned, "we bury a man who served his country in war . . . and then came home to serve his community in a time of peace. His death saddens our hearts . . . but his bravery elevates our spirits. He wore the uniform of the Kickapoo County Sheriff's Department with the same pride that he wore the uniform of the United States Marine Corps. It was my honor to know him. My privilege to command him."

I squeezed off one last round. The blast echoed through the woods. "Do you think Sheriff Zimmer shot Hess?"

Alex strained her eyes to see the last bullet hole I had made in the target. "Do you?"

"You're the big-shot detective from Scotland Yard . . . you tell me."

"I think it's a possibility. What did the autopsy say?"

"The slugs that killed him were nine millimeter. The kind of bullets that come out of a German Luger."

"Were both shots fired from the same pistol?"

"According to the markings . . . yes."

An all-points bulletin was put out for Wolf Stangl, but in agreement with the Secret Service, no mention of his Nazi past was included. It was our hope that newspeople would not connect the dots now running between myself, Stangl, and President Kennedy's visit to St. Paul. My offer to back out of the Mass had been graciously rejected by the White House. In fact, the Secret Service seemed to treat the entire threat as almost routine. Promised me a meeting.

I reloaded. Handed the gun to Alex. She examined it as a curiosity.

"It's a 1903 Springfield," I told her. "It fires a 30.06, fed to it by a five-round magazine. In sixty years, nobody has made a better rifle."

"Really?" A fresh target was pinned into place. Alex LaChapelle put the Springfield to her shoulder like a pro. Stiffened in anticipation. She was wearing a stylish field jacket. Her hair was still down from the funeral, blowing free in the autumn breeze. In fact, I thought her hair might have been in her eyes when she squeezed the trigger. A gaping hole appeared in the chest of the target. She fired again. The hole widened. A third shot just about obliterated the chest region.

Needless to say, I was impressed. A woman of never-ending surprises. "Where did you learn how to shoot?"

"Boarding school, mostly. We used a Gewehr 41. Chambered in 7.9 millimeter with a ten-round box magazine."

"That's a German rifle," I said.

"Yes, our instructor preferred it. He always said if there are two things the Germans do well . . . it is making guns, and making war." She nodded at the Springfield in her arms. "But this is nice." Then she handed it back to me.

"That must have been one hell of a boarding school." I laid the rifle over my shoulder and we walked the path away from the target range, along the ridgeline overlooking the Wisconsin River and the Kickapoo

Gunn Club. The clubhouse stood on a hill above the sixteenth green. Canadian geese frolicked in the ponds below. The fairways were resplendent. "Fats always wanted me to join," I told her.

"Why didn't you?"

"Truthfully? For years, I thought they were silly. Pretentious. Fats never really fit in, you know. They needed the county sheriff in their pocket, so they treated him like gold. They treated me like shit."

"What makes you believe they're involved in this?"

"I suspect they took a shot at our President once before."

"Your wheat field case?"

"Yes."

"But you can't prove it?"

"No. That's the beauty of conspiracies . . . they force you to peel away the layers."

"How so?"

"Peel way Stangl . . . maybe you find Zimmer. Peel away Zimmer . . . you find the Gunn Club. Peel away the Gunn Club, God only knows what you'll find."

"I must tell you, Deputy Pennington, it simply looks like a golf club to me."

"What does that mean?"

She stepped in front of me in that way that she had. Stuck her beauty in my face. It was her feminine and highly effective way of making a point. "It means others in your town do not share your negative view of the Gunn Club . . . and they are no closer to being a member than are you."

"It's all in my head?"

"Since when does one need some grand, evil conspiracy to take a shot at an American President? With the exception of John Wilkes Booth and the ghost of the Lost Cause, most of the men who have taken shots at your Presidents have been petty criminals, or lunatics.

Wolf Stangl doesn't want President Kennedy dead . . . he wants you dead."

"Maybe he wants us both dead."

"Do you believe in vigilante justice?" she asked.

"The Gunn Club isn't about vigilante justice," I explained. "It's not about golf, or hunting. It's about power, and about the lengths men will go to preserve their access to power."

"But that isn't what I asked you, Deputy. I asked if you believed in vigilante justice."

"I believe some men need to be shot."

"And how many of these men have you shot?"

"Apparently, not enough."

30 | ON THE ROAD AGAIN

Once again I made the drive down to Madison. Not that I ever minded. It was a beautiful drive and, as I've said, I always did my best thinking on the road. If I was about to accuse my sheriff and political rival of murder, I needed some dirt with which to bury him.

I also needed a day away from the lovely detective from Scotland Yard. Alex LaChapelle was getting to me in more ways than one. She had a point about some of the losers who had assassinated or attempted to assassinate American Presidents, but her implication that the high crimes of the Kickapoo Gunn Club were all in my head really stuck in my craw. These were power-hungry men in radically changing times. They would not stand idly by while their power slowly slipped away.

Something else was bothering me about Alex LaChapelle. Something I couldn't quite put my finger on. It was the funny way she referred to the man in her life—that anonymous face back in London she claimed to have slept with on several occasions. The relationship she described had a strange ring to it. Off-key. Maybe it was just my jealousy kicking in. I wondered if there was a way to check on her life in England without her knowing about it. I was pretty good at spying on people, but I'd never done it from across the ocean.

I was also having fantasies about her. Dreams, if you will. Strange as it sounds coming from me, they were not sexual. At least, I don't think they were sexual. One in particular seemed innocent enough. Yes, I was watching her from a secret vantage point in the nearby woods, but nothing happened.

It is noontime bright. Summertime warm. She is seated by the edge of a sky-blue lake. Maybe it's in England. Maybe it's in Wisconsin. Doesn't really matter. She is dressed in canary-yellow shorts with a white cotton top. A necklace of red beads is draped about her neck. Her hair is tied back in a way that is more casual than formal. Silver earrings dangle from her lobes. Elegant, but not flashy. She is wearing sunglasses. The way she is sitting is very ladylike. Her bare feet are flat on the grass. Her knees are together, angling up to her chest. Her arms are balanced over her knees. It is a very relaxed posture. Her legs are gorgeous. Flawless. Her arms are long and slender. Her fine, lissome hands, one atop the other, are manicured. Polished in pink. But what stands out is the pensive air of her countenance as she stares into the sparkling blue water before her. A troubled woman, deep in thought. A sad little smile graces her face, the kind of smile that might precede a tear. The beautiful face she shows to the world conceals something. She seems oblivious to her picturesque surroundings, and yet very much a part of them. I watch her sit this way for an hour.

So begins and ends my fantasy of Alex LaChapelle. There were times in my life when I would have killed to be married to a woman like that.

I came into Madison on the Middleton Road. Wound my way through the ever-sprawling UW campus to State Street, and then up the hill. Madison is one of America's unique cities. A hidden gem I had always hoped would remain hidden. Not too big. Not too small. The state capitol was built on an isthmus between two great bodies of water—Lake Monona and Lake Mendota. The city clusters around them. The Wisconsin capital is particularly striking during the summer and autumn months. In fact, the only thing I didn't like about the place was its nickname: Mad City. Gave the town a petty reputation it didn't deserve. Still, as much as I liked visiting, I could never shake the feeling I wasn't good enough for Madison. Part of it may have been my small-town inferiority complex. Part of it may have been the college atmosphere. Or maybe it was the imposing white marble dome of the state capitol building always glaring down at me.

I walked over to a state office building across the street from the capitol. It was a typical government building of the time. Nondescript. A five-story file cabinet. Unlike my last trip, I had made this trip in full uniform. I had always found it easier to obtain records with my hat in my hand, a badge on my chest, and a large gun on my hip. Back in those days, people didn't question cops.

She was a sweet, round woman. Had probably worked there for years. I handed her a request form over the countertop. I didn't mention that the subject of my search was a county sheriff. It was my hope she would not recognize the name. "I need the employment records of a J. D. Zimmer with the State of Wisconsin," I told her.

"Do you want just the public records, or would you like to see the personnel files?"

"If it's not too much bother," I said with a smile, "I'd like to see everything you have."

"Is this a criminal investigation?"

I dropped the smile. "Yes, ma'am, it is."

It was a good twenty minutes before she returned to me. "I'm sorry for the wait," she said. "There really wasn't a lot." She handed me two files. They were a lot thinner than I had expected, considering the man had risen to the office of sheriff.

I found a metal table beside a window overlooking Lake Monona. Paused a few seconds to soak in the autumnal beauty of Madison before opening the book on acting sheriff J. D. Zimmer.

I really believe the one reason my career in law enforcement ended so successfully was because I was able to change with times that were changing. Not easy for a cop. Most cops I knew clung stubbornly to their whims and their ways. It's not that they tried forever to hang on to their youthful days on the police force. It went much deeper than that. Most of them clung to the view of cops they held as a child. They grew up wanting to wear that badge and gun. Chase the bad guys. Protect the innocent. Punish the guilty. It was a vision of police work that was never real to begin with. But all of their lives, they clung to that vision nonetheless.

I was a bit different. You see, I never really wanted to be a cop. In fact, after the war, I went to school in Madison on the GI bill. I thought I was going to be some kind of scientist. After flunking out the first year, I attended a seminary school in St. Paul. But that was even harder than college, and I didn't have the courage it takes to be a priest.

Sheriff Fats made things simple. "I've seen your military record. You're a cop, son. You've got police work in your veins."

I sat at the table, and with the autumn sun streaming through the glass, I opened the files on the man who stood between me and the office of sheriff. In rough order, this is what I found:

Born: John David Zimmer, Oak Park, Illinois, 1919
Attended University of Chicago, 1936–1939
Prison guard, State Prison at Janesville, Wisconsin, 1950
Patrolman, Fort Atkinson, Wisconsin, 1953
Deputy Sheriff, Jefferson County, Wisconsin, 1955
Member, Governor's Commission on Penal Reform, 1960

There were other odds and ends, but overall it was a pretty slim file. In fact, plain and simple, it was just a pretty file. Almost sterile. What jumped out at me was what was missing. Again in rough order:

Why does a man smart enough to go to the University of Chicago become a cop?

Why did he drop out of college after three years?

Where was he from 1939 to 1950?

How does a lowly deputy sheriff win an appointment to a prestigious governor's commission?

And most importantly, why was he named acting sheriff of Kickapoo County?

Deputy Hess had said he had a hunch. Now, so did I.

During the wheat field case I had met a Professor Levine from the University of Chicago. A visiting physics professor teaching at UW Madison. I presented him with some of the more interesting aspects of the murder scene. He took it as a challenge. A chance to play detective. He put a lot of students and a lot of brainpower on the problem and, in the end, he helped me solve the case. I was so pleased, I offered to drive him home to Chicago from Madison.

On the road to the windy city, the brainy physics professor seemed fascinated with crime—almost as impressed with my line of work as I was with his. In particular, he was forever enthralled with Chicago's famous Leopold and Loeb case, where two brilliant students of immense wealth kidnapped and murdered a fourteen-year-old boy just to see if they could get away with it. "Evil walking hand in hand with intellect astounds me," he said. "There has to be an explanation . . . a scientific explanation."

"You're dealing with people, Professor. And with all respect to our friend Marilou Stephens, I'm not sure you can apply simple science to the complexities of the human mind and come up with accurate answers."

"Well, it's certainly a challenge, Deputy."

Now, studying the antiseptic file before me, I wondered if I might place a call to the professor in Chicago and challenge him once again.

31 | DEVIL'S LAKE

Sometimes, in looking back, it seems like all of the women in Kickapoo County had big tits. Amy Spellman had the biggest tits of all. They weren't big to the point of being ridiculous. They were just big to the point of being sexy as hell. She never endeavored to show them off. She never tried to hide them. I'm sure, to Amy Spellman, those gorgeous tits were just two pieces to the puzzle of who she was.

She was the classic Scandinavian blonde. Her maiden name had been Nelsen. She was tall for a woman, with baby-white skin and a natural smile. She was kind of shy, and everybody who knew her liked her. All in all, just one of our local beauties.

Her husband's name was John. I didn't know much about him. He was originally from Eau Claire. I think Amy had gone to school up there. After they married, they settled into a small farmhouse on the edge of the thick pines near Devil's Lake. I'm pretty sure they were only renting. Seemed too young to be buyers.

I was driving home from Madison after a long and frustrating day of trying to pick up some kind of paper trail on J. D. Zimmer. Usually, I was pretty good with documents. It was the lack of documents in

Sheriff Zimmer's file that was gnawing at me. The man behind the sunglasses, I suspected, was not the man he claimed to be. Perhaps Deputy Hess had had the same hunch.

Anyway, I had been my good little altar-boy self for several months, and now I was feeling edgy. Working day in and day out with the goddesslike Alex might have had something to do with it, but then I never really needed much of an excuse.

The autumn days were getting considerably shorter. It was dark as I neared the Devil's Lake area. I checked my watch. Near 9 p.m. The timing seemed perfect. At that point, I was like the dupe in that old comic routine—where there was a little devil standing on one shoulder, and a little angel standing on the other. Each of them screaming the opposite advice into opposite ears.

"Do it."

"Don't do it."

"Do it."

"Don't do it."

"Do it."

The little Catholic angel always carried the day. But, I confess, it was usually the devil who carried the night.

One of the things you learn in years of patrolling a rural county is that farm people don't care much about pulling down their bedroom shades. Or even turning off the lights. Why should they? There's nobody out there. Well, there's not supposed to be anybody out there. But as far back as when we were growing up town boys, our gang was cutting through cornfields, crossing country roads, and sneaking up on farmhouses to see what we could see.

I steered off the county highway and rolled down a bumpy old fire road. Killed my headlights. Deep into the woods, I brought the squad to a halt and shut off the engine. It was another warm night. The car windows were down. I sat and listened to the concert of crickets.

Again, I checked my watch. Now it was 9:15. I stepped from the squad.

There is nothing quite as dark as dark in the woods. I carried with me my trusty flashlight. One of those heavy steel five-battery suckers. In those days our flashlights doubled as nightsticks. I kept it off. Step by step, I inched my way through the ancient forest. It was the best time of the year to be in the woods. The weather was still gorgeous, the trees were in bloom, and the first frost had killed off most of the flying insects. A state park was nearby, and the tall trees in this particular neck of the woods had been spared the axes and saws of the nineteenth century.

They were a young couple. Newlyweds with no children. Quite frankly, they fucked a lot. It was an old house they were living in—two-story clapboard in need of a fresh coat of paint. There was no air conditioning, so it was not unusual that the bed would be pushed near the window. By the time I reached the tree line, the bedroom light upstairs had already been turned on. The downstairs was dark. I could see the two of them passing in and out of the room as they prepared for bed. Finally, Amy came into the bedroom to stay. She was wearing a dark bathrobe, which set off her thick blond hair. She tossed a wet towel onto the bed and then stood before the open window. Her arms were folded just below those wonderfully large breasts. Every now and then she would rub away the first chills of the evening as she stared up at the stars. Believe me, out in the country, far from the city lights, the stars on a clear and dry Wisconsin night are a considerable sight.

At last, the husband entered the bedroom. No shirt. Probably no shoes. Just a pair of blue jeans. He was a handsome man, a little taller than Amy, with a wide hairy chest. He, too, walked to the window. Came up behind and put his arms around her. Locked her in a poignant bear hug. They stood together staring into the night.

I leaned up against a tree and folded my own arms to ward off the goose bumps. I was as close as I could comfortably get without being spotted. Yet, I was pretty close. If you really know how to hide, and keep in mind I was trained how to hide, your target should be able to stare directly at your hiding spot and still not be able to see you.

My heart picked up the pace to the point where I could hear it thumping. Every now and then, through the woods, came the sound of a night owl searching for prey. Other than that, the old forest was unusually quiet. Or maybe it just seemed quiet to me because my ears were tuning in to the attractive young couple in the bedroom window.

It wasn't long before the big stud made a move on his beautiful wife. From behind, he draped his arm over her shoulder and plunged his hand beneath her bathrobe. Fondled a breast. She leaned back into him. He kissed her neck. In another minute, he had that big tit out of her bathrobe, exposing it to the night air. Exposing it to me. I swear, I could hear Amy moaning with delight. Finally, he spun her around and they kissed as he stripped her of the robe. Let it drop to the floor.

Her naked back was to me now. She was still in her panties. He usually threw her onto the bed, but this night he spun her around and placed her up against the window. It was almost like the guy knew I was out there. I was ecstatic. This had the potential to be the best night ever.

Standing only in her panties, she had one hand on each side of the window, exposing both of those magnificent tits to me. Her husband, John, seemed to disappear, until I realized he had dropped to his knees behind her. He was kissing her ass, or something like that. I could see her panties slipping down her hips. She was smiling with delight. I thought for sure he would lay her across the bed, but instead he stood up behind her. Kept her arms spread against the window. He spread her legs. That's when she let out her first scream. He was inside of her. I was sure of it. He reached his arms around her and grabbed a tit with each hand. Then he squeezed. He was fucking her hard. I mean, really hard. Intense. I couldn't really say if Amy was enjoying it as much as he was. She was certainly moaning with sexual pleasure, but she didn't seem all that comfortable doing it in that standing position. On the other hand, her stud of a husband couldn't have been happier. He was screaming louder than she was. I had the feeling this was their first time in a vertical position, because he was coming fast.

Perhaps because I was never a direct participant, I had always found the sounds of lovemaking more erotic than the sights. Even before his wife's screams could reach their high octave peak, John Spellman was spent.

Amy was moaning with relief. She appeared glad it was over. Most of the young pigs I had watched fuck over the years would have been done with her at that point. But this guy was something of a tender lover. She turned in to him, and he held her tight. I watched him put her to bed. Then he walked across the room and turned out the light.

At that point, I wanted to smoke a cigarette, but I had given up smoking when the first reports linked it to cancer. So I just stood there. Blowing air through my lips. Staring up at the dark window. That's when I noticed it. Something was wrong. It wasn't anything I heard. It's what I didn't hear. The crickets had stopped. In fact, everything had stopped. Suddenly, dead silence pervaded the entire forest.

For a thousand years people have been telling tales of the dark woods. The tale I tell of that voyeuristic evening is to me as chilling as any story I have ever heard. What broke the unearthly silence was a scream so frightening, it shot through me with the force of an electrical shock. I wasn't one to freeze in the line of duty, but I froze that night. For what I heard resembled the high-pitched scream of a wolf. The cry of the banshee. It was a scream of bloody murder emanating from somewhere deep in the woods. In truth, it was so loud and so ungodly that I could not even tell from which direction it was coming. I don't think I'd ever been as scared as I was at that moment. All of my senses intensified. Magnified. The spit in my mouth turned to dust. Then the scream trailed off to silence. Ran out of breath. Now my heart was lodged somewhere deep in my throat. Probably why I couldn't breathe. Finally, I forced myself to move. I plunged directly into the woods, into the deep shadows of the rustling pines. I drew my service revolver. Kept my flashlight off, but at the ready. The gun in my hand could stop a Mack truck, but I didn't know what good it would be up against a ghost. There had to be a reason they named the area Devil's Lake.

It came again. Even louder this time, cutting through the night air like a hot knife. I squashed my fear and tried to reason. Great horned owls were known for their lunatic screams, but they only screamed like lunatics during their mating season, which was early spring. Again, I couldn't determine its direction. In fact, I couldn't see a damn thing. The problem for me was this—as animalistic as *it* pretended to sound, that screaming in the woods possessed a human element—though it was hard to believe anything human could scream that loud. Still, there were no wolves in Wisconsin. The beast of a thousand legends had been hunted to extinction in the Dairy State.

When all was quiet again, I rechecked my position. In a crunch, I could break for the darkened house before me, though if the Spellmans heard what I was hearing, I'd probably be greeted with a shotgun blast. I could also backtrack through the black forest to my squad. It seemed to me, the squad was the better bet. I had the cover of dark and the shelter of the woods.

Just then I thought I glimpsed something shapeless steal through the trees. I held my gun at the ready. Strained my eyes to the point of pain. But it was my ears that were once again assaulted. By laughter this time. Mad laughter. Feline laughter. The laughter was closer than the scream. I put it somewhere in the shadows between me and the house. I leveled the .38 in that direction.

I was within a heartbeat of squeezing off a round when *it* finally spoke in that electronic foreign-sounding voice that had been haunting me for years. It was some kind of loudspeaker, and the speech emanating from it was German. Nazi German. *"Es ist ein guter Tag gewesen. Alle Züge waren rechtzeitig."*

It was the amplified voice of Colonel Stangl, tearing through the deep Wisconsin woods the way it once tore through Wolf Pass. The way it once echoed across his prison camp, like the devil in Dante's *Inferno.*

I couldn't understand the German words, but that wasn't important, because he wasn't talking to me. He was talking at me. That I knew he was out there seemed more important to him than anything he might say.

I would not have believed it was possible for him to have followed me at night without my noticing. If I had been out on patrol, it never would have happened. But I wasn't out on patrol. I was out in the woods in the dead of night trying to satisfy some inexplicable need. Living with my weakness. Ironically, if the madman had his rifle with him, I was about to die of my strength.

I knew about where he was standing. My guess was, he knew about the same. It had to be some kind of bullhorn he was holding. He was sounding cockier than he actually was, because he couldn't possibly spot me through the trees. It must have been especially frustrating if he was planning to take a shot at me.

I decided not to engage him in conversation. In fact, I decided not to engage him at all that evening. I would silently withdraw from the dark field of battle and fight him another day. There was no question that up until then he had been winning the psychological war. But I think I scored at least a few points as I quietly slipped away from him that night. The same way I had slipped through his fingers at Wolf Pass.

32 | THE SURRENDER: *1944*

Thanks to my rifle and my handiwork, no train again reached Wolf Pass before the winter snows. By the spring thaw, Germany had surrendered. But long before that happened, it was I who gave myself up. The decision to surrender was hard, but actually doing it was torture. Nothing in the world is more humiliating. That must be why they don't teach you how to surrender in the United States Army.

The mountains of Bavaria are treacherous. There is nothing comparable anywhere near Wisconsin. I was like a frightened deer, hiding in a stand of pines above a gravel road. For five days I had limped, sometimes crawled, in the direction of Switzerland—dodging German patrols, one bloody boulder at a time. I was making little progress. I was out of food. Out of energy. My wounds were getting the best of me. My stomach felt as if I had been stabbed. I was dragging my left leg. To top it all off, I was lost. Compass and all. I couldn't help but wonder, lying there in the morning cold, if that was how the deer back home had felt as I stalked them through the pines. They had to instinctively know that I was out to kill them. In fact, I used to think deer had a sixth sense when it came to me. That I was different from other hunters. A legend in the North Woods. My prey had no room for error. But now I was the hunted, and I confess, I hated it. Even with my rifle and a few remaining rounds, I hated it. For me deer hunting would never be the same.

I grabbed hold of the crucifix around my neck. It was made of pewter and had belonged to my mother. She had worn it around her neck until the day she died. I was just a little boy when my father removed it from her body and looped it over my head. Now in the Bavarian Alps, with the cross of Jesus clenched in my fist, I prayed to the mother of all mothers for advice. Tell me what to do.

It was a circular road that ran beneath me. I may have crossed it once before. The gravel was thick with the tire tracks of German patrols. They must have wanted me awfully bad. Still, I felt I had traveled far enough from Wolf Pass to give myself plausible deniability. All that was left to do was surrender and play stupid.

If captivity seems inevitable, I was told, get rid of the rifle and the ammunition. Get rid of anything that would hint you are a sniper. You were a gunner on a B-17. You were on a bombing run. Your plane was hit. You bailed out. End of story. Never reveal the scope of your mission. Never.

I felt as if I was parting with my best friend. I actually kissed my rifle goodbye. Then I ditched the Springfield in the woods. Threw some fallen branches over it. Scattered the few cartridges I had left.

When I finally toppled down to the gravel, I forced myself up again and started limping down the road, like I was on my last stroll in the country. I reasoned a German patrol would be by soon enough. Besides, the war was near its end. How long would I be a prisoner? How bad could it be?

I was on the road an hour, having second thoughts about giving myself up, when the rumble of trucks could be heard lumbering up the mountain. Troop trucks. At the first sight of the patrol, I limped to the center of the road and threw my hands high in the air.

I must have been the first American soldier some of the younger Germans had ever encountered. Some of them looked as young as fifteen. Considering my appearance, it had to make them wonder how they were losing the war. I was ordered to sit in the middle of the road. Not easy to do with a broken leg. There was a lot of nervous chatter on walkie-talkies. My German was limited to about a dozen words picked up during the war. None of their soldiers spoke English. We were obviously waiting for somebody. One of the kids offered me a swig of water. As my thirst was quenched for the first time in hours, I remember thinking that captivity wasn't going to be so bad. That's when the Nazi monkey arrived.

He had on a gray SS uniform. I guessed his rank at captain. He was a wiry little fellow. Nasty, with thick spectacles. His English was lousy, but to the point. "*Auf* feet!"

I stood, but he knocked me right back down with the back of his hand. From the looks on the faces of the German soldiers, they, too, were afraid of the little bastard.

"*Wo ist* rifle?"

"I'm a gunner," I told him. "My guns went down with the plane."

"Sie lügen!" He put the boot to me. *"Wo ist* rifle?"

"On the plane."

"No plane," he screamed. *"Zeigen Sie mir* rifle."

I didn't show him squat. I did, however, get the shit kicked out of me. It felt like when I was beaten up as a kid. Even though I was bruised and bloody, I kept thinking to myself that it wasn't all that bad. I'd survive.

The Nazi monkey had his men scour the nearby woods for an hour, but I had traveled far enough to believe my rifle was safely hidden.

"Wirf ihn in den Lastwagen," the captain yelled.

I was hoisted to my feet and thrown into the back of a truck for the long ride down the mountain.

33 | PORTRAIT OF A PSYCHOPATH

For as long as anybody can remember, farmers have been bringing their produce to Madison and selling it on the sidewalks that surround the state capitol. The farmer's market. It is America at its best. Country meets city. Still, as much as I enjoyed the tomatoes and the apples and the corn on the cob, not to mention the sunny Saturday mornings, it was Marilou Stephens I sought out in Madison. The maniacal scream in the woods and the Nazi bullhorn had unnerved me. It was frightening that this ghost of the Third Reich was able to shadow me so easily. That he was able to prey on my weaknesses without end. I needed some kind of ammunition to steel myself against a force I couldn't see, much less understand.

As we walked up the isthmus to the market, I leveled with the brainy beauty. Revealed my suspicions about Sheriff Zimmer. Told her of the public records I had found, and not found, and of the photograph and packet that I had sent to Professor Levine at the University of Chicago, where Zimmer claimed to have been a student. I told her of my hunt for Wolf Stangl. That I believed the Nazi war criminal was in Wisconsin. That he was shadowing me, and that he would probably follow me to St. Paul. Now armed with more specifics, she told me in no uncertain terms what kind of man I was up against.

The market was pleasantly crowded. We moved easily among the fruit and vegetable stands. Marilou held up a big red apple. "A man like that would eat his own children and not feel any remorse. There is no boundary he won't cross. The suffering of others has no effect on him."

"I already know that he's a monster."

"You're not going to catch him believing in ghosts and goblins. Get clinical. He is almost certainly a psychopath."

"Aren't all criminals crazy?"

"No. That's a very dangerous assumption. True psychopaths are not crazy men suffering hallucinations . . . incapable of self-control. Quite the contrary. They are chillingly in command of their emotions. They are aware of what they are doing, and why. Their behavior is the result of choice. Freely exercised. That's why we send psychopaths to prison instead of a mental hospital."

Beneath the shadow of the state house, we walked on.

"Tell me more."

"He has his own moral code. Besides being deceitful, he is highly manipulative and highly persuasive, with good social skills."

"I was in his prison camp. I've seen his social skills."

She continued. "What he likes best is exercising his power over others. He will lie endlessly. He will lie even when the truth won't hurt him. If one lie is exposed, he will make up another on the spot. He is narcissistic. He sees himself as a superior being justified in living according to his own rules. He will justify his actions all way to the hangman's noose."

"When he calls me on the phone . . . can I reason with him?"

"No. He sees no reason to change his behavior. All of his life, he has probably been protected from the consequences of his actions by well-meaning family members . . . usually women . . . his mother, his wife, his daughter. As a result, his behavior goes unchecked and unpunished."

"Cold, calculating, and ruthless," I said.

"And that's his bright side, Deputy Pennington. He will never recover. He cannot be rehabilitated. He can only be killed."

The talk of killing sounded sickening coming from such an attractive and intelligent woman, like profanity from a Christian. I was almost sorry that I had dragged her into the story. We sat on the steps of the capitol building and watched the shoppers parade past.

Where the postwar woman was supposed to get married and have babies, Marilou Stephens got an education and had a career. And from what I could tell, she did it over the objections of her family.

"My father was that way," she said, almost to herself. "Cold and calculating. Not a psychopath, but a manipulative old bastard. If I could crawl into a time tunnel, I'd go back and see to it that I got different parents."

"There's a paradox in that statement," I told her, "but I don't have the intellect to discuss it."

She smiled at that, but it was a sorrowful little smile. "It's called the 'grandfather paradox.' The most innocent of time travel nudges the tiniest of butterflies, who flutters his wings and begins the wind that becomes a hurricane that kills your grandfather."

"No more you."

"That's right," she said. "I would never be born."

It was the only time I ever heard Marilou mention her father, but it was the second time that she had mentioned a time tunnel, as if she knew of a secret passage in the earth where one could go back and start over.

The variety and the abundance of food surrounding the capitol were remarkable. So many of us in the capitol square that morning had survived the Depression. Survived the war. Did anybody remember what it was like to be hungry?

I tried to take in all of the things Marilou had told me about the kind of evil I was up against. Again I thought of canceling my trip to St. Paul. Why play into his hands?

"I have a security meeting with the Secret Service tomorrow," I informed her. "Zimmer and Captain Hargrow are going to be there."

"And your detective friend from London . . . will she be at this meeting?"

That was the woman I heard speaking, not the psychologist. "How did you know about her?"

"That rumor made it all the way through the hills. I heard she's striking."

"I suppose she is," I said, faking indifference. "Yes, I expect she'll be there. She wants Stangl as bad as I do."

"Why?"

"Because he killed her father."

"That might make her a little too close to the case. Do you trust her?"

"Yes, I trust her."

"Do you love her?"

34 | THE MEETING

We gathered in the sheriff's office. J. D. Zimmer was seated at his desk, right between the American flag and the Wisconsin state flag. He was wearing his damn sunglasses. Captain Hargrow parked his ass on the edge of the desk, again looking down at me in the chair. Outside the window were great bursts of leaves. Explosions of color. The autumn sky couldn't have been bluer. My mood couldn't have been grayer.

Mr. Andersen of the Secret Service introduced himself to us. He was a solid no-nonsense man with slick, dark hair. Impeccably dressed. He smelled of an Ivy League education. He got right down to business. "I'll be in charge of the St. Paul leg of the President's trip."

"Where's Alex?" I asked, interrupting.

Zimmer glanced over at me. "I saw no need for her to attend."

"This is the Scotland Yard detective?" asked Mr. Andersen of Captain Hargrow.

Hargrow threw up his hands. "Don't look at me . . . I've never met her."

Zimmer spoke up. "Yes. She's been assisting our investigation."

Mr. Andersen seemed puzzled. "I thought Captain Hargrow was assisting your investigation."

"No," I told the Secret Service man, "Captain Hargrow is investigating me. Detective LaChapelle is assisting the investigation."

By the look on his face, Mr. Andersen wasn't happy with my sarcasm. "I see. Is she traveling to St. Paul?"

Again Zimmer spoke without hesitation. "No."

That came as news to me. "When did she tell you that?" I asked.

"This morning."

"You talked to her?"

Zimmer gave me that cold, blank stare of his. The man could freeze water with just a dirty look. "I talk to her quite often. I *am* the sheriff."

That he talked to her often also came as news to me.

Mr. Andersen not only sensed the tension in the room, he seemed fed up with the whole mess. He seized the conversation. "The reason I'm here, gentlemen, is because of the conflicting accounts we're getting on the two homicide investigations in Kickapoo County."

"There are three homicides now," Zimmer reminded him.

"Three homicides then," confirmed Mr. Andersen. "Personally, I wouldn't give a damn if Richard Nixon were your killer . . . except that your lead investigator, Deputy Pennington here, is about to attend Mass with the President of the United States. Now, do you have a suspect?"

"Yes," I told him.

"No," argued Zimmer.

Mr. Andersen shook his head in disgust. "I'm guessing this brings us to the infamous Wolf Stangl debate."

Captain Hargrow grinned and nodded his head.

Sheriff Zimmer used his fingers to count off his points. "There have been no reported sightings of strangers or suspicious characters in Kickapoo County before or after the murders . . . much less a Nazi war criminal known to the FBI, military intelligence, and the Secret Service. Not even Deputy Pennington, who once knew him personally, has caught a glimpse of this so-called madman. If he's here . . . he's a ghost."

Mr. Andersen chewed on those facts. "I don't believe in ghosts. Can I take your argument to the bank, Sheriff?"

"Yes, sir, you can."

"More importantly, can I take it to my superiors?"

"Yes, sir, you can."

The meeting was short and humiliating. I stood to leave. "Mr. Andersen," I said, "may we speak alone?"

We moved into the stairwell with the tall windows that overlooked Courthouse Square. The tree-lined park that stretched before us was magnificent in its glory. I spoke to the Secret Service man with as much earnestness in my voice as was possible without sounding desperate. "I can appreciate that you're a professional, Mr. Andersen, but you're going to have to take this threat a lot more seriously." I gestured back to the sheriff's office. "I won't be dismissed."

"We take all threats seriously, Deputy Pennington. The problem here is finding the threat. Did this Stangl character threaten the life of the President?"

"No . . . not specifically."

"In these alleged phone calls to you—"

"What do you mean, 'alleged?'" I argued, interrupting. "I have the man on tape."

"Captain Hargrow seems to think what you have on tape is good theater. He checked with the phone company. There was indeed a call placed to your house from the phone booth where the deputy was killed that night . . . but the call never went through. Whoever you have on tape did not call from that location."

The evidence hit me like a brick, partly because I was getting the information secondhand.

Mr. Andersen continued. "In these phone calls, did your suspect make any mention of the President?"

"No."

"Any mention of St. Paul?"

"No."

"Do you see my dilemma, Deputy? Captain Hargrow is somewhat skeptical. Your sheriff seems almost dumbfounded. Your assistant from Scotland Yard didn't even show up. I also understand that you're a candidate for the sheriff's job?"

I was flabbergasted. "What . . . you think this is just politics?"

The Secret Service man shrugged his wide shoulders. "Politics does have a tendency to follow the President of the United States. Aside from that, we have a confidential FBI report in hand stating there is 'no credible evidence' your man Stangl is in the country. Fact is, there is no credible evidence the man is alive . . . and if he is alive, what flimsy evidence we have points to his living in South America. I'm going to have a hard time convincing the brass he's visiting the Wisconsin Dells."

35 | CAMP KICKAPOO: *The Trial*

German POW Paul Friedrich Stangl surrendered himself to Sheriff Fats on a country road outside Kickapoo Falls. He was tired and hungry. And lost. He finally stopped by a farm and asked the farmer's wife if she would call the legendary sheriff for him. Asked if he could have some food and water while he waited. He told the family he had done no wrong. He was no threat.

True to his word, that's where Fats found the young man, sitting beside the mailbox on the dirt road that ran by the farm. "There was no blood on him," the sheriff would later testify. "He was wearing the same old prisoner uniform he had escaped in. It was dirty and sweaty from his running . . . but there was no blood on it. Don't know how he could have killed our Patty that way and not got blood on himself."

Word had spread down Main Street that the escaped prisoner and accused murderer of Patty Best was in the county jail beneath the courthouse, and that he was being transferred. A large crowd gathered in the square out front. There was no talk of lynching, or anything like that, but the tension in town that day was palpable. A combination of military police vehicles and sheriff's cars surrounded the Kickapoo

County Courthouse. It was by far the most dramatic convoy ever seen in our neck of the woods.

Fats led the way, strutting out the double doors of the courthouse like a bull moose. Behind him came two army MPs. Each of them had hold of an arm of the prisoner. *Soldat* Stangl was shackled at the wrists and feet. Other MPs and sheriff's deputies followed behind, some of them carrying shotguns. The most striking thing about the scene was that young Stangl was now wearing his uniform—the sun-bleached, shrunken gray wool uniform of the once proud Afrika Korps. Fats said he had requested it. They had to wait while it was driven down from the logging camp. Perhaps the prisoner's German-Austrian pride had kicked in. Or it could be that uniform was the only shred of protest he could muster while in the hands of an enemy bent on destroying him.

The heavily guarded convoy proceeded slowly out of town. Sheriff Fats personally escorted them to the borders of his county. They left without incident, through the hills, toward the United States Disciplinary Barracks at Camp McCoy, Wisconsin. During World War II, it contained a maximum-security military prison where some of the worst-of-the-worst Nazis were held until nearly a year after the war's end.

Between Fats's position as county sheriff, and my father's position as the YMCA representative, I was able to penetrate some of the secrecy that surrounded the murder trial of young Stangl. In later years, through the Freedom of Information Act, I was able to obtain some of the records. But to this day, a lot of the documentation concerning the German POWs remains sealed—and in some cases, lost.

Criminal trials, as practiced by the military, often seem a puzzle to American civilians. This was especially true during the war years, when it appeared the rules were being made up as the war went on. Yet even in peacetime, military courts have an extremely low rate of acquittal. In the case of the U.S. Army *vs.* Paul Friedrich Stangl, there were to be no shades of gray. It was murder, or it wasn't anything.

The trial was held in secret, but as the YMCA representative, my father was allowed to wait in the anteroom of the courtroom at Camp McCoy. It was there one day that he encountered Nazi Frick. "His eyes were a taunt to the human condition," Dad told me. "If ever a man fit the image of an ax murderer, it was that damned Frick."

Frick was one of the few prisoners at Camp Kickapoo who spoke English, and he had come to the trial to testify against Stangl. No record of his testimony is available, but it must have been devastating for the jury to hear a Nazi prisoner testifying for the American prosecution.

Not long after Frick's testimony came one of those bizarre announcements only the army could put out—that if the defendant should be acquitted, the verdict would be announced publicly. But should the judgment of the military court be guilty, there would be no announcement. Silence would signal a verdict of guilty.

Since it's virtually impossible to penetrate the thinking of the United States Army, the reasons for all of the secrecy can only be guessed at. My father believed several issues were involved. As the trial of *Soldat* Stangl got underway in the late winter snows of 1945, thousands and thousands of German combatants were being interned in the United States. To have it known that one of their own had been found guilty in a military court of raping and murdering an American girl could be devastating to their morale. Could have caused a lot of problems in a large POW population that now stretched from coast to coast. Also, it was not lost on our government that thousands of American soldiers were still being held behind barbed wire in Germany and in the Pacific. At the time, it was difficult to say what a ruthless enemy facing imminent defeat might do to its prisoners. They certainly needed no further provocation.

Anyway, after a three-day trial and six hours of jury deliberation, a secret ballot was taken and a verdict was reached. But the President of the United States directed "that the verdict and the sentence of the accused be not announced." The sentence was then sealed and classified.

Murder was by definition a capital crime. The penalty was death.

Still, the secret would be kept from the condemned man himself. He would not be told the day, the place, or the manner of his execution until his last hours.

My father was allowed to visit with him in his solitary cell shortly after the verdict was not announced. "This is wrong," Dad told him. "Frick lied. Not even our sheriff believed him. We can launch our own investigation . . . we can get you a new trial. There have to be appeals . . . even in the army."

"No, it is better this way," young Stangl assured him.

"How can that be? Your life is at stake."

"You do not understand, Mr. Pennington. I have family in Germany. A mother, a father, my little sister. I pray they are still alive. The Nazis have promised they will leave them alone, if only I go quietly."

"The Nazis can't get to your family. By the end of the year, there will be no Third Reich."

"You are wrong, my friend. There will still be a Third Reich, and there will always be the *Heilige Geist.* Let me warn you, Mr. Pennington . . . they like your Wisconsin."

"Who?"

"The Holy Ghost."

My father never realized the meaning of that warning. He left young Stangl that day shaken by the military injustice. On his way out of the camp he ran into one of the army captains who had assisted in the prosecution. "Does the death penalty in a military case mean death by a firing squad?"

Reluctant to talk, the captain shook his head. "In the United States Army, no."

"What then?" Dad asked.

"Well," the captain told him, glancing over his shoulder, "let's just say, if I lived in Wisconsin right now . . . I wouldn't go sit under the old apple tree."

36 | THE DIRTY SHERIFF

I watched from the squad room window as the twilight descended on Kickapoo Falls. The evening was fairly quiet. The night watch was on the road. The sheriff had gone home. His office was empty. I tried Alex at the hotel, but there was no answer. I hadn't seen her in two days. I was about to call it a day myself, go home and get out of my uniform, when the omnipresent telephone rang.

I turned toward my desk and eyed it suspiciously. Phone calls were fast becoming my undoing. Finally, after letting it ring five loud, annoying times, I picked up the receiver. "Deputy Pennington."

"Deputy Pennington . . . for a small-town cop, you sure do get some interesting cases."

"I swear, I don't go looking for them." The pleasant voice was familiar, but still I couldn't place it. "Who is this?"

"I'm sorry, Deputy, this is Professor Levine at the University of Chicago. I got the packet you sent to me."

"Hello, Professor. It's nice of you to call." I stared into Zimmer's empty office, the office I so badly wanted. "So tell me, did our unelected sheriff really attend the University of Chicago?"

"These records you gathered are a combination of fact and fiction. If you were a student of mine . . . I'd give you an incomplete."

"Fact and fiction are kissing cousins in this neck of the woods. Were they of any help at all?"

"Actually, it was the man's photograph that stirred my memory . . . take away the mustache, and twenty-some years."

"And then what have you got?"

"The eyes. The eyes gave him away."

"So you remember him?"

"He was a student of ours before the war . . . but his name wasn't Zimmer. His name was Frick."

The name hit me head-on, like an eighteen-wheeler on a darkened highway. *Frick!* My father had told me endless stories of a rabid Nazi at the POW camp by the name of Frick.

The professor went on. *"Gerhard Frick was his name. We called him Gary Frick, just to get under his skin. Some of our more creative professors called him Frick the dick . . . for obvious reasons."*

"What do you mean?"

"He was a German exchange student. He didn't particularly like having Jewish professors."

"When did you last see him?"

"Just like the records here say . . . he disappeared in 1939 . . . right after England declared war on Germany. We figured he went running home to the motherland."

37 | CHAPEL GORGE

I grew up believing in ghosts and goblins. In the Wisconsin Dells the stories are endless. Legendary. During the sunlight hours, the amber river that knifes through the tall cliffs and narrow gorges is mesmerizing. Awesome and inspiring. The place can't help but elevate your spirits. But at nighttime, the enchanting fifteen-mile stretch of water belongs to other spirits. Vengeful and malicious. To me, the Dells after dark is the spookiest place on earth. So, it was with a great deal of trepidation that I found myself inching upstream in a sheriff's boat, a lifetime of haunting tales coming back to me in a flood.

I had gone to her hotel room with the news. Pounded on her door. There was no answer. I hadn't heard from her in nearly two days, and in a small town, it's not easy to avoid somebody for two days. I pulled a pocketknife from my gun belt and picked the lock. They were pretty easy pickings back then. The room was empty. Pristine. The bed was made. The linen was untouched. Nobody had been there since housekeeping.

Detective LaChapelle's notebooks and papers were stacked neatly on a small desk. I flipped through them, not really sure what it was I was looking for. It was then I came across the note. The scribble was

Zimmer's—block-print capital letters. I'd seen it a hundred times in the past year.

AFTER SUNSET
ON THE TIP OF BLACK HAWK ISLAND
ACROSS FROM CHAPEL GORGE
BE ALONE

Alex had been pestering me to show her the Narrows—the haunted Narrows—but I never thought she'd be foolish enough to head upriver on her own, after dark, to meet with Zimmer. Of course, she had no way of knowing of his Nazi past, and she was an adventurous spirit.

Somehow, I believed, Zimmer had gotten to her. Scared her off the meeting with the Secret Service. Lured her up the river. Or maybe, just maybe, the beauty from Scotland Yard had been working both sides of the fence from the beginning. How often, I wondered, when she was not with me, had she been sharing secrets with Sheriff Zimmer? The question Marilou Stephens had put to me in Madison now followed me upstream:

"Do you trust her?"

The sheriff's department had two boats on the Upper Dells. One was missing. I had the other. I entered the Narrows at High Rock, the giant cliff looming over me like a Cyclops. The moon was nearing full. White clouds scudded the face. The darkened water was moving fast, making the boat difficult to maneuver. Still, I hoped the sound of the rushing water would mask the sound of the motor.

The river widened considerably on the approach to Black Hawk Island. Chapel Gorge lay to my right. The water over there was as smooth as ebony glass. I tried to put out of my mind tales of the resident ghost. I cut the engine and guided the boat gently to the shore. I docked at the point where the old whorehouse had once stood. In the dark, I couldn't see any other boats.

Once on the island, I crouched down in hunting mode and just listened to the myriad noises the woods and the river make after dark. That's when I heard it. Faintly at first, but then more clearly. For a combat veteran of the Second World War, and a former prisoner to boot, it was a chilling sound. More frightening than any ghost story. It was the sound of the German language being spoken in the distant woods. As a sniper, I had learned to listen for such voices. Judge the distance. Then fight, flee, or just freeze.

I had my trusty flashlight, but I kept the light off. I drew my service revolver and moved toward the woods. Toward the sound of the spoken German.

With every soft step through the trees, it became more and more clear that it was Zimmer's voice I was hearing. It was Zimmer who had been feeding information to Wolf Stangl. Like who was sleeping with whom in Kickapoo Falls. It was Zimmer who selected the targets. Stangl pulled the trigger, no doubt, but it was Zimmer who lined them up in his sights. And it was undoubtedly Zimmer who lured Deputy Hess to the truck stop, and then ambushed him. Zimmer had placed the phone call to my house. Got a busy signal, the confirmation he was expecting. Stangl had called me from a second location.

Now, on Black Hawk Island, the advantage was mine. Zimmer would not be expecting me. I had docked without a noticeable sound. I had pretty much located my prey. I was moving in for the arrest, or the kill, when there came a piercing cry out over the water. It was the kind of cry an Indian warrior might make going into battle. The haunting cry had come out of Chapel Gorge. I turned and leveled my gun in that direction. But there was no follow-up sound. There was nothing to see. All was quiet again. Maybe it had been some kind of hawk. I turned my attention back to the woods, but the German voice had stopped.

Now the woods before me were dark and silent. Every tree seemed to possess a pair of shifty eyes. There had also been a noticeable shift in power. Suddenly, I felt more like the hunted than the hunter. I made sure my boat was still in my sight line, and then I crept into a stand of pines. The bed of needles crunching beneath my feet sounded almost like an announcement: *Here comes Pennington.*

If you're a cop, there can be no greater humiliation than having somebody sneak up behind you in the dark and put a gun to your head—even if it's a fellow cop, and especially when you think you're being so damn sly.

"Herr Frick, I presume?"

"You've been doing your homework, Deputy Pennington." He pressed the cold barrel into my neck. "Throw down the gun."

I dropped my revolver, but hung on to my flashlight.

"Give me some light, and step out here," he ordered.

I shined a path out of the woods, and we stepped into the moonlight on the tip of the island. Zimmer was in his sheriff's uniform. The same uniform in which Fats had taken so much pride. The thought that it had been corrupted sickened me. I could see Chapel Gorge directly over his shoulder. "Where's Alex?" I asked.

"She hasn't arrived yet."

"I heard you talking to her."

"Then you've heard way too much."

That's when the frightening realization hit me. Zimmer had been speaking German. He hadn't been talking to Alex. He'd been talking to Wolf Stangl. The former SS officer was probably watching us from deep in the woods—the same way he had watched me that night at Devil's Lake. Still, I found it hard to believe the Nazi war criminal had come all the way to Wisconsin only to allow Zimmer to do his dirty work for him. "Get Colonel Stangl out here," I demanded. "I want to talk with him. I want to see his face."

Zimmer only chuckled. Spoke his native German. *"Denken Sie, dass er allein arbeitet?"*

"What does that mean?" I asked him.

"Do you think he works alone?"

The question seemed trite at the time. Rhetorical. But it would return to haunt me in both languages.

"Gerhard Frick . . . Gary Frick . . . Frick the dick . . ."

"Watch your mouth, Deputy."

"You murdered Patty Best when you were a POW at the logging camp up in the hills. Raped her, and then took an ax to her. Then you framed the Stangl boy."

In the dark of night with the bright moon overhead, he possessed the eyes of a snake. Dark and darting. "The colonel warned me about you. You are as he suggested, very clever, Deputy Pennington. But in the end, you're no smarter than your father was."

"Tell me, Herr Frick, does the colonel know that it was you who framed his son?"

"Raise your voice, and I'll put a bullet in your head."

"No, you won't, because the colonel needs me alive. I'm his ticket to St. Paul." I began slowly to circle the acting sheriff. "You stayed here after the war because there was nothing to go home to. The Third Reich was in ashes. So your German friends at the Gunn Club got you a new identity. A new career. From a Wehrmacht officer in Germany, to a county sheriff in the heart of America. But in the end, you're the same old Nazi."

"And you, Mr. Pennington, are the same old thorn in our side."

It was my sense that he might pull the trigger no matter what I said. I was just about to swing my flashlight in self-defense when again that wild and eerie battle cry rang out over Chapel Gorge. Shot through the trees like an arrow.

It startled us both, and Zimmer turned toward the river.

Out over the water floated an apparition right out of a horror movie. It was white and translucent. The moonlight shone right through it. It took the form of a screaming old woman. Then the infamous ghost of Chapel Gorge swirled madly above the waves, before it dissipated.

This all happened incredibly fast. Still, it gave me time to whack Zimmer across the jaw with the head of my flashlight. I could hear a bone break in his face. He tumbled to his back, but managed to hang on to his gun. He leveled the revolver at my head in a fit of rage. I dove to the ground. Heard a shot. I heard a second shot. Then a third, and a fourth.

I know gunshots, and those shots hadn't come from Zimmer's police revolver. Besides, I was still alive. I got to my knees and shone the flashlight on the appointed sheriff of Kickapoo County. He was prostrate. He was bullet-riddled. He was dead. Good and dead.

The shots that killed him had come out of the woods, and they had come from a Walther P38. I shone my light into the trees and saw the gun extending from a bony white hand. Then the ghostly shooter stepped into the light. The hand on the Walther belonged to Detective Alex LaChapelle of Scotland Yard.

She walked right past me, as if in a trance. Fire shone in her blue eyes. She stood over the body of J. D. Zimmer, alias Gerhard Frick.

I came up behind her. "I don't know if this is the proper time to ask this, Detective, but have you ever killed a man before?"

She was still pointing the gun at Zimmer, but her police poise had vanished. She appeared possessed, as if at last she had taken a measure of revenge. She let the gun rest at her side. Looked out upon Chapel Gorge. "What was that strange light out over the water?"

I, too, stared over at the blackened water at the foot of the Narrows. "Maybe it was swamp gas," I told her. "Might have been fog. But it sure looked like a ghost to me."

"I don't believe in ghosts," she murmured.

I turned back to Black Hawk Island and peered into the deep woods. "I do."

38 | THE INTERROGATION: *1944*

Colonel Stangl spoke with a Bavarian growl. Other than that, he spoke near-perfect English. The Nazi monkey had brought me to the colonel's office and left me alone with him. He was wearing an immaculate white coat. Though it had a military look, it appeared more like riding clothes. I'd never seen an outfit quite like it. He was the camp commandant. He towered above me. Even when he was sitting on the edge of his desk, he was looking down at me. I was just a boy soldier on crutches. I'd spent two days in the camp hospital, and two weeks in isolation. I was dirty and hungry. I'd been beaten, and I was scared. I didn't know exactly where I was. It seemed to be some kind of makeshift prison camp, somewhere between Wolf Pass and Munich.

On the wall behind his desk was a rifle rack, and displayed across that rack was one of the most beautiful sniper rifles I had ever seen. A German-made rifle cleaned and polished to the shine of a championship trophy. On Stangl's desk, to my horror, was my Springfield '03, Unertl scope and all. It was stained with dirt and blood. In the days after my capture, they had obviously returned to the mountain determined to find it. Like good cops in dogged search of evidence.

As the colonel spoke, I tried to stand at attention in the center of the room. Not easy on crutches. "So you are the young Herr Pennington," he said. He was standing behind his desk, reading from some papers before him. "Private First-Class P. A. Pennington. U.S. Army Air Forces. You were a tail gunner. You were on a bombing run. Your plane was hit, and you bailed out over Germany. That is what you told your captors . . . yes?"

"Yes, sir."

"Where are you from, Herr Pennington?"

"I'm required only to give you my name, rank, and serial number . . . sir."

"This is true . . . and admirable . . . but let us not be so formal. Are you a Catholic?"

The question surprised me. My shirt was open. My crucifix must have been showing. Still, I saw no harm in answering. "Yes."

"I am Catholic, also. So let us speak to one another as Christians." He moved to some kind of buffet and grabbed a bottle of wine and two glasses. I remained frozen in the middle of the room. The office was stark, more like a glorified shack. Like the entire camp, it had a temporary look—the office of a man who didn't want to be there and didn't plan on staying long. "It's a Bordeaux," he said as he poured. He held out the glass to me. "It's quite good."

I took the glass from his hand. Sniffed it. I wasn't a wine drinker, but it smelled okay. Then I smelled it again, highly suspicious.

Stangl seemed amused. "Please, Herr Pennington, if I was going to kill you, it wouldn't be by poison." He tipped his glass to me and then took a hearty sip of wine.

I watched him swallow and smile, a bemused smile emanating from a man with no lips. I sipped my wine. It was delicious.

The thing to remember about the interrogation that day was my age. I wasn't yet twenty-one years old. Stangl was in his forties. He was a high-ranking officer in a powerful enemy army. He was dressed in some kind of white spit-and-polish Nazi uniform that made him look like God. He had menacing scars up and down his face. Plus, he spoke to me in a polite and highly civilized manner, which I found extremely intimidating. That I handled myself as well as I did that day still amazes me.

He sat on the edge of his desk in a nonthreatening manner. "Pennington . . . that's an old English name, is it not?"

"Yes."

"So please, Herr Pennington, which one of the United States do you come from?"

"Wisconsin," I finally told him.

"Wisconsin . . . that's a western state, is it not?"

"Midwestern."

"A young soldier, no older than yourself and very dear to me, was captured in North Africa. He's now imprisoned in America at a place called Camp McCoy . . . in Wisconsin. Do you know of it?"

"I believe it's new, sir."

"So . . . it seems they have one of mine . . . and I have one of theirs."

"Well, Wisconsin is a big state."

"And before Wisconsin, where did the Penningtons come from?"

"Nantucket."

"The island of the great whale hunters. So you have in you the blood of a great hunter." He tugged on his sparkling white coat. "Perhaps, Herr Pennington, I am your white whale."

Moby-Dick being the most boring fucking book I'd ever read in my life, I got the joke. If it was a joke.

"This Wisconsin," he asked, "is it near Minnesota?"

"Yes, they border."

"I have cousins in New Ulm, Minnesota. Do you know of it?"

"I've heard of it."

"Yes, it's a German-Austrian community in the middle of America."

The wine was tasting mighty fine. The conversation seemed friendly enough. "That's not unusual," I said to him. "A lot of people in my hometown are German. Many of them still speak your language."

"And what town is that?"

"It's called Kickapoo Falls. It was named after the Kickapoo Indians, who once lived there."

"I love American names. I think someday I would like to see Wisconsin. Tell me, Herr Pennington, is there a young girl waiting for you back home in this Kickapoo Falls?"

I shook my head. "No, not really."

"Ah, but you smile."

"Well . . . I like her, but I don't think she likes me."

"Women at that age can be very cruel."

I couldn't argue with that. I sipped more wine.

"There is much hunting in Wisconsin, is there not?"

"Everybody in Wisconsin hunts."

"So you have in you the blood of a hunter. You come from a state of hunters. And you were captured in the very mountains where an enemy hunter was shooting at my trains."

The wine suddenly took on a bitter taste. "I'm a tail gunner," I stated, as emphatically as possible. "Our plane was hit. I bailed out."

"And the others?"

"What others?"

"The other men in your plane . . . what became of them?"

"I don't know . . . I hope they made it to Switzerland."

"Yes, let us hope." He turned and picked up the Springfield from the desk. "The problem I have is this . . . why would such a young boy from Wisconsin be sent to do such an important and dangerous job . . . stopping my trains?"

I assumed the question to be rhetorical. I didn't answer it. Nor did he seem to be bothered by my lack of a response. He just studied the Springfield, as if he'd never seen one before. He nodded to the sniper rifle on the wall. "Our rifles are far superior. However, I see you use the Unertl scope. Do you know who invented the Unertl scope?"

"No, sir, I don't."

"John Unertl, a German sniper in the First World War." He cradled the Springfield in his arms. "I carried a rifle in that war. I was just a boy, even younger than you are now. Which is why I admire your shooting skills. I particularly admire how you waited for train noise before squeezing the trigger. It masked the gunshots very well. You were able to kill . . . what? . . . four or five of our finest men before we realized what was happening. You must be a man of great patience. That's unusual at your age."

I remained silent. I kept thinking, *Name, rank, and serial number. Name, rank, and serial number.*

"Herr Pennington, this rifle has fingerprints on it. I believe those fingerprints to be your fingerprints. Do you know who invented fingerprinting for identifying villains? Scotland Yard. Yes, the British do some things very well. Unfortunately, mountain climbing isn't one of them. Anyway, I will simply send your fingerprints off to the Gestapo in Berlin. They will compare them to the prints on the rifle, and I will have my sniper. But the Gestapo is very busy these days . . . that would take time. Please help me."

I swallowed a mouthful of wine getting up my nerve. "With all respect, Colonel, why don't you save all of us the rigamarole and just claim the fingerprints are mine? I mean, who's going to question you?"

Stangl laughed, a nasty laugh. "'Rigamarole' . . . what a wonderful word. I'll have to remember it . . . along with the words 'Kickapoo Falls.'" He turned deadly serious. Stood and stepped toward me, the rifle in his arms. Bored a hole in my head with his menacing stare. "The reason I go through all of the rigamarole, Herr Pennington, is because I must know. I must satisfy myself. Do you understand that? What is it they say in those wonderful American gangster movies? *'I've been framed.'* No, Wolfgang Stangl does not frame villains. You see in my native Austria, I was a *Kriminalbeamte*. A police officer. The Austrian police were very professional. Our job was to uphold the law of the land. Yes, punishment was swift and harsh, but I always made sure I punished the right man. Always. Perhaps someday you will understand that, too. Now, why don't you save me the fingerprint rigamarole and confess that you were the sniper in the pass."

I finished my glass of wine. Swallowed hard. "I was a tail gunner," I said, tilting my head back and looking him straight in the eye. "Our plane got hit. I bailed out."

Stangl reached for my throat. I thought for sure he was going to strangle me with his bare hands. Instead, he ripped the crucifix from my neck. It hurt coming off.

He stared at the small pewter icon in his hands. "You are Catholic. I am Catholic . . ."

"Then you'll understand, Colonel, when I tell you . . . that belonged to my mother. She's dead now."

He dangled the crucifix before my face. "Do you swear before God . . . that you were not the sniper in the pass?"

I choked out the words. "I do."

"Do you swear on the grave of your blessed mother, that you were not the sniper in the pass?"

My throat was parched. "I do."

"Such an interesting young man you are, Herr Pennington."

"May I have my crucifix back . . . sir?"

"Someday I will return it to you, Herr Pennington. This, I promise. But today, I am very disappointed in you."

39 | THE ROAD TO ST. PAUL

Beneath his sheriff's uniform, J. D. Zimmer had hidden the telltale arm tattoo of the SS. At first, it seemed impossible to me that years later Gerhard Frick could have returned to Kickapoo County, to the very place where he had once been held prisoner, as an appointed sheriff, without anybody recognizing him. But remember, very few civilians were ever allowed inside the prison camp, and the prisoners themselves spent most of their days deep in the woods chopping trees. The guards in the camp were to a man from out of state, and they returned to their homes after the war. The years went by and added age and weight to Frick's disguise as Sheriff Zimmer, not to mention the mustache and the ubiquitous sunglasses. In all probability, the only man in Kickapoo Falls who could have fingered Frick for who he really was would have been my father. And he had been dead for years.

The interstate took us all the way to Hudson. Golden trees and fire-colored leaves lined the route through the rolling hills and past the farms of cornucopia. The deadly events in Kickapoo Falls were two days behind us. Still, I kept hearing Zimmer's words:

"Denken Sie, dass er allein arbeitet?"

"Do you think he works alone?"

Now I would be running for sheriff against a dead man. Already word around town was that my new girlfriend had literally killed the competition. Some were openly scoffing at the idea of Zimmer having a Nazi past. It was all politics. At the Gunn Club they were saying I must have wanted that job awfully bad, because I had just killed my second sheriff in two years. Truth was, I was standing *close* to both men when they were killed. But in a small town, *close* is true enough.

In the western Wisconsin town of Hudson, we crossed the bridge over the St. Croix River into Minnesota, where we followed the wheat fields strung along Highway 12 into the city of St. Paul. But something peculiar happened as we crossed that bridge. I remember it because my senses have always been attuned to such things, and because it had been such a beautiful autumn. The sun disappeared. Right there at the scenic river that divided the two great states, the sun slipped behind the dark clouds. I don't remember seeing sunshine again that fall.

It was Friday afternoon when we pulled into town. When he arrived on Saturday, President Kennedy would be staying across the river in Minneapolis. Since I wouldn't be joining the President until his cathedral visit on Sunday, Alex and I were put up at the Buckingham Hotel—a monster brick building kitty-corner from the church, and only half a hill away. It was a grand hotel, located at the foot of the cathedral, but above the bustling city. Still, I think it had seen better days. Had a musty smell. It was the kind of large dowdy hotel, half residential, that in America was literally coming down, while the sleek Hiltons, Sheratons, and Holiday Inns were going up.

Alex's room was just down the hall from mine, on the sixth floor. She had been fairly quiet during the three-hour ride. Not her usual smart-aleck self. Of course, she had just killed a man. But the closer we got to the Minnesota capital, the deeper her silence seemed to become. At the time, it didn't really bother me. I was used to driving in silence.

It was my job. I watched her walk down the long hallway and press her key into the door. Before disappearing into her room, she turned and smiled at me, as if to confirm she was all right.

I tossed my suitcase onto the largest four-poster bed I'd ever seen. The room was spacious. High ceiling. Large closets. A big bath. The furniture was Victorian. The paintings on the wall were of old Europe. Still, the once grand room had a shabby feel to it. The carpeting was threadbare in places. Plaster cracks showed on the ceiling. Wallpaper was curling at the edges. The young man behind the front desk said the hotel was scheduled to be razed—to make way for an entrance ramp to a new interstate that would link Minneapolis and St. Paul to Madison and Milwaukee.

On a table was a complimentary collection of booze. On the floor was a complimentary newspaper. I passed on the booze, picked up the newspaper, and walked to the windows. It was a corner room, with great views south and west. I parted the curtain on one of the tall windows to my left and took in the southern view. The city that had been named for a saint hadn't changed a whole lot since I had attended a seminary school in the west end of town. In those days, we'd ride the electric streetcars to the movie theaters downtown. There must have been ten theaters and ten ice cream parlors in a crowded four-block area. I saw *The Best Years of Our Lives* in St. Paul. And *The Lost Weekend* and *The Razor's Edge*.

Though their days were numbered, most of the big movie houses were still around. But the streetcars were gone. Only their rusting tracks remained, embedded like souvenirs in the brick streets that crisscrossed the city. Smelly, noisy buses now plied the busy roadways.

Directly beneath my window, at the foot of the hill, was a seedy intersection called Seven Corners. Seven streets managed to cross paths at the same place. A maze to strangers. I could see the Mississippi River, and atop its bluffs, Rice Park, reminiscent of the cozy public squares I'd seen in Europe during the war. On one end of the park stood the elegant James J. Hill Reference Library. On the other end was the castle-like federal courthouse.

I stepped over to the other wall and parted another curtain. Now I was looking west. High on the hill beneath overcast skies was the point of my trip, the Cathedral of Saint Paul. Its great green domes could be seen from every corner of the city. For a small-town Catholic boy who had once tried to become a priest, the sight was humbling.

I made a mental note to scope out the hotel from the street. The face of the Buckingham was filled with windows, and its sight lines faced the front steps of the cathedral.

Tired from the long drive, I turned away. Thought about a nap. Standing at the hotel windows with my back to the church, I opened the local newspaper, more out of habit than curiosity. What I saw shocked me. Sickened me. Even by the innocent security of the times, I was dumbfounded to the point of nausea.

ST. PAUL NORTH STAR PRESS

Friday, October 5, 1962

THOUSANDS EXPECTED TO WELCOME KENNEDY

Extra Security to Handle Crowds

Directly beneath the headline was a detailed map. Complete with arrows. It was captioned ROUTE OF THE PRESIDENT'S TWIN CITIES TOUR. Off in the right-hand corner, as if it were a cruel joke, the newspaper had stamped PRICE 10 CENTS.

Yes, for ten cents, anybody who wanted to take a shot at the President of the United States could get a detailed map of his motorcade and a full article about his schedule, including arrival and departure times for each and every stop.

It was joked that during the Cold War, spies operating in America had only to read the damn newspapers. Well, I wasn't laughing. Reading by the light of the cloudy day, I found the newspaper's attention to detail incredible. Filled with contradictions. The paper went on and on about extra police and Secret Service. Even special telephones. All of the protections afforded the President. Then in the next paragraph, in the very next breath, it gave out extraordinarily detailed information about exactly where the President would be, and when he would be there. In most cases, it even listed the names of the people he would be with—including at the cathedral Mass a sheriff's deputy named P. A. Pennington of Kickapoo Falls, Wisconsin.

And then there was the damn map. Splashed on the front page above the fold, it came off like a neon billboard that said SHOOT ME, I'M IRISH.

According to the map, President Kennedy would arrive at Wold-Chamberlain Field on Saturday at 4:30 p.m. After shaking a few hands, the President would get into his limousine and head north on Highway 55 to Minnehaha Parkway. Then the motorcade would turn east along Minnehaha to Park Avenue, and follow Park Avenue all the way into downtown Minneapolis, to the Leamington Hotel.

There was even a paragraph on the President's car, which was flown in separately. The paper reported that the specially built presidential Lincoln had a glass top, which could be opened or closed to suit the vagaries of the weather. It also noted, to my astonishment, that the bubble top was not bulletproof.

Once at the Leamington Hotel, the presidential party would take over twenty rooms of the fourteenth floor, including the five-room presidential suite. The presidential suite, it said, was brand-new and covered the entire north end of the fourteenth floor.

For his appearance at the state fairgrounds that night and the next day at the cathedral, times and routes were also printed, including the exact entrance the President would be using at his arrival. I later discovered the Minneapolis paper was more of the same. An assassin's road map. A sniper's picnic. I shook my head in disbelief. The thought of the Nazi war criminal poring over the daily newspapers made my skin crawl. You have to understand, I was a cop, but it wasn't my job to protect the President. It was my job to arrest Wolf Stangl.

After hurriedly unpacking, I marched down the hall and knocked at Alex's door, newspaper in hand. There was no answer. Figuring she had stepped out, I returned to my room and caught a quick nap. Well, I lay there with my eyes closed, anyway, but I don't think I actually slept. I tried her door again before dinner, but again there was no answer.

I grabbed dinner alone at a greasy spoon called the Idle Hour. Watched the light go out of the cloudy sky behind the church as I ate my ham and eggs. It was dark when I walked back up the hill to the hotel. A light rain was falling. I checked at the front desk for messages. There were none. I passed on the elevator because the hotel had a winding staircase. Plush red carpeting. Gold rails. I just liked climbing it.

On the sixth floor, I tried the detective's door one more time, but again her room returned only the hollow echo of my knocking.

I returned to my own room. It was too early for bed. So I pulled a chair up to the corner windows and let my mind work the case. I studied the map of the President's motorcade printed in the newspaper.

"Denken Sie, dab er allein arbeiten?"

Finally, I shut off all of the lights in the room and watched the rain fall over the city. And the illuminated cathedral that graced the city.

40 | THE TARGET: *1944*

Do you know what it's like to be scared for your life twenty-four hours a day, seven days a week? Wake up scared. Muddle through the day scared. Go to bed scared. That's what it was like to be a prisoner of war in Nazi Germany. Then there was that damn P.A. system. Colonel Stangl's voice barking at us over a scratchy loudspeaker every morning. Every night.

That September morning started as usual in the camp. At 5:45, we were rousted from our bunks for roll call on the parade ground. When the Germans had accounted for every last one of us, we were dismissed for a meager breakfast. Usually weak coffee or bad tea, and some kind of German biscuit. Soon after breakfast, something out of the ordinary happened. We were once again ordered to the parade ground and assembled for roll call. We knew something bad was about to happen because Stangl stood before us in his sinister white coat and riding breeches, and his shiny black boots. Like he was going on a foxhunt. Then two guards set up a shooting target on a wood cross right between the men in the front line. In fact, their shoulders were actually touching the edge of the target as they stood at attention under the gaze of the tower machine guns.

I had gleaned this much from the prison camp grapevine—Colonel Stangl had been demoted. Assigned, if not confined, to commandant of the small camp. So Stangl ordered that the sniper in Wolf Pass was to be apprehended at all costs. Alive if possible. He was going to deliver him personally to Berlin. It was the only way the SS officer could save face.

Stangl barked an order and his little Nazi monkey came running with a rifle. It was my Springfield. I went cold inside.

"Herr Pennington," he called.

I limped forward. Stangl made a great show of loading the 30.06 cartridges. "I have cleaned it myself," he said. "It was very dirty." Then with great fanfare he handed me the rifle, as if I were a fellow Nazi. "Follow me," he ordered.

The arrogant bastard then turned his back on me and marched through the front gate. I had a loaded weapon. I could have shot him right through the back. Sent his heart exploding through his chest. Of course, with all of the guns trained on me, it would have been the last thing I ever did. So instead, I followed the son of a bitch. I was off my crutches, but still limping. The Nazi monkey and several other guards fell in behind me. We marched out the front gate and up a hill overlooking the camp.

When we had reached the crest of the hill, Stangl turned and looked down at the camp. Down at all of the prisoners lined up like ducks in a shooting gallery. "Herr Pennington," he said, pointing at the camp, "hit the target."

I strained my eyes to even see the target. I had been preparing myself for some kind of physical torture, but nothing could have prepared me for the hell the Nazi colonel was about to put me through. I kneeled, in a shooting position. My leg hurt. I had nothing to rest the rifle upon. I put my scope to the target, my finger hooked on the trigger. I guessed it to be a little over eight hundred yards to the bull's-eye. Up against each side of the target was an American soldier, frozen at attention. Behind the target, the frightened soldiers were lined up four deep. If I shot high, one of them could get his head blown off. I squeezed the trigger. The 30.06 kicked up dirt in front of the target and sent a line of soldiers scrambling left and right. I heard the guards order them back into formation. Straight lines, standing at attention. It was the ricochet that I worried about, but thankfully nobody had been hurt.

Stangl spoke over my shoulder. "That's not very good shooting, Herr Pennington. On the other hand, it might be very good acting. Take your time, Herr Pennington, but this time hit the target."

I had orders from high command. Never reveal the scope of my mission. Again, I shouldered the rifle. Allowed it to quiver in my arms. Then I squeezed off round two. That shot went high. Way high. I saw the men dip their shoulders as they heard the bullet whiz overhead.

"Perhaps," said Stangl, "it's the rifle. Let me try." He jerked the rifle from my hands. Stood perfectly erect. Put the Springfield to his shoulder. Rested his index finger on the cold crescent of metal. Sighted his target with an intense rage I had rarely seen in a rifleman. Then he fired. Again, I was straining to see the target. What I saw instead was a soldier standing at attention two feet from the target. Suddenly, and without warning, the top of his head exploded. Blood everywhere. There were screams and shouts as the prisoners hit the ground in acts of self-preservation. Then their German captors were barking orders at them. Threatening them at gunpoint. Getting them on their feet and lined up at attention. The dead soldier lay on the ground before them. Bloody and broken. All but headless.

"No, Herr Pennington," said Stangl, "the rifle works fine." He reloaded it and coldly handed it back to me. "Hit the target."

The early morning sun was peeking through the pines. A slight breeze rustled the hairs on the back of my neck. Once again, as slowly and as awkwardly as I possibly could, I put the rifle on the target. What was I to do? I was running out of options. Should I hit the bull's-eye? Prove his point? Cost me my life? Or should I hit one of my own men? He would certainly be suspicious if with every shot I missed both the target and the men. With almost a blind jerk, I pulled the trigger. I didn't care what I hit. But again, I hit nothing.

Stangl ripped the rifle from my hands. "My turn." He ejected the shell and shot the bolt home. Again he put the stock to his shoulder with a purpose so evil I was having a hard time believing it. Again, a shot rang out and an American GI crumpled to the ground amidst shrieks of horror, the top of his head gone. "I have more bullets than prisoners, Herr Pennington." He threw the rifle down at me. "Hit the target."

I was sick. "This isn't right," I choked out. "This is murder."

"I'm sorry, Herr Pennington, you do not enjoy watching your men being shot down? Neither did I. Hit the target."

Every night before lights-out, the men in my barracks would gather around a couple of bunks. Share precious cigarettes and talk about the day. It's what kept them going. I hadn't been in the camp long. I had made few acquaintances. Still, that day I had watched as American soldiers were murdered. One by one. How many? Hard to say. I stopped counting. You see, I had orders. Never reveal the scope of my mission. Not to the enemy. Not even to the American officers.

That night in the barracks, I lay in a top bunk staring up at the rotting wood ceiling. I couldn't look down at their faces, meet their eyes, so I lay there in total silence and listened to their voices. Right below me. All around me. Bitter voices. Scared voices. If there was such a thing as angry cigarette smoke, I could smell it, wafting up from below. In ways, I was more afraid of them that night than I was of Stangl.

"If he's the goddamned sniper they're looking for . . . we should just tell the crazy Kraut. Give him up before he gets us all killed."

"C'mon, he tried his best to hit the target . . . leave him alone."

"I say he faked it. Missed on purpose."

"There's not a man in this camp who could've hit that target from that distance."

"A sniper could have."

"A sniper, my ass . . . the kid doesn't even shave yet."

"He sure as hell ain't no tail gunner."

"That's right . . . and there was no killing in this camp until Pennington arrived."

"There was no killing in this camp until Stangl arrived. When this war is over, Stangl and his kind will have to answer. Now, leave the kid alone and go on to bed . . . all of yas."

The men had a point. I was trouble. As long as I remained there, their lives were in imminent danger. At lights-out that night, Colonel Stangl's voice came godlike over the loudspeaker. *"You have a Judas among you. What will you do? What will you do?"*

Something moral snapped inside of me that horrid day, because I had actually done some of my best shooting. With every soldier of ours that the monster Stangl coldly assassinated, I would with the next shot miss the target with a purpose so clear and accurate, he would know both that I was the sniper in Wolf Pass—and that he would never be able to prove it.

41 | SEX LA CHAPELLE

A cathedral is a church in which is located a bishop's chair, or *cathedra*. In 1851, a year after the official establishment of the Diocese of Saint Paul, a simple log chapel built atop a bluff on the Mississippi River was formally blessed the Cathedral of Saint Paul. A second and third cathedral would eventually replace the log chapel, before the great church was constructed on a hill overlooking the city. Like a good little Catholic boy, I had again read up on the cathedral before making the trip.

The dimensions were enormous. While its twin towers reached a height of 150 feet, the great dome rose to 280 feet. Twenty-four large windows at the base of the dome flooded the sanctuary with light.

Down the hill from the great church stood the Buckingham Hotel, where I stayed two nights before the Mass. It was late. I couldn't sleep. I sat at the window in trousers and a T-shirt staring at the illuminated cross atop the dome. Then I heard a gentle rapping at the door.

I was startled. Got up and reached for my revolver hanging from the hook on the door. Took a deep breath. "Who is it?"

"It's your favorite British detective."

I slipped the gun back into its holster. Opened the door. Peeked out.

She was wet from the rain. Her eyes had a bloodshot look to them. Maybe she was tired. Perhaps she'd been crying. She might have had a drink. "Come in," I said to her. "Let me take your coat." I hung her wet coat on the hook, over my gun. "I knocked earlier, but you were out."

"Why?"

"Why what?"

"Why did you come knocking?" she wanted to know.

"I just thought I'd stop by and see if your room was all right."

"The cop from Kickapoo Falls is an expert on hotel rooms?"

"Point taken."

She was wearing a cream-colored blouse that was tucked neatly into an expensive black skirt. The woman had style. Maybe too much style for a cop. The comfortable shoes she'd purchased in Kickapoo Falls were wet from the rain.

"Where have you been?" I asked, as politely as possible.

"Walking, mostly."

"You're still upset. You should go to bed."

She smiled. "That's a good idea." Motioning to the collection of booze on the table, she said, "They've apparently sent you some refreshments. I could use a good stiff drink. Join me?"

"Any Wisconsin beer?" I asked.

She pawed through the bottles. "Apparently not allowed in Minnesota."

"I'll pass."

She raised an empty glass. "If you don't mind . . . ?"

"No," I said, "go right ahead."

Alex poured herself a Scotch and water.

I strolled to the tall windows, happy she was with me. Parted the sheer white curtain and gazed out. It was still raining. A steady drizzle.

Small-town people are forever fascinated with the size and pace of city life. "It's a nice town," I said to her. "Not too big."

Alex stood behind me, peering over my shoulder, the drink in her hand. "It's actually very European in style. I was told St. Paul was built on seven hills. Just like Rome."

"Really?"

"Oh, yes," she said. "I think I climbed all seven of them tonight." She sipped her drink and went on. "The medieval architecture, the winding streets, the domes, the rivers, the great church on the hill . . . it's a city that would be right at home on the Continent. Of course, that's probably not the Europe you saw."

I shook my head in sad resignation. "No, there wasn't much left of the Europe that I saw." I continued to gaze out the window at the Cathedral of Saint Paul, fully illuminated atop the hill. The design, enormous in shape, was a modified Renaissance style. Twentieth-century in its purpose and ambience, but medieval in many of its features. The pews of the cathedral could seat twenty-five hundred worshippers. With the addition of folding chairs and standing room, as many as five thousand people were expected to attend Mass with the President. St. Paul's F. Scott Fitzgerald, never the most devout of Catholics, said the cathedral looked like a giant, angry bulldog, sitting on its haunches, growling down at the city below. I dropped my hand, let the curtain fall.

"Leave it open," she said. "I like the view . . . it's much better than my room."

I parted the curtain again and let the rainy night rush in. "I don't know, Alex . . . a Roman Catholic boy and a girl from the Church of England, alone together in a hotel room . . ."

"We'll roast in hell together . . . you and I."

"Yes, perhaps."

She moved to the window. Stared up at the church, its massive dome staring back at us. I took a seat in a winged-back chair, equal distance from the window and the bed. A great view of the church. A great view of the detective. A great view of the bed. After a moment, Alex turned and looked at me. She was stunning, standing before the tall window, backlit by the misty glow of the night—including the street lamps, the preternatural light of the church, and the occasional shot of cloud-to-cloud lightning.

She looked as if she might want to talk. Something was on her mind. I tried to get things started. "Have you called your boyfriend . . . in London?"

"He's not my boyfriend."

"I just thought . . . since you'd slept together on several occasions."

"It's complicated."

"You mean, he's married?"

She laughed, a sad little laugh. "We're all a little corrupt, in our own way." She stared into her Scotch. "Tell me about her," she said.

"About who?" I asked.

"You know who."

"Maggie?"

"No," she said, swirling her drink. "Maggie was an obsession. Your lifelong fantasy. Tell me about Lisa. The woman with whom you claim to have had a nonsexual sexual relationship."

"What's to tell?"

"The specifics. What did you do? How did you do it, considering your so-called wounds?"

I shrugged my shoulders, as if it had been no big deal. "She would tell me what to do, you know, kind of coach me along."

"How so?"

"We'd play a game . . . it was silly."

"What kind of game?"

"She'd make me repeat after her. Then after I'd say it . . . she'd do it."

"Give me an example."

I squirmed in my chair. Alex had that playful look in her eyes. The same look Lisa used to give me. "She'd say, 'Unbutton the top button of your blouse.' Then I'd repeat, 'Unbutton the top button of your blouse.' Then she'd unbutton the top button of her blouse."

"Do you mean like this . . ." Alex reached up with her free hand and undid the top button of her cream-colored blouse, opening the flow of her neckline to me. It gave her a casual, sexy look. Very American. "Then what would she do?"

I smiled an embarrassed smile. "She'd say something else."

"Such as?"

"Such as, 'Now the button below it.' "

Again Alex reached up and undid a button on her creamy blouse. With the opening of the second button, the top of her lacy white brassiere was exposed. I cleared my throat as a wide grin spread across my face, wondering how far the British detective was prepared to go. The game was juvenile, but I enjoyed playing it. I didn't believe she would go very far.

"Kick off your shoes," I told her.

Alex playfully sent her new Pennington shoes flying in my direction. Now she was barefoot with her blouse partly open. I was running out of innocent options. If the game continued, things were sure to get more serious.

"Go on, Deputy," she said to me, "I'm listening."

"You're supposed to be telling me what to say. It doesn't take any guts for a woman to do what a man tells her to do."

She took a drink. "I see . . . but it does take guts for a woman to do what she tells a man to tell her to do?"

I laughed. "I'm not sure I followed that . . . but, hey, I didn't make up the rules."

"Repeat after me . . . open another button."

"You're playing with fire, Detective."

"Repeat after me," she ordered. "Open another button."

I hesitated. Maybe out of respect. Probably out of a sense of fear. "Open another button," I muttered.

"A bit more emphatic, Deputy Pennington."

"Open another button," I said, emphatically.

Alex LaChapelle placed her drink on a small table. Then her manicured fingers went to her blouse and peeled off button number three. Now the entire front of her brassiere was exposed to me. Her cleavage was showing. Only one button was left fastened, and then we would be to the top of her skirt.

"Repeat after me," she said. "Let's do that last button."

Again, I hesitated. She was gorgeous, standing there in her bare feet, with her blouse wide open, the perfect shape of her breasts exposed to me. Still, I didn't think she would go much further. It didn't feel like she was teasing me. It felt more like she was testing me.

"What's the matter, Deputy . . . no guts?"

"Okay, Detective. Let's do that last button."

Alex reached down to her navel and popped open the last button. It didn't really expose that much more skin. What it did was put us at a crossroads. From the sexy but steely look in her eyes, she wasn't backing down. "Repeat after me," she said. "Drop the skirt."

I stared her straight in the eye. "Drop the skirt, Detective."

There was a button along the side. And a zipper. She didn't fumble with them. In fact, there was no hesitation in any of her movements. She simply responded to what I told her. Or rather, what she told me to tell her. When the zipper had run its length, she let the dark skirt slip to the floor. Stepped out of it. Then she did that wonderful thing that women do with their hair. With her long, lissome legs showing beneath the open blouse, she reached both of her hands behind her neck and sent her hair flying in opposite directions. Shook it loose. Then she just stood there, staring back at me. The cream-colored blouse was so long I couldn't even tell if she was wearing panties. I guess she was reading my mind.

"Repeat after me," she said. "Are you wearing panties?"

"Are you wearing panties?"

"Yes," she answered. "Show them to me," she ordered.

"Show them to me," I repeated.

Alex turned her back about three quarters. Reached down and lifted her blouse to her hip. I could see the delicate white panties outlining her buttocks. She dropped her blouse back into place and crossed in front of me, slowly and deliberately. Picked up her drink as she passed. She sat on the edge of the bed, one gorgeous leg tucked beneath her, the other leg dangling free from the bedspread. She stole another taste of the Scotch. Licked her lips. "You see, this is the part I don't quite understand." She stared at me with those inquisitive blue eyes. "What did she tell you to do that was so erotic, you virtually had a sexual relationship without ever touching her?"

Again, I shrugged my shoulders, feigning indifference. "She touched. I watched."

"She touched you?"

"No . . . she touched herself."

For the first time in the game, the momentum shifted. She was trying to figure out in her head what came next. It was obviously something she'd never before done with a man. The question was whether I was going to take over the game, or not. Considering her beauty, considering her sexuality, it wasn't a difficult decision. But would she really go on playing?

"Lie across the bed," I ordered her, "your feet facing me."

At first, she hesitated. Then Alex placed her drink on the nightstand. She slowly positioned herself across the bedspread, her blouse wide open, her knees tucked together.

There was a soft quiver in her voice. A sexy nervousness. "Now what?" she wanted to know. With that one little question, power was shifting.

"Now you do exactly what I tell you to do."

"I see."

"No, you don't see . . . not yet, anyway. Drop the strap on your bra and show me your nipple. The left breast."

Alex was right-handed, so it would have been easy for her to reach across and pull the strap of her bra down her shoulder, exposing a breast. But again, she hesitated. Paused a second to think about what she was about to do. Still, she went ahead and did it. Slipped off the strap. Pulled down on the cup, exposing a large, dark nipple on a small breast.

"Now play with it," I told her.

"What do you mean?"

I pretended I was mad. "I mean, put your fingers on your nipple and toy with it."

And that's what she did for me. When she appeared to be enjoying it, I made my move. I really didn't think it would reach that point, but I sensed she was ready. "Alex, I want you to lie very still now. I'm going to strip you of your panties."

This time she had no response. She simply lay still, staring up at the ceiling.

I rose from the chair, stepped toward the bed, and reached for the waistline of her panties. I suppose because of the things I couldn't do in bed, removing a woman's panties was to me like the climax. The end-all.

I stripped the tight, white panties from her hips, from her legs and her feet. I let them drop to the floor. Then I returned to my seat.

Again, she let her knees fall together.

"Alex, I want you to spread your legs and show me."

She took her eyes off of the ceiling and shot me a doubtful glance.

"Do it, Alex. Spread your legs."

Alex LaChapelle allowed her legs to spill open, exposing herself to me.

"Now I want you to put your fingers inside of you and play with yourself . . . while I watch."

Again, she seemed doubtful. She was back to staring at the ceiling.

"Alex, you've done this before. You know it, and I know it. You've just never done it with a man watching you. Now do it."

I was emphatic. I was in charge. I sat back and waited.

It didn't take her long. The beautiful woman from London reached her right hand down to her legs. Ran a finger up her thigh until she was barely brushing herself.

"Put them inside of you," I ordered.

At last, she responded. She slipped two fingers inside of her and began toying with herself. And I watched. Watched as she thrust them deeper and deeper. Faster and faster. It took only a few minutes for Alex to reach her climax. But she wasn't a screamer. She was the kind of woman who tried not to scream, which to me made her even more erotic. Still, there seemed a deeper guilt to her sexual silence. But then sex thrives on secrets. With that, she curled up on the bed, in the fetal position, and we talked small talk until she fell asleep. In the wee hours of the morning, I slipped into bed beside Alex LaChapelle, put an arm around her, and closed my eyes to sleep.

42 | A VOICE FROM THE PAST:

Penultimate Call

It was Saturday morning. When I finally opened my eyes, Alex was gone. I felt foolish that she had been able to slip away without my waking. I checked the clock. It stood at 8:35. I stumbled from bed and shuffled to the window. Stared up the hill at the church. An ominous tone colored the morning sky. No rain. No wind. Just dark, brooding clouds hanging over the cathedral like a sodden blanket, blocking the sun from the city.

President Kennedy would be landing at Wold-Chamberlain Field in less than eight hours. I was actually praying it would rain. The President would be a lot safer. The top would be up on the limousine helping obscure the President as a target. And with fewer people standing in the weather, the motorcade would move swiftly through the streets.

I showered and dressed. Breakfast was toast and coffee from room service. I threw on a light jacket and ventured out for a walk. Though I considered knocking at her door, I wasn't quite ready to see the brainy British beauty.

I really had twenty-four hours to kill, because I had no official role until the Sunday Mass. So I followed the sidewalks down the hill to

Seven Corners. Then I negotiated traffic until I found myself among the huge department stores—Dayton's, Donaldson's, The Emporium, and The Golden Rule. I chose Dayton's, and stopped in to buy a dark suit. I hated suits. They never fit right, and I only wore them to funerals and weddings. I finally found something quasi-handsome, halfway between cheap and inexpensive.

I was trying to think of something nice to get for Alex. A present. But what does a man from a small town in Wisconsin who is visiting a big city in Minnesota buy for a sophisticated woman who is visiting from London? In the end, I figured no gift was better than a bad gift. At least that's the conclusion I reached over a hot dog at the lunch counter in Woolworth's.

The state capitol building in St. Paul looked remarkably like the state capitol building in Madison, white marble dome and all. So I passed on a tour. Instead, I found myself up behind the cathedral, strolling the parkway before the great mansions that graced Summit Avenue. The Victorian boulevard went on for miles, shadowing the Mississippi River all the way to Minneapolis. But I only followed the opulent street to the park on Ramsey Hill that overlooked the river. The High Bridge before me was strung like an iron necklace between two bluffs over the Mississippi. I watched the cars parade over it, north and south. It was said if you were going to kill yourself in St. Paul, the High Bridge was the place to do it. Cops in the city had told me stories about people leaping from the bridge, or in some cases being helped over the rail. Few survived. Most broke their necks when they hit the water. It was rumored that in the good old days the cops would dangle suspects from the bridge until they literally spilled their guts. I loved old cops telling old stories. Little did I know then that when I reached my own golden years, the stories I would tell of life and death in Kickapoo County would match or surpass them all.

The rain held off, but the temperature actually dropped as the day wore on. I knocked at her door in the afternoon. But Alex was out.

Where was she? What was she feeling? Was she embarrassed? Was she in love? I returned to my room. Flopped down on the giant bed and thought about what had happened there the night before.

I needed to talk to her. To see her face. Hear her voice. I was just about to step out the door again when the phone rang.

I picked up the receiver, hoping it was Alex. "Hello."

"Herr Pennington, how did you sleep last night?"

The blood drained from my face. He was calling from the street. City noises cluttered the background. The connection was as bad as ever. Still, the sound of his voice cut me like a razor. Somehow in my Alex LaChapelle euphoria, I had convinced myself that Wolf Stangl had been left behind in Kickapoo Falls.

"I slept fine . . . thank you for asking."

"Did you enjoy how she stripped for you? Because I enjoyed it very much."

I turned to the windows. We were high on a hill. The only possible place from where he could have spied my room would have been from the towers of the church.

"You're bluffing," I told him.

"Her back was to me as she unbuttoned her pretty blouse . . . but then, when she sat on the edge of the bed, the way her bare legs dangled before you . . . certainly you felt the same thing as I. We are so much alike that way. Or when you stripped her of her underwear . . . was the feeling you enjoyed at that moment the same as mine? As a man, I'm curious."

I was inclined to hang up. To not engage him in conversation. Back away, the way I did that night at Devil's Lake. But then he went on, and I was forced to listen.

"And so we are all in St. Paul. We only await the guest of honor."

"They know about you."

"Who knows about me, Herr Pennington?"

"The Secret Service, the FBI, Scotland Yard . . . all of them."

"Please do not forget the Kickapoo County Sheriff's Department. You mustn't be modest, Deputy. Your chances of becoming sheriff have greatly

improved with the death of Mr. Zimmer . . . though talk about town says just slightly."

Just then, the carillon bells in the cathedral towers began their hourly hymn. Westminster chimes. Then the carillonneur tolled the hour. It was 4 p.m. Stangl, too, heard the ringing of the bells.

"You have exactly thirty minutes, Herr Pennington."

"Thirty minutes till what?"

"You once asked to meet me . . . remember?"

"Anywhere, anytime, that was the deal. Let's leave this between me and you."

"When he leaves the airport, your President's motorcade will start down Highway Fifty-five. There is a large round tower made of stone . . . part of an old abandoned fort. From the top, I will have a clear shot at the motorcade. I put the distance at three hundred yards . . . a moving target. But still, I like my chances. Unless, of course, you can get to the tower first. Then it will be just you and I, Herr Pennington . . . like old times."

It angered me no end, the way he could get me to drop a telephone at his whim and run like hell to wherever it was he wanted me to be. But what choice did I have? I dropped the phone, grabbed my gun, and I was off and running.

43 | THE FORT

At the front door of the hotel, I jumped into the backseat of a yellow cab. I shouted, "I'm a cop. Fort Snelling . . . and step on it."

The cabby popped out of his afternoon slumber and dropped his big Ford into drive. "I'll step on it, Mac, but lots of traffic out that way." He was a heavyset man with slick gray hair. Had probably been on the job for years. His cab reeked of cigarette smoke and stale food, like he might have lived in the damn thing. "The President is coming."

"Yes, I know the President is coming. That's why you have to hurry."

I checked my watch. It was 4:02.

"What police you with?" the cabby asked.

"St. Paul . . . now move it."

Well, of course I lied. What was I supposed to tell him—Kickapoo County? We rolled quickly down the steep hill to the maze of streets that skirted downtown, a labyrinth so intricate even white mice could get turned around. Fortunately, the cabby knew where he was headed, but there was nothing he could do about the traffic. We melted into the congestion of West Seventh Street and started for the fort. The time was 4:10.

In my seminary days, I could often see the drab buildings of Fort Snelling sprawled along the bluffs across the river. I confess, I never visited the place, but I did know the basics. Fort Snelling was where the Twin Cities began. The original fort, including the Round Tower, was built at the confluence of the Minnesota River and the Mississippi River to protect American interests after the Louisiana Purchase. During World War II, Fort Snelling and Wold-Chamberlain Field were used as training grounds. Now as we raced that way, Wold-Chamberlain was well on its way to becoming Minneapolis/St. Paul International Airport, but there hadn't been a whole lot of activity at the fort since the end of the war.

My cabby sped out one of the city's main arteries, weaving in and out of heavy traffic. Blaring horns cursed as we passed. I got the feeling the cabby was enjoying the ride, as if playing his part in one of those old Hollywood movies. We finally came up to the bridge that crossed the river to the fort. The high bluffs were ablaze in a forest fire of leaves. Orange leaves, yellow leaves, brilliant displays of red and gold. A church spire was spiriting out of the treetops. Only the clouds kept the scenery from being spectacular. I could see the Round Tower to the east, but the main body of the fort seemed to lie to the west. There were no planes in the sky over the airport. Probably put on hold until after the President landed. Again, I checked my watch. The minute hand was passing 4:20.

I tried to remember some of the things that had been printed in the newspapers. They said President Kennedy would not exactly be coming to Minnesota first class. In fact, the President would arrive aboard a prosaic propeller-driven DC6. The reason he was flying in a simple DC6 is because he was out stumping for Democratic candidates, and some of the airports in communities along the way did not have runways long enough to handle his official Air Force 707 jet. His plane, the papers said, would taxi up to a ramp on the south side of the main terminal building. There President Kennedy was expected to deplane and spend a few minutes shaking hands. When he left the Twin Cities on Sunday, he would depart aboard his official 707, which was being flown to Minnesota to pick him up for the return trip to Washington.

I had the window down for a clearer view. The air smelled of rain. I kept my eyes on the cloudy sky as we crossed the river, but still there were no planes in sight. Barricades littered the side of the highway, and up ahead state patrol cars were expected to close the road at any minute.

Once across the water my cab driver turned west, toward the fort. But the Round Tower, standing atop the bluff like a lighthouse, was over my shoulder to the east. "No," I yelled. "I want to go over there . . . to the tower. Turn around."

"I can't," he argued. "There ain't no public roads over that way. That part of the fort has been abandoned for years. They're gonna build that new highway right through there."

The fort and the airport sat directly between the two cities. There were still arguments as to which city they actually belonged. In fact, the four-lane highway we were now on splits near the airport. Two lanes to Minneapolis. Two lanes to St. Paul.

I pulled out my revolver. "Stop the damn car."

The cabby skidded to a halt on the side of the highway. Looked over his shoulder and saw the .38/.44 Probably thought I was going to shoot him. "Jesus," he screamed.

Now I was out of the cab and dancing across the busy highway that ran by the fort to the airport. In my wake, I left cars honking in anger. I had hoped I'd caught the attention of the state patrol down the road. I sprinted through deserted parking lots and past crumbling stone buildings. Fort Snelling was still in operation, but the old fort, the original fort, had been left to ruins. Only the huge Round Tower of the once venerable fort was still standing, and it stood among a summertime's growth of weeds and brush. A bare flagpole was planted on top of it.

The tower had been built of rough limestone quarried near the river. Its walls, complete with musket slits, were six feet thick. I stood outside the tower's old wood door. Checked my watch—4:25. I checked the sky. No planes. With police revolver in hand, I kicked open the door and stepped inside, gun at the ready.

It was dark and damp. Smelled of soil and moss. I found myself at the foot of a spiral staircase. Giving my eyes a second to adjust to the darkness, I started up the stone steps.

I really had the fighting feeling this was it. That I was about to confront Wolf Stangl for the very last time. I promised myself while creeping up those steps that I would shoot the son of a bitch on sight. No more talk. No more games. Aim for the widest part of his body and fire three to four times. Until I saw the Nazi drop.

At the top of the stairs, a rotting log door was flapping open. Somebody had been there. I took a deep breath and stepped quickly onto the roof. It was windy. The only sound was a rusty chain slapping against the flagpole. I searched around, literally, my gun out before me. Around and around in a perfect circle. But I saw only stone and sky. I was alone atop the tower.

I actually heard it before I saw it. The sound of an airplane coming in low. I turned to the south and east. It was a DC6. As it passed overhead, I could hear car horns blaring and see people pointing out their windows. It was 4:30. The President was landing.

I raced back down the stairs and searched the rest of the tower. The musket slits on the different levels offered perfect cover for a sniper, but the rooms were deserted. Had been for years. I scoped out the basement, but there was nobody. I couldn't have been more alone. I even felt alone. I crept back up the steps to the roof to see what I could see. Again I circled the tower. The view was incredible. I was at the zenith of the fort on the peak of the bluff where two great rivers and two great cities came together. St. Paul was behind me. Minneapolis out in front of me. I could look down at the mighty Mississippi River having just spilled over St. Anthony Falls, and then I could turn my head and see the oncoming Minnesota River. I stared across the highway at the airport, but the main terminal building blocked my view of the President's arrival.

The sound of the rusty chain slapping the flagpole was beginning to annoy me. Or beckon me. I turned that way. That's when I spotted it, hanging above me. A fine metal chain was wrapped around the large rusty chain. The ghost of Wolf Stangl had been there, all right. As I walked toward the two chains, my eyes began to fill with tears. There was a cross dangling before me. Though I hadn't seen it in years, I recognized the icon right away. It was the pewter crucifix I had worn around my neck nearly half my life. The crucifix that had once draped the neck of my mother. The same crucifix Colonel Stangl had ripped from my neck that day in his office. Made me swear to God, swear to my dead mother, that I was not the deadly sniper in Wolf Pass. I untied the crucifix from the flagpole and held it between my fingers.

Out the corner of my eye, I caught the flashing lights of squad cars leaving the airport. The motorcade had begun. I walked to the edge and looked over the stone wall. Like Stangl, I put the distance to the highway at three hundred yards. Even for a moving target, it was a pretty even shot for a sniper.

I stood there with my mother's crucifix in my hand and watched as President Kennedy's motorcade passed by me on the highway below. The clouds in the sky were still thick and gray, but no rain was forthcoming. The top of the presidential limousine was down. I caught a good look at Mr. Kennedy's shock of brown hair as he sailed by. Then the motorcade turned away from me and started for Minnehaha Parkway, where eighty thousand people lined the route, waiting to get a glimpse of the young American President.

44 | THE ESCAPE: *1944*

Surrendering had been a mistake. After the "target" slaughter, escape was all I could think about. Dream about. I could not sit idly by and wait for the next murderous round of Stangl's sniper game. The man had me in his sights. It was just a question of what he was going to do with me. And when. I also feared the other men in the camp. Some of them were wasting away mentally, as well as physically. Two of the prisoners counted the total number of barbs on the fence that held them prisoner—54,397. All of the prisoners viewed me as an outsider. At the very least, to them I was bad luck.

Even as my leg healed, I could feel my strength draining away. Still, bum leg and all, I was in much better condition than the other prisoners. I had only to look at their gaunt faces to see the effects of near-starvation and everlasting fear. There was less food with every passing day. That meant every day that I spent in captivity, I would be one day weaker. Escape would require all of the strength I could muster.

Also, there was talk of closing the small compound that housed us and transferring us to a notoriously overcrowded camp called Bad Orb, northeast of Frankfurt. It was said on the prison grapevine that we were living in the "Fritz Ritz" compared to Bad Orb.

I knew where Switzerland was. I figured as long as I had a rifle in my hands, I would have a fighting chance. That was the most audacious part of my plan. I was determined to leave with my Springfield, *Kriminalbeamte* Stangl's only piece of evidence.

Because the camp was only meant to be temporary, and the war had taken a heavy toll on the German army, security seemed to be lax. There were the usual guard towers, machine guns, and barbed wire, but most prisoners believed the minefields supposedly surrounding the camp were fake. The guards were slovenly and third-rate, if not fourth-rate. The seasoned German soldiers were either fighting at the front, or they were already dead. To help deter escape, Colonel Stangl had implemented a new and lethal policy. Nobody yet had had the nerve to test it.

It was a camp ritual. Once a week Stangl's Nazi monkey, who spoke halting English, would visit each barracks and deliver his infamous escape speech. "For each prisoner who escapes," he barked out, "we will execute the man who sleeps in the bunk beside him. Johnson, if you escape, we will execute Benson. If Benson escapes, we will execute Hostettler. If Hostettler escapes, we will execute Pennington. If Pennington escapes . . ."

I blocked out the name.

It is written into the Geneva Convention—a prisoner has a duty to escape. Late one night, I dropped through loosened floorboards to the dirt beneath the barracks. In my pocket was a pair of pliers sharpened to a crude wire cutter. I had stolen it from a lower bunk. I crawled to the edge of the barracks. Peeked out at the grounds. There were no sweeping searchlights. No roving guards. No German shepherds. We were in a simple holding pen. It was only starvation and Stangl's murderous escape policy that prevented breakouts. When I felt all was clear, I scurried like a frightened dog to the headquarters shack. It was the last place they'd expect an escapee to go.

The night air was still warm. The window to Stangl's office was unlocked. Inside, all was dark. I slithered through the window. My rifle lay across the desk, like some kind of trophy. I rummaged through the drawers until I came across a box of 30.06 cartridges. I loaded the rifle. Loaded my pockets. I am a changed man with a rifle in my hands. I never felt so good in my life. I felt as if I could liberate the entire camp. Liberate all of Europe. It was dark in the office, but I pawed through his desk in the hopes of recovering my crucifix. I had no such luck. I turned to see the haunting silhouette of the German sniper rifle hanging on the wall. Thought about stealing it. Then I forgot about it, and back out the window I went.

I was an hour getting through the wire. The pliers were barely passable as cutters. Once through the fence, I spent the next hour crawling on my belly. Prayed with all of my heart the so-called minefield was fake. You see, ultimately, war is about survival. I was in survival mode. Did I think of my fellow prisoners? I thought of them a lot. But I couldn't see how a soldier acting passively would be doing anybody any good. If those men had had my health, my rifle, they, too, would have gone through that fence. I believe in my heart they understood that. It's not like any of the Americans in that camp came looking for me after the war.

Once through the field, I scrambled up the hill outside the camp. Lay there, exhausted. I can't remember if I dozed off or not, but before I knew it, the sun was peeking through the forest.

Now I was wide awake. I was hungry and scared, but scared in a wonderfully alert sort of way. I was lying on top of the hill where I had been ordered to *"hit the target."* The camp below me was just coming to life. This is what I saw:

Colonel Stangl stormed out of his headquarters building in just a white T-shirt. The little Nazi monkey was beside him, more flustered than I'd ever seen him. They were furious. On Stangl's orders the prisoners were rousted from their bunks. Guards stormed into my barracks.

Finally, when all of the prisoners were assembled on the parade ground, and it was obvious I was not among them, Stangl turned my way. Looked up the hill. I put him in my sights. Goddamn me to hell, I had the evil son of a bitch right in my crosshairs.

No, I didn't shoot him. My ego had a point to prove. I moved the gun a foot to the right and sent a 30.06 through the head of the little Nazi monkey—the SS captain who had beaten me the day I surrendered. Got the little bastard right between the eyes. His brains exploded over Stangl's white T-shirt. It was sniper vanity. Perhaps the mistake of my life. I had Stangl's head in my sights, but I let him go. It was a mistake I vowed I would never repeat. If ever again I found evil, any evil, locked in my crosshairs, I would, without hesitation, pull the trigger.

Stangl ducked behind the front line of prisoners and put a chokehold on one of the men, just to shield himself from my aim. A good sniper has to be aware of the shot he cannot make. I gave up on Stangl. Trained my sights on the west tower. Took out the guard behind the machine gun. I ejected the shell and moved to the east tower. Took out that guard. Now there was pandemonium in the camp. Bullets were whizzing over my head, and peppering the hillside before me. I calmly reloaded my Springfield and took a long last look at the small compound. I couldn't locate the coward Stangl among all of the scrambling men. So I turned and disappeared into the pines.

45 | SECRET SERVICE MAN

We talked in a quiet corner of the spacious lobby of the Buckingham Hotel. The overstuffed, overwrought couches and matching chairs were mostly empty. The crimson carpeting that stretched from wall to wall had faded to a pale red, exposing frayed edges and numerous cigarette burns. The Saturday night dinner crowd was just arriving, and piano music was spilling out of the restaurant and bar. Mr. Andersen, the Secret Service agent in charge of the President's Minnesota visit, leaned up against a wall and smoked a Camel. He eyed everybody who passed as our tense conversation heated up. Still clutching it in my hand, I told him the story of the long-lost crucifix.

"Did you actually spot him?" he asked.

"No," I told him, with a deep sigh. I knew what was coming.

"And back in Wisconsin, did you actually see him there?"

"No."

"Has anybody in the United States reported seeing this ghost of Nazi Germany?"

"No."

He shook his head in resignation. "It's not that we don't take you seriously, Deputy Pennington . . . we do."

The patronizing tone in his voice irked me. "Well, you couldn't prove it by me, Mr. Andersen."

His habit of looking elsewhere while talking to me was irritating, though I didn't think he was a bad guy. In fact, he seemed very professional. "May we speak off the record?" he asked.

I rolled my eyes. While investigating the wheat field murders two years earlier, everybody in town had wanted to speak *off the record.* In Kickapoo Falls, the phrase had become a running joke. "Okay," I told him. "Off the record."

He blew a long stream of smoke toward the wide spiral staircase. Finally, he looked me straight in the eye. Lowered his voice a hair. "Israeli intelligence puts Stangl in Brazil. They have no evidence he's left South America."

"I've talked to him on the phone."

"Yes, we believe you have . . . but did it ever occur to you that he's been calling you from Brazil?"

"That's ridiculous."

"Is it?"

Now I was mad, or just frustrated. "I've got a murdered train engineer and his murdered wife buried in Wisconsin. Do you think he shot them from Brazil?"

He took another long, slow drag on his cigarette. "Captain Hargrow of your state police thinks Zimmer might have shot them." Then he paused before adding the kicker. "And quite frankly, there are still a few people in your hometown who think you might have pulled the trigger. You see, Deputy, we've been taking your reports very seriously." He finished his smoke then snuffed it out in a nearby ashtray. "By the way, Deputy Pennington, when you meet the President tomorrow . . . will you be armed?"

"As a rule, Mr. Andersen, I don't carry a gun to church."

"Good. Let's not start. Now, why don't you enjoy the Mass tomorrow morning, and let us worry about the President's security. We haven't lost a man in sixty years."

46 | LAST SUPPER

Before ascending the spiral staircase to my room, I checked the front desk for messages, hoping for something from Captain Hargrow back in Kickapoo Falls. Perhaps he had found something in the search of Zimmer's papers. He'd obviously been talking to the Secret Service. Why wasn't he talking to me?

"You're sure there's nothing?" I asked the young man behind the desk.

"Nothing, Mr. Pennington." I was about to turn and go when he added, "Your ladyfriend just got in, though. She must have been shopping. I saw her carrying some boxes."

I smiled at the thought. "Thank you," I said.

I spotted Alex down the hall, smoking a cigarette outside her door. I walked that way, trying in vain to conceal my frustrations. "I didn't know you smoked."

"Bloody bad habit. But then there are a lot of things you don't know about me, Deputy Pennington."

"The last woman who said that to me tried to kill me."

"He called, didn't he?"

"Yes," I admitted, "he called."

"More games?"

I nodded my head. "Yes, more games."

"Tell me about it at dinner?"

"Dinner would be nice. I heard you went shopping."

"Yes . . . a department store called Dayton's."

"Better than Harrods?"

She laughed. "Nice, but no, not better than Harrods."

A misty drizzle fell outside our restaurant window. The bar and grill off the hotel lobby was comfortable and free of crowds. All of the action was across town at the state fairgrounds, where the President was speaking at a Democratic fundraiser. Our table was aglow in candlelight, and across from me Alex was nothing short of radiant. I couldn't help but think of how far above Wisconsin women she held her head. Not even Maggie Butler, the angel of my dreams, could have held a candle to the woman from London. In grace and style, in beauty and in speech, she was out of their league back in Kickapoo Falls. Which meant she was out of my league.

"Chapelle means 'chapel' in French," she told me. "La Chapelle . . . 'the chapel.' "

"Alex the Chapel," I echoed. "Sounds like someone on the right side of the law."

"Yes, it does, doesn't it? Of course, you seem to believe I'm in love with a married man . . . and I think you're in love with a dead woman. Or two dead women. We're both doing something wrong here."

"What an odd pair we make, Detective. Will you sleep with me tonight?"

She smiled, genuinely surprised at my boldness. "I confess . . . I haven't quite recovered from last night, Deputy."

"No, I mean, just sleep." I tried to explain. "No sex. No games. Just go to bed with me at night, and wake up with me in the morning."

"No games?"

"I promise."

The smile left her face as fast as it had appeared. "I have to make an important telephone call."

"I understand."

"I'm not saying no."

"I didn't hear a yes."

"You don't know much about women, do you, Deputy?"

Now it was my turn to smile, and a rueful smile at that. "Lisa said that exact same thing to me . . . seems like a long time ago."

We ate our dinner in a mostly pleasant silence. The drizzle continued to spot our window, reminding Alex of London. Reminding me of the morning Mass.

Again she was reading my mind. "Do you think he'll strike tomorrow?"

"He has to . . . or what was this all about?"

She thought about that for a minute, the candle flickering in her face as she worked the case. "I could again argue he's not out to kill your President. He's out to kill you. For that . . . he can wait until you return home."

"And I could again argue he's not out to kill me. He's out to humiliate me . . . the way I humiliated him. And what could be more humiliating to an American police officer than being responsible for the death of an American President? Just as I'm about to get the job I've always dreamed of . . . my career would be over. My name would be infamous, linked forever with an assassination."

"Why do you think he returned your crucifix?"

"To let me know he really is in town. That he really can put himself in a position to shoot the President."

"And the Secret Service?"

"They think I'm chasing a ghost. A phantom. They're convinced he's not in the country. But they've assured me they've added security. I've gotten a little more cooperation out of the St. Paul cops. Besides that,

I've blanketed our hotel with photographs and a detailed description of Wolf Stangl."

"Where will he strike?"

"At the church. That's the only place the President and I will be together."

"But he knows that we're expecting him there. Why would he risk it? To date, he's played it so safe nobody has even seen his face."

"So you, too, think I'm chasing a ghost?"

"I think your dangers are back in Kickapoo Falls. I have never completely bought into your assassination theory."

That night, the skeptical detective came to my room dressed in white—an elegant white bathrobe concealing a silky white nightgown. On such a figure, she must have appeared saintly floating down the hallway. Outside the windows was a slow despondent drizzle. I pulled the drapes to block our view of the church. Or to block its view of us.

"You look like an angel," I told her.

She smiled, that sad smile of hers. "No, I'm the devil, I assure you."

I nodded at the huge Victorian bed. "Which side do you prefer, Detective?"

"Apparently, the wrong side, Deputy."

"Well then, I'll take the right side."

She shed her bathrobe and we climbed into bed. Pulled the blankets over our laps and sat there like children at a slumber party.

She laughed, a nervous laugh. "We're being reckless when we should be at our best."

"We're being human."

She glanced over at me. "Just sleep, right? None of that other rigamarole."

I paused a second. "Yes," I told her. "Just sleep."

I turned out the lamp and rested my head on the pillow. Now only a sliver of light from the illuminated cathedral slipped through the curtains. Fell across Alex. In the dark, she continued to sit in the bed. I marveled at the transformation her personality had undergone since the day she had stepped off the train in Kickapoo Falls. The brainy, energetic, and smart-alecky woman from Scotland Yard had evolved into the introspective, almost forlorn woman sitting beside me in the bed. My ego allowed that I had something to do with it. Or maybe it's what happens to all foreigners who come to America. The Coca-Colanization gets to them and they long for home. Or even worse, they long to stay.

Anyway, that night it was hard to say what was on her troubled mind. Perhaps like me she believed the morrow would culminate in the long-delayed capture of Wolf Stangl, the man who had supposedly killed her father—even though I suspected Stangl had used fatherhood to play games with her mind, the same way he had played games with mine.

After a long half-hour of silence, Alex LaChapelle at last laid her lovely head down on the pillow, her back to me. I gently reached out and stroked her long, beautiful hair, as if she were a little girl. She turned in to me. Crawled into my arms. I held her tight. She was not sobbing, but I had the distinct feeling tears were falling from her eyes. I kissed the top of her head. And we fell asleep that way, knowing not of the horror the next day would bring.

47 | COME THE MORNING

She was still there in the morning. I had half expected her to be gone. Alex woke before me. She stood at the window, the drapes wide open, revealing the incessant rain and the cathedral up on the hill. Again I was struck by her saintly appearance. The flowing white robe, the long dark hair, the tall windows, and the great church out before her all combined to paint a striking tableau in black and white.

I crawled out of bed and moved up behind her. Put my hands on her shoulders. Spoke to her the way a man would speak to his lover. "Do you want to attend Mass with the President? I'm sure I'd be allowed a guest."

She turned in to me. "Sorry, Church of England, and all that rot. But if you don't mind, I'll watch from your room. You have a much better view."

"No, I don't mind. In fact, it would be comforting knowing that you're up here."

"Yes, don't worry, I'll be keeping an eye on you."

"I'd appreciate that."

We had coffee and toast in the room as I dressed for Mass. The decision was made to wear the damn suit. I had wanted to wear the uniform of which I was so proud, but the uniform of the Kickapoo County Sheriff's Department would look totally naked without a service revolver—and like hell if I was going to carry a gun into the church. So I left the loaded revolver hanging on the back of the door. Put on the new dark suit instead. Felt as awkward as a teenager at the prom. I came to her for last-minute help. "Is my tie straight?"

She reached up and pulled it tight. "You have never looked better, Deputy Pennington. Do you have a hat?"

"No hats. The President hates hats."

"But it's raining."

"This may seem like an odd time to ask," I said, staring into those mysterious blue eyes of hers, "but I was hoping we could spend the last night together. You know . . . dinner . . . then maybe here."

"Yes, that might be nice."

"It's just that . . . I don't think you should be alone."

"You don't need an excuse to want to spend the night with me, Deputy."

"Thank you, Detective. That may be the nicest thing you've ever said to me."

48 | THE MOTORCADE

Needless to say, I arrived at the steps of the cathedral feeling mighty proud of myself. I had just spent the entire night with the most beautiful woman I'd ever seen, and now I was about to attend Mass with the President of the United States. Not bad for a man from Kickapoo Falls.

The weather hadn't changed a whole lot in twelve hours. Still no sunshine. No blue skies or fluffy white clouds. Just that slow, dispiriting drizzle that turned everything gray. Umbrellas floated up and down the street, and around the block. Still, I thought the President would be safer in the rain. Despite the gloomy weather, I estimated the crowd surrounding the church to be about two thousand. And that didn't count the thousands who were pouring into the cathedral for the Mass.

Directly across the boulevard from the church steps, at a respectful distance, were the protesters. Like everyone else, they were mostly silent and wet. From what I could see of their signs, their two biggest complaints seemed to be the integration of schools in Mississippi, and a lack of military action in Cuba. I could read two signs very clearly. IS OLE MISS AN EXAMPLE OF FEDERAL AID TO EDUCATION? Next to that, an even larger sign read TROOPS FOR MISSISSIPPI BUT NONE FOR CUBA.

On the other end of the political spectrum, the Student Peace Union from the University of Minnesota carried smaller signs opposing any use of military force against Cuba. They were also against American aid to Vietnamese troops resisting communist guerrilla forces, and they were opposed to nuclear testing. But all in all, average Minnesotans who just wanted to catch a glimpse of our thirty-fifth President overshadowed those who came to protest.

Using my badge and a special pass, I made my way through the police barricades to my assigned spot on the front steps of the cathedral. Mr. Andersen of the Secret Service was waiting for me. The gathering of umbrellas was so thick, I really couldn't tell whose umbrella I was standing beneath. Sometimes I was stuck between two of them as they dripped rainwater over my shoulders.

"Is there anything we need to know, Deputy Pennington?"

"No," I assured the Secret Service man. "Is there anything I should know?"

"No, I think we've covered all of the angles."

It was 9:30 when I took up my position on the welcoming committee. Then came word that due to the weather, the President would miss the ten o'clock Mass. He would now be attending eleven o'clock Mass. So for another hour, we stood in the continuous light rain and waited. It was as if nobody wanted to lose his precious spot. Not a single person exercised an ounce of common sense by suggesting we go inside to wait where it was warm and dry.

I could see the Buckingham Hotel just down the hill. The old Victorian structure was huge, with faces at nearly every window. Too many faces to see Alex on the sixth floor through the rain. I shifted from umbrella to umbrella and made small talk with the other guests. But I was never much good at small talk. I thought of the larger issues at hand. The President's security. The hunt for Wolf Stangl. My growing relationship with Alex LaChapelle. And I thought about the little things. My new suit was getting wet. Rainwater was seeping into my socks. Why did it seem the Secret Service guys were watching me like hawks? I grew weary and apprehensive. Restless. Finally, word spread through the crowd that he was coming.

The motorcade swung off Summit Avenue. St. Paul police cars led the way, the cherries atop their squad cars spinning red and white light. Motorcycle cops, miserable in the rain, but bursting with pride, rode shotgun. Then came the limousines. I counted at least five of them. There were probably more. Secret Service men seemed to emerge from the crowd and ran alongside the cars as they slowed for their approach to the cathedral.

The black presidential Lincoln with its bubble top pulled up to the curb in front of us, and suddenly we could see the ghostly image of John F. Kennedy through the rain-splattered glass. It's hard to describe my feelings at the time because they were so unprofessional. What I mean to say is this: as President Kennedy stepped from his limousine surrounded by Secret Service men holding umbrellas over him, I forgot I was a cop. I forgot all about Alex across the street at the Buckingham Hotel. It didn't even bother me that I had been on my feet for two hours, and that I was wet, cold, and miserable. At that moment, I was just another giddy American about to meet the President of the United States. I was as excited as a schoolkid. I remember watching the faces of those around me light up as he stood on the sidewalk and then started up the stairs. I wondered if my own face was as animated as theirs. Probably more. There was a loud continuous cheer from the crowd as the President began his greetings. Almost everyone he shook hands with apologized for the weather.

He was taller than I had remembered, but just as handsome. A man's man. He wouldn't remember my name, so as he approached, a gleam of recognition in his eyes, I thought to reintroduce myself. He reached out to shake my hand, and I stepped three quarters around him, so that my back was to the Buckingham Hotel.

"Deputy Pennington," the President said, "we meet again."

"Mr. President, I'm surprised you remember me."

"One does not forget a visit to Kickapoo Falls."

"You've been promoted since then."

"Hopefully, come next month, you, too, will be promoted."

"I hope so."

At that moment, I was the most important person in the world. In fact, the whole crowd around us was straining to hear what the leader of the free world was saying to the small-town cop from Wisconsin. Press photographers were snapping pictures. As we started up the steps to the massive doors of the cathedral, the President laid an arm across my shoulder. Lowered his voice. Almost intimate. "Jackie and I especially want to thank you for all of your help on election night," he said. "We were told about what went on in the harbor."

"I'm glad I could be there, Mr. President."

"We don't forget our people."

The entire conversation was over in less than a minute, but over the years I've played that talk over and over in my head. Maybe I even embellished it a bit, but I don't think so. The President moved on to other dignitaries as we rose as a group to the terrace before the main portals. I couldn't help but look up at the great arch as we passed beneath it. Chiseled in the pediment was a sixty-foot-wide rendition of Christ and the twelve apostles. Beneath this rendition, carved in Latin, was Mathew 28:19. *"Go therefore and make disciples of all nations."* Flanking the inscription on either side of the monumental arch were the figures of Saint Peter and Saint Paul. I found their presence somehow reassuring. Soon we were all in the narthex of the great church. Out of the weather. And out of sight of evil's eye.

49 | CAMP KICKAPOO: *The Execution*

Under the terms of the Geneva Convention, no prisoner of war convicted of a capital crime could be executed until at least three months after the date on which his own government was notified of the sentence. So it was that a full month after the guns in Europe had fallen silent and his homeland lay in ruins that *Soldat* Paul Friedrich Stangl was finally read his verdict and given his sentence. The counsel for the defense, an army captain, performed the perfunctory ritual through the bars of his cell. He was cold and aloof. And brief. "On the charge and specification of murder . . . *guilty.* The accused . . . Private Paul Friedrich Stangl . . . *to be hanged by the neck until dead.*"

His date with death was set for the coming Friday, the traditional day of execution, because Good Friday was the day that Christ died. That put the date of the execution just two days away. Friday night, July 6, 1945. All that was left was the approval of the Secretary of War, and the President of the United States.

My father drove down a day early for the execution. He thought it important that he be there. He stood behind a barbed-wire fence and watched the condemned man take his one hour in the exercise yard. It was sunny and hot, the middle of a wonderful Wisconsin summer. Only the day before, he had been celebrating the Fourth of July back in Kickapoo Falls. It was a joyous celebration. The parade down Main Street was the largest in the town's history. The war in Europe was over. The Allies were preparing an invasion of Japan. And his son, yours truly, was safe at a hospital in Switzerland.

Besides the military guards, one other man stood at the fence that day watching young Stangl. A darkly clad civilian. Don't ask me how, but Dad was pretty sure he knew who the man was.

The stranger was dressed in country garb. A floppy black hat with a long gray coat. But it was not a farmer's clothes. More western, like a rancher. "Are you the preacher?" the stranger asked my father, in a gravelly voice.

"No, not really," Dad told him. "I'm with the YMCA. I worked with the boy at the camp. I'm here to witness. Are you the . . . ?"

"Yes, I am. Kansas, mostly. The army brought me in for this job. Never been to Wisconsin before. Pretty country. Nice folks."

"Do you always watch them before you . . . ?"

"Before I hang them? Yes, I do. It's part of the job."

"How so?"

"So I can make out his drop. Every man has a different drop, you know. I have to have his age . . . his height and his weight. Is he a strong man, or a weak man? It has to be perfect, you know. Death has to be instantaneous. So I add more inches on the drop for a stronger man."

"And what will you do for Private Stangl?"

"He looks to be a strong lad. Probably set his drop at eight feet."

"Will that make it quick and clean?"

"You care for the boy, do you?"

"Yes, I do."

"Yes, it'll be quick and clean. It's much quicker than shooting, and certainly a lot cleaner. I consider it foolproof, actually, provided an experienced man is doing the job."

"Guess I always thought anybody could do it."

"Oh, no. Most of the botched jobs, they get the knot wrong. The knot is the secret to it, you know. We have to put it on the left-hand side . . . beneath the left lower jaw. At the drop, it finishes up in front and throws the chin back and breaks the neck. The bones collapse on the spinal cord. Cuts off oxygen to the brain. Paralyzes the rest of the body. Average man be dead in about seventeen seconds."

"And if it's done wrong?"

"If you had the knot on the right-hand side, then at the drop it comes back behind the neck, and throws the neck forward, which would make for strangulation. Man might live on the rope a quarter of an hour then."

"When their time comes . . . do most of them go calmly?"

"From my experience, ninety-nine out of every hundred go that way."

"And do you pull the lever yourself?"

"Yes, the executioner must do it. That's the executioner's job."

There had never been a hanging in the disciplinary barracks at Camp McCoy. The army did most of their hanging at Fort Leavenworth in Kansas. But there was a war on and allowances had to be made, so a makeshift gallows was constructed in the elevator shaft of an adjoining warehouse. From a specially built platform on the first floor, the prisoner would drop eight feet through the first floor into the basement.

My father's last visitation with *Soldat* Stangl came on Friday morning. They were alone in his cell. The prisoner was emaciated. His hour in the bright summer sun every day left his ghostly white skin blotched. Red and burned. He was sullen. Reflective. Mostly Dad let the boy talk—about growing up in Austria and Germany. About how strict his father had been. About rebelling. Getting in and out of trouble. Going off to war.

"We were nine-ninety-nine," he said in a delicate voice. "Petty criminals. I never killed a soul, Mr. Pennington . . . not even in the war. We surrendered the first chance we were given. Few of us were Nazis. We looked at the Americans in front of us, then we looked at the Nazi officers behind us. Seemed to us we had more in common with the Americans . . . so we threw up our hands." Then he choked back a rueful little laugh. "We Germans make the best Americans, you know . . . but we make lousy Germans."

Germany, England, Italy, and even the Vatican formally protested the hanging of a prisoner found guilty of murder in a secret trial with secret transcripts. In fact, Tokyo Rose was said to be cracking wise about American justice to the boys who were still fighting in the Pacific. What was the war about if it wasn't about moral justice? But with young Stangl's father already a war criminal and on the run, there was little hope of a reprieve. The army judge advocate general and the Secretary of War studied the record and affirmed the sentence. President Truman signed the death warrant.

On Friday evening, with the sun gone from the sky, POW Paul Friedrich Stangl, flanked by two MPs and trailed by a Catholic priest, was escorted into the warehouse. He wore the gray field jacket of the Afrika Korps. When *Soldat* Stangl reached the gallows, he sat down on the first step and removed his shoes. With manacled hands he put on a clean pair of socks. Then, in his white stocking feet, he padded up the thirteen stairs to the hangman's noose.

My father was down below, as was Sheriff Fats. The two men from Kickapoo Falls must have felt as if they were watching their own son being paraded to his death. No reporters were allowed at the hanging. A man from the state department was there, along with one man each from the German and Swiss consulates. Everybody else present that evening was military.

Dad mumbled, "This is wrong . . . so damn wrong."

Fats weakly replied, "There are larger issues."

Young Stangl stepped onto the trapdoors. The executioner, still in his dark hat and long coat, wrapped a heavy leather strap around the prisoner's ankles. Another strap was wrapped around his thighs. A third strap was wound around his arms and chest. A heavy hemp noose, oiled to make the knot tighten swiftly, was placed around his neck.

The fort commander stepped forward. One step behind him was a first lieutenant. It was the lieutenant who read the execution orders to the prisoner. First in English, and then in German.

"Do you have any final words?" the commander asked.

Young Stangl stared down at my father and Sheriff Fats. A natural smile creased his face. "I love Wisconsin. I should like to have stayed longer."

"Anything else?"

He shook his head. *"Nein."*

The Catholic priest administered last rites, and then stepped away, his Latin words echoing through the warehouse. With that, *Soldat* Stangl calmly submitted to the black hood. All was deathly quiet. The fort commander nodded to the executioner. The executioner crossed himself. Then he pulled the lever on the trapdoor.

The prisoner dropped eight feet into the cellar. The hangman's noose tightened instantly and the boy swung only slightly at its end, his neck broken, his head bent sharply, almost touching his right shoulder. The only sound to be heard was the thick, slick rope, groaning and creaking as it stretched on the gallows. My father silently counted off seventeen seconds. Whispered a prayer.

At the end of a rope in a deserted warehouse in the heart of Wisconsin, the war was over.

50 | THE MASS

It strikes me that in a story about good versus evil, I have said very little of my relationship to God. That's because I wasn't all that good. Besides, being a Catholic meant that I had to go through the Church to get to God. I attended Mass maybe once or twice a month, plus Christmas and Easter. I confessed my sins a couple of times a year. Well, I confessed most of my sins. I had mixed feelings about sharing the juicy ones. Point is, the Catholic Church was a constant throughout my life. It was always there. The Church never changed. That was both its strength and its weakness. At least in America. Because America under John F. Kennedy was changing, and it was changing fast. I really believe that it was those of us in law enforcement who felt the changes first, and felt them the most. The Sixties were not kind to those of us who wore a badge and a gun. Still, even in those confusing and turbulent times, there was always the Church. I found comfort there.

We were led to three reserved pews in front of the pulpit. The President and his party sat in the second pew. Senator Eugene McCarthy was there with his wife, but other than the Minnesota senator, I didn't recognize any of the faces. My group was ushered into the third pew. I was directed in first, but as I started down the pew I noticed a man already seated on the far end. I moved all the way down and sat beside him. It was obvious to me he was Secret Service. Two other Secret Service agents stood in the aisle beside the President throughout the Mass.

If the exterior of the cathedral was overwhelming, everything about the interior design was grand in scale. At heart, I was still a small-town boy from Wisconsin, but I'm willing to bet that on that particular Sunday the Cathedral of Saint Paul would have awed even the devil himself. As the organ played and the choir sang, I was nearly overcome by the pageantry. With a slight turn of my head, I could see the President of the United States in a state of worship. With a tilt of my head, I could look straight up into the great dome, a hundred seventy-five feet in inner height. The effect was as if staring into the gates of heaven. Around the altar before us were six tall columns of black and gold Italian marble, like black-robed guardians. And at the crest of the altar, fifty-seven feet above the congregation, was implanted the largest crucifix I had ever seen. The same symbol of the Holy Spirit that my mother had worn around her neck. That had been stolen from me during the war. That had been recovered at Fort Snelling only the day before, and was now draped unceremoniously about my own neck.

I have one other strange memory of the eleven o'clock Mass that day. As soon as President Kennedy was seated, after they had gotten their glimpse, almost half of the people in attendance got up and left. As the service began, they streamed out of the church. There were actually empty pews behind me. Granted, a lot of them had sat through the ten o'clock Mass, expecting the President then. It's hard to ask even a good Catholic to sit through two Masses in one morning. Still, I suspect there were a lot of admiring Protestants and curious Republicans at the cathedral that morning.

I have the bishop listed as Gerald O'Keefe. I remember that from the pulpit he acknowledged the President's attendance on that rather rainy morning, and he asked his flock to pray that God would give the first Catholic President of the United Sates the strength and the courage to carry out the weighty responsibilities of his office.

There was a doorway to my right. It was an exit near the pulpit. Several of President Kennedy's top aides waited for him there. They could be seen constantly poking their heads around the corner. I recognized Press Secretary Pierre Salinger from television. There was also a telephone engineer, who stood right in the entrance near two specially installed telephones. I was told one of the phones was connected directly to the White House. Apparently the other phone belonged to the Secret Service. I watched as agents used the phone several times during the Mass. Which brings me to one last note about the people in that particular doorway. Mr. Andersen was over there.

As we marched through the ritual like good Christian soldiers, I confess I glanced at my watch on more than one occasion. I wanted only for it to be over. To say goodbye to the President. Wish him well. To return to the hotel and the beautiful woman that waited for me there. To return to Kickapoo County and convince the people that I was ready to be their county sheriff.

In that magnificent cathedral literally surrounded by Secret Service men, the threat to President Kennedy seemed a distant memory. Almost ridiculous. Possibly an exaggeration on my part. It was then, near the end of the service, that my company with the President of the United States came to an abrupt end.

After talking on one of the special telephones, Mr. Andersen stepped from the doorway beside the pulpit and moved my way. In fact, he came toward me with such decisiveness that I thought he was going to arrest me. He leaned into the pew. "Deputy Pennington, will you come with me, please."

I was embarrassed. I stole a last glance at the President, but his attention was on the pulpit. Nobody else seemed overly concerned, either. Apparently, Secret Service men dragging people out of Mass was fairly routine. I got up and followed the man-in-charge the short distance down the aisle. We stepped into the doorway. Once there, Mr. Andersen took the telephone receiver from the hand of another agent and held it out to me, a look of disgust in his eyes. He didn't come right out and say it, but he was no doubt thinking it: *This had better be good.*

That's when it hit me. The moment when the whole case came flooding back. I feared it was Wolf Stangl calling. The war was on.

I grabbed the receiver from Mr. Andersen, took a deep breath, and then put it up to my ear. "Pennington," I said. My heart was racing. The call was long distance. In those days you could tell. The connection was always scratchy.

"Deputy Pennington, this is Captain Hargrow . . ."

I was both relieved and confused. Mad even. It was not Stangl calling, it was the state police back in Wisconsin.

". . . We're here searching Zimmer's office, and you're not going to believe what we just found."

"What," I demanded to know, "could possibly be so important that I had to be reached immediately? Pulled away from the President?"

"It's a telegram from Western Union . . . dated September 15, 1962."

I'm a smart man. I was a smart cop. The problem that plagued me throughout my career is that I was not fast. What I mean is, I didn't think fast. I did my best thinking over time. Like behind the wheel of a squad car on long, lonely stretches of road. Or lying in bed at night, alone, waiting for sleep to come. That's when the clues all came together. That's when I solved mysteries. The only times when I was quick and decisive was when I had a rifle in my hands. It's a wonder I survived so long. That Sunday morning in the cathedral was one of those days when my brain was working the case without my being conscious of it. The telegram from Western Union, devastating as it was, set off a chain reaction, and the whole story of Wolf Pass mushroomed in my mind.

Captain Hargrow read me the telegram verbatim, but in my memories of that rainy day, I do not hear his voice over a scratchy telephone line. Instead, I see the actual telegram, as if posted to a cathedral wall. Nailed to the church door. It is staring me in the face. It is taunting me. Haunting me. Like an indictment.

OFFICE OF SHERIFF KICKAPOO COUNTY
REGRET THAT DUE TO MY WIFE'S ILLNESS
WILL NOT BE ABLE TO TRAVEL
TO STATES TO ASSIST IN HUNT FOR WOLF STANGL
INTELLIGENCE PUTS STANGL IN BRAZIL
NO CREDIBLE REPORTS HE HAS LEFT BRAZIL
PLEASE KEEP US INFORMED
SIGNED DETECTIVE ALEX LACHAPELLE
SCOTLAND YARD

51 | THE DENOUEMENT

There were maybe ten minutes left in the Mass. Zimmer's haunting words spoken on Black Hawk Island had returned like a curse. *"Do you think he works alone?"*

I bolted out the north door. People were everywhere. A sea of dark umbrellas was floating up and down the boulevard that graced the church. Many people were just milling about, waiting to see the President leave. Others were leaving themselves. I looked over at the Buckingham Hotel, but the steady rain and dark skies obscured the people crowding the windows. I think I spotted my room. From what I could tell, there was nobody up there. I rushed past the police barricades and across the boulevard. I was certainly hurrying, but I can't say I was running. I had more than enough time to get to my room, and I didn't want to panic. Or start a panic. The problem was, I didn't know what kind of ghost or monster I was going to find waiting for me when I got up there. I berated myself for not wearing a gun. I had to be the only cop in town that day who was unarmed.

The rain had only intensified during the Mass. By the time I pushed through the lobby doors of the hotel, I was good and wet. I raced to the large spiral staircase. Took the stairs two at a time, all the way to the sixth floor. The carpeting was a blessing. I couldn't be heard rushing down the hallway. I stopped directly outside my door, my breath coming in sharp spurts. I held the key in my hand. I think I counted to three. Then I pressed the key into the lock, gave it a good turn, and pushed. The chain was on the door. I stepped back and kicked it in. The chain snapped. The door flew open. And I stepped into the room.

I didn't know if she would be there or not, but I still half-expected to find Wolf Stangl there, pointing his rifle down at the crowd. It was the same dreadful but exciting feeling I had experienced while creeping up the spiral staircase at Fort Snelling. But as was the case at the abandoned fort, upon entering my room I found not the Nazi war criminal—only his ghost.

She was seated on the floor facing me, beside an open window that overlooked the stone steps of the cathedral. The rain was splashing in. Propped between her knees was a World War II German sniper rifle. Specifically, a Gewehr 41 with a Unertl scope. It was probably the same damn rifle I had last seen hanging on the wall of the office at Colonel Stangl's prison camp. She gripped the long rifle with both her hands, more like a crutch than a weapon. As striking and frightening as the tableau was that presented itself to me that day, it was the haunting stare in her face that I'll always remember. There were tears in her eyes, but not the kind of tears that run down a woman's face. These tears went much deeper than that. Almost flowed backward. Inward. Toward her mind. Down to her heart. The glistening shell that surrounded the iris reflected my image.

I was dripping rainwater. I was perspiring. I was cold. I was speechless. I allowed a second to catch my breath. To collect my thoughts. I wanted to sound as calm as was humanly possible, given the situation. "What are you doing, Miss Stangl?"

Her voice was hoarse. Almost gone. "You've figured it all out."

"Yes," I told her. "As soon as I found out who you weren't . . . I figured out who you were."

She laughed, that omnipresent sad little laugh of hers. "Pray tell, who am I, Deputy Pennington? Please tell me. I wish to know."

"You are not the daughter of Captain LaChapelle, that's for certain. I suspect you are the long-lost daughter of Colonel Stangl . . . adopted and raised in England, no doubt."

"Father told me over and over . . . do not underestimate him."

"And would *Father* be the same man you have referred to on several occasions?"

That one got through to her. Cracked the ice of her stare. Cracked her voice. "You have no idea what some men are capable of . . . or what a father's love is worth to a woman."

"When did he come for you?"

She ran a finger up the barrel of the rifle. "They brought me to him . . . when I was twelve. When I was fourteen. When I was sixteen . . . until I was old enough to stay with him."

"Who brought you to him?"

"The Third Reich. The Nazis who still walk among us . . . in London, in Germany, and here in America."

She had a point. People forget how many Nazi sympathizers there were in England and America before the war—including people with names like Lindbergh, and Kennedy. After the war, they simply melted into the woodwork.

"They sent me the fake telegram," I told her, "right after Zimmer intercepted the real one. They had Zimmer planted in America as soon as the war was over. Of course, Zimmer didn't know he was being set up . . . that the wily colonel and his friends knew all along who had framed his son. If he could get Zimmer to Kickapoo Falls, the colonel could kill two birds with one daughter. They raised you and brainwashed you from the time you were a little girl. From the day your mother was killed in the bombing."

"I suppose."

I watched her caress her father's rifle. My own gun was hanging right where I had left it, on the back of the broken door. Within my reach. I shot a quick glance that way, then turned my attention back to the mysterious assassin on the floor before me.

I was still trying to piece it all together. Still breathing hard. "So they were right all along," I said, more to myself than to her. "He's never left South America. You were the one feeding him the information. Then he would make the phone calls from Brazil, or wherever the hell the gutless bastard is hiding."

"No," she said, shaking her head. "He's here."

"Only in spirit. It was you who killed Frank Prager at the train station. You murdered Lisa. You helped set up Deputy Hess. You had the loudspeaker and a tape recording of your father's voice at Devil's Lake. You set up Zimmer on Black Hawk Island, and then took revenge for your brother. You left the crucifix at the fort. You've been a very busy girl, Miss Stangl."

She only shrugged. "I'm afraid the ghosts that roam Kickapoo County are all too real."

That's when we heard the bells of the church up on cathedral hill. It was noon. Mass was over. President Kennedy would be leaving any minute. She listened to the bells as if they were an alarm clock. Her wakeup call.

"Westminster chimes," she said to me, glancing up at the open window. "I summon the living . . . I mourn the dead."

I held out my hand in warning. "Stay right where you are."

"I have to finish my father's work. Do you want to watch?"

"Why the President . . . why not me?"

"I'm to be allowed three shots . . . two for the President and one for you. Or was it one for the President and two for you. There's been so much killing . . . I forget."

"What would possess you to follow through with such a mad plan?"

"My father possesses me."

"No more. With every killing, he's been dying inside of you. I can see it. Where he thrives on murder . . . it is tearing you apart. You weren't born evil like him . . . he had to drill it into you."

Seems curious to discuss her beauty at such a dangerous moment, or perhaps it was the sense of danger she presented that made her so beautiful, but she was never more striking than that moment when I witnessed her struggling with the ghost of her father. Wrestling with her conscience. Her long hair was safely tied back so as not to obstruct her vision. Her face was red with anguish. Her khaki field jacket hugged her slender figure, lending an arrogant grace to her persona. It took all of the strength she had, but she pulled herself to her feet, the rifle out before her. When she spoke, she was barely audible. "I have to shoot him, don't you see?"

I reached for my revolver hanging on the door. Leveled it at her. "Put the rifle down."

"No, it's the only way."

A cheer went up from the crowd on the street below. I could visualize the President walking down the cathedral steps, his limousine waiting at the curb. The cheers of the crowd grew louder and louder, rising above the rain.

I was torn between Marilou Stephens's definition of a psychopath, and my love for the woman I had come to know as Alex. I pleaded with her. Tried to reason. "Did the colonel tell you about everything my father did for your brother? Practically held his hand all the way to the hangman's noose. Prayed for him. Cried for him. Did he tell you where Paul is buried? I'll take you there."

A lone tear spilled down her cheek. "I've been there."

She turned away from me. Turned toward the window. Raised the sniper's rifle to her shoulder. As soon as I saw the tip of the barrel reach the windowpane—I took aim.

"Please, Alex . . . I will shoot you."

"I'm counting on it."

The cheering from the crowd reached its zenith. The President had to be nearing the street. When she wouldn't stop, when she swung the tip of the long barrel out into the rain, I squeezed the trigger.

I fired just that one shot that bloody day. Her father's rifle fell from her hands as the bullet slammed her against the wall. The cheering below continued uninterrupted. Then sirens began to wail and motorcycles kicked into gear as the presidential motorcade quite routinely slipped from the grasp of the cathedral, and then sped away down Summit Avenue.

The would-be assassin was still on her feet, her back to the wall. Blood coated the entire left shoulder of her field jacket. I kept my gun leveled at her chest, even though it was obvious she was through.

She stared me straight in the eye. Laughed a little, that kind of laugh a person makes just before she cries. "You're a very dangerous man for a woman to know, Deputy Pennington." Then she slumped to the floor, bleeding profusely. Sat there like a sad little rag doll.

For a sniper, I was never very good with a revolver. I had aimed for her shoulder, but I nicked her heart. She lingered in the county hospital for two days, never regaining consciousness. I sat by her bedside the whole time. In the middle of the night, a nurse woke me and told me that she was gone.

For I, the Lord your God, am a jealous God, visiting
the iniquity of the fathers upon the children . . .

—EXODUS 20:5

EPILOGUE I

A VOICE FROM THE PAST: LAST CALL

I left St. Paul much as I had arrived. In the rain. I drove east in a daze, the miles slipping by me like a morning mist before a weak breeze. I had attended Mass with the President of the United States. What was supposed to have been the honor of a lifetime was now but a sorry chapter in the life of a small-town cop. Rightly or wrongly, the Secret Service stepped in to literally clean up the mess. There was little press about the woman who had been shot at the Buckingham Hotel.

I arrived home well past dark. Kickapoo Falls was in bed. The street lamps along Courthouse Square shone on wet, deserted sidewalks. The falling leaves drifted through an empty park. Down on Ash Street, I poured myself a glass of red wine and swallowed two aspirin. I turned out the lights and slumped into the chair next to the fireplace. Closed my eyes. Listened to the steel wheels of the old Milwaukee Road as it rolled through town. Felt a haunting loneliness.

It wasn't long before the phone rang on the table beside me. I wasn't startled. Wasn't even surprised. You see, he didn't scare me anymore. In fact, I felt sorry for the son of a bitch. I picked up the receiver with genuine indifference. "Hello."

"Herr Pennington . . . it was my hope you would not be around to answer your telephone."

"I suppose."

"Is it over?"

"Yes, it's over."

"And is she . . . captured?"

"She's dead."

"I see. And she died at your hand, no doubt."

"Isn't that the way you planned it?"

"I had planned for you to be gone now . . . your memory shamed before your nation."

"When is it over for you, Colonel? You poison your own people. You eat your own children . . ."

"Of all men, certainly you should understand the power of the gun . . . and the weakness of the flesh. I tip my hat to you, Herr Pennington. You need not fear me any longer."

"I do not fear you."

"Your fear should be that you are so much like me."

The Nazis were like a virus that would lie in wait for a hundred years, slowly evolving into a fresh force. I knew they walked among us. Lived inside of us. Even in the heart of America. I would remain forever vigilant. Every small town has its share of evil. Kickapoo Falls just got the lion's share.

EPILOGUE II

FINAL THOUGHTS

I should like to write that our personal little war went on for years. That Wolf Stangl became my archenemy. My Professor Moriarty. That with our bullets finally exhausted, we used our sniper rifles as clubs, and we struggled like gladiators at the brink of Reichenbach Falls, or perhaps some waterfall in Wisconsin. But I'm afraid our final confrontation was far less dramatic. In 1971, Wolf Stangl was arrested at a Volkswagen plant by Brazilian authorities. He was extradited to Germany to stand trial for war crimes.

I flew halfway around the world to see him. Why, I'm still not sure. To gloat? To reason? To ask him a hundred questions to which there were no acceptable answers?

He was being held in solitary confinement in the Düsseldorf remand prison. Great Britain wanted him to answer for Captain LaChapelle and the missing commandos. America wanted him to stand trial for the cold-blooded assassination of American prisoners. The Austrians wanted him for the execution of fellow policemen, and the West German government wanted him in order to prove a point—that they could try their own.

We sat across a metal table in a sterile visitors' room where lawyers talk to their clients. In a strange way, he seemed almost glad to see me. He smiled. Don't ask me why, but I smiled back. He was by then a sick old man. He was balding. What hair he had left was dirty-water gray. Over his gray flannel trousers he wore a white shirt under a ratty gray sweater. He'd been locked up for a year in a six-by-twelve-foot cell, and his chalky white skin with its pocks and scars reflected a lack of sunshine. A lack of exercise. He reportedly received death threats daily. He had been kept in total isolation. I was his first visitor in months.

"You are getting old, Herr Pennington."

"As are you, Colonel."

"You were just a boy . . . yet you stopped my trains."

"Yes, I stopped your trains."

What do you say when you are finally face to face with true evil? Truth is, there was nothing to say. The conversation for the most part was meaningless. Trite. Any philosophical questions I might have had about the meaning of it all faded away in the face of his pathetic condition. We talked for less than an hour, and then it was time to go.

"One last question," I said to him.

"What is it, Herr Pennington?"

"What really became of Captain LaChapelle and his men?"

His eyes lit up, as if he were recalling old friends. "The British commandos? We captured them above the pass. The captain and his men were chained together, marched to the side of a pit and shot one by one."

"On your orders, no doubt?"

"I believe they died an honorable death."

While Germany, Austria, America, and Great Britain continued to fight over him, Christian Wolfgang Stangl died of heart disease in his prison cell. He was seventy-three years old.

His daughter's real name was Vera Stangl. We traced her travels from Brazil to London, and then to Chicago, where she had spent the summer before beginning her reign of terror in Kickapoo County. But unlike her father, she lacked the killer instinct. With each murder she committed, the *Svengali* effect wore away, and her conscience haunted her to the point where I found her crumpled on the floor beneath the sixth-floor window at the Buckingham Hotel.

I saw her again, but her stay was brief. She came to me one night in a dream. She was dressed all in white. Winter white coat. White pillbox hat. Had that angel look. That Jackie look. In reality, she had been dead a good ten years. Her father was gone. President Kennedy had been assassinated. But in the dream her name was Alex, and it was 1962 all over again. We were at the train station in Kickapoo Falls. It was snowing, that bright, fluffy kind of snow that floats slowly to the earth in the melancholy of early December. Her bags were aboard. The case was solved. She was going home to England.

"It's amazing," I said.

"What?"

"The effects that trains have had on my life."

"You're not going to cry, are you?"

I shrugged. "It's just that I don't think these old trains have much of a future."

"Don't worry about it. You're going to do just fine." The whistle sounded. She held her hand out to me. "Goodbye, Sheriff Pennington."

I held her hand and smiled. "Goodbye, Inspector."

She liked that. The train pulled slowly out of the station. She stood in the doorway waving to me, before disappearing into the snow, and then fading from my life. I had aimed for her shoulder, but I nicked her heart.

On Memorial Day of the following year, I went out to the small Catholic cemetery on the edge of town. I wore my new sheriff's uniform for my father to see. Placed some flowers on his grave. Crossed myself and whispered a prayer. Then I stood in the spring sun. Interrupted by war, I thought of all the things a young man never gets to say to his father.

I had saved one solitary flower. Dad would have liked that. From his grave, I made my way across the lawn to a lonely corner of the cemetery. The few headstones there sat in the comforting shade of an American elm. I found the stone I was looking for. Placed the lone flower on the ground before it. It read simply:

PAUL FRIEDRICH STANGL

1922–1945

A cross was carved into the stone above the name. Dad must have cashed in all of his chips with the church, but he got young Stangl a Christian burial. The boy had wanted to stay longer. Dad saw to it he would stay forever.

Just as often as I was forced to wrestle with my own conscience, the people of Kickapoo County were forced to wrestle with me. That I was one of their own made it doubly hard. In 1962, I ran for sheriff against a dead man. I won by less than fifty votes. Actually, that was the year I ran against two dead men, because I was also running against the ghost of Sheriff Fats. I ended up serving as sheriff of Kickapoo County for more than thirty years. The first few elections were close. In the last elections, I ran unopposed.

Often, as happens in squad rooms, the young deputies would gather around a desk on a late autumn afternoon between shifts and swap tales of a legendary sheriff. By the time I retired to my island, I could not recall if the stories they told were of Sheriff Fats, or if their stories were about me.

And so here ends another chapter of my life. I lay down this pen in hopes of laying to rest the ghosts of Wolf Pass. But I suspect they will haunt me still. There were too many betrayals. Too many deaths. Sometimes, late at night, when the Lake Michigan waves keep me awake as they break against the rocks, I hear voices. Screams. I hear the blunt sounds bullets make when they penetrate the flesh. The screams are loud, like the winds off the water. But the voices are faint, as if out to sea. Still, as I grow older, they seem to grow louder. They are demanding voices. I only hope that when my soul finally sets sail, I will have some answers.

ACKNOWLEDGMENTS

There aren't a lot of books written on German prisoners held in America during World War II, so I am grateful for the work of the following authors: *Stark Decency: German Prisoners of War in a New England Village* by Allen V. Koop, University Press of New England; *Stalag U.S.A.* by Judith M. Gansberg, Crowell; *Behind Barbed Wire: German Prisoners of War in Minnesota During World War II* by Anita Albrecht Buck, North Star Press of St. Cloud, Inc.; *The Killing of Corporal Kunze* by Wilma Parnell, with Robert Taber, L. Stuart; and on the subject of Nazi war criminals, *Into That Darkness* by Gitta Sereny, Vintage Books.

Special thanks are owed to my friend Celeste Gervais for her critiques along the way, and to my friend Mary Mauskosir for her help with and her translations of the German language.

I began writing *Wolf Pass* in June of 2001. It was completed in July of 2002. A special thank-you to Elaine Koster of the Elaine Koster Literary Agency, and to senior editor Doug Grad of Penguin Putnam, both of whom made publication possible.

S. T.

ABOUT THE AUTHOR

Steve Thayer was born and raised in St. Paul, Minnesota. He is the author of six novels, including the *New York Times* bestsellers *The Weatherman* and *Silent Snow*. He lives in Edina, Minnesota.